SIMON'S DEATH

SIMON'S DEATH

JACK B.S. NORTH

For those in despair,

may they be heard.

1

PLEASE PASS THE PEAS

"Please pass the peas, Michael."

"Simon, Phyllis wants her peas."

Simon lifts his head up from contemplating the pea he's chasing desultorily around his plate with his fork. He turns his head, stares at his older brother Michael.

Michael elbows his sunken shoulder. He bays, "C'mon, Simon, you know how to pass the peas."

"Michael," their mother Phyllis says. "I asked *you* to pass me the peas." Her eyes bore down her long nose, along the length of the table dressed in its whitest tablecloth at him until Michael drops his own eyes.

Michael picks up the shallow Doulton bowl with its roses twirling madly around the rim, filled with peas glistening in butter, its silver serving spoon leaning against its gold-lined white rim, and stretches his arm toward Phyllis across Simon, who is back to chuffing one pea around his dinner plate with his fork. Phyllis grasps the fine china bowl. Michael lets go. She holds it over her plate as she spoons up a generous portion of peas, letting them roll out of the spoon onto her plate. She slips the empty spoon underneath the mound of green peas and leans its graceful handle back precisely in the curve of the bowl. She hands the bowl back to Michael, who lays it back down on the table where it had been.

For a few minutes, silverplate rings Doulton plates and voices are still.

"Hey guys! Knock, knock," chirps the boys' sister, the middle sibling, Sarah, suddenly from her seat across from Michael and Simon.

"Not now," her mother and father say in unison, their eyes on their food.

Sarah sinks back into her padded chair and exaggeratedly chews her last bite of roast beef, making mm sounds of gustatory delight. Continuing to be ignored, she mushes her peas with the back of her fork so that they will stick to the silver and puts the whole in her mouth, pulling the fork out from between her closed lips with a grand upward gesture and an ostentatious slurp. No one responds. She frowns and glares down at her plate. She has no more mashed potatoes to play with, having eaten them first.

Michael elbows Simon's shoulder and, with a mouth full of peas, potatoes, and beef, asks, "So man, you going to work tomorrow. You look like you could join Gramps."

"Enough Michael," Phyllis admonishes him. "I don't want any unpleasantness at the table. It's best to ignore him when he's in this mood," she instructs him.

"He needs to toughen up," their father Fred chimes in, as if he's said this about Simon many, many times before.

Simon mutters to his plate, "Why do I need toughening up? It's normal to miss the dead." He raises his head and scowls at Michael, "Don't you miss Gramps? We just buried him!"

Michael shrugs, "Hey man, life goes on, you know."

"Don't use those vulgar common phrases, Michael. How many times have I adjured you?" Phyllis remonstrates.

Sarah chokes on her last mouthful of peas. Michael waggles his eyebrows in response at her. Simon glowers at his plate and recommences chasing his pea. Michael schools his eyebrows and turns a contrite face to Phyllis. "Sorry, Phyllis."

They continue to eat in silence.

"Michael, when do you get back to residency?" Fred asks as he places his knife and fork together on his plate to signify he's done with eating and it's time to talk.

"Tomorrow. They gave me a couple of grief days off."

"Quite right. Are you still on the same rotation?"

"Nah, I mean, no. They switched yesterday."

"Which one are you on?"

A dramatic sigh from the other end of the table makes Michael hesitate.

"Your mother is sensitive about this topic. But we two are talking here. Go ahead," Fred instructs Michael.

Michael replies, with a swift sideways glance at Phyllis, "Um, gynecology."

"Oh, must we?" Phyllis expostulates. "Really Fred. Can we talk about something more suitable for the dinner table." It's not a question.

Fred replies, "Nothing wrong with me and my son talking about his future." To Michael: "I think your mother likes poking her sensitive ears into our conversation. It gives her a nice frisson of outrage." To Phyllis again: "It isn't Michael's fault his rotation has taken him to . . . gynecology." Fred smiles and fixes Phyllis with his amused eyes.

Phyllis drops her eyelids and tells her plate as she swivels her own knife and fork toward each other, "Of course, Fred. But let's switch topics."

Sarah promptly pipes up, "I thought the huge flower thing the Smiths sent were gorgeous. Did you see all that work the florist did? And then they just dumped it on the dirt. What a waste, eh?"

Phyllis sighs, "Sarah must you be so common in your language."

"Yes."

Michael chokes; Fred allows a small smile to appear and disappear; Simon steams at the pea he's chasing. How can Phyllis talk about language on this day? How can Fred talk about Michael's work as if nothing has happened? Don't they miss Gramps? Is he the only one to notice the empty seat across from him, the one Gramps sat in next to Sarah only last Sunday.

Only last Sunday.

A whole week, Simon ruminates, five days since he'd last heard his grandfather's rough voice. Simon sinks into memory as Fred consents to Phyllis's request and the other four begin to discuss the weather. Every morning for years his grandfather had called him to check in, to say Hi, to ask him what was up for the day, Simon remembers. Jawing, as Gramps had put it, for only five minutes. But that was Simon's cue that his day had begun, of knowing that his day would be okay because Gramps had called.

Gramps called only him. No one else was interested. Sarah complained Gramps timed his calls for the moment when they were heading out to work. Michael's complaint was that he was usually with a patient. Didn't the old man know they were busy, the two would moan and roll their eyes.

One time, Simon had asked Michael: "You have time to see your friends, why don't you have time to talk to Gramps? It's only five minutes." Michael had exclaimed: "Hey man, Gramps doesn't give me a chance to call him. The old bugger always beats me to it. Why doesn't he chill and wait? I'll call when it's convenient, man."

Sarah had barged into their conversation, whining that Gramps calls all the time. Every. Single. Day. And who has that kind of time to waste? Sarah had said she had her life and he had his and why did he want to call her anyway? Just because they were family? Family were supposed to be there in times of crisis, but that didn't mean she had to talk to him while she was running for her bus. It was inconsiderate. Just like an old man to be inconsiderate, she'd said.

Simon stops pushing his lone pea in its endless circle around his plate as he tries to recall how he'd replied to their excuses. With shame, he remembers he'd been silent. He should've said that giving Gramps a time window would've been easy; he should've said if you don't talk during the peace times, how can you be there during the crisis times?

Like now.

Heat flares in his chest, and bile spurts up into his dry mouth. He lifts his head up into the small talk flowing back and forth over him and interrupts: "Does no one miss Gramps?" he yells.

Talk stops. Phyllis draws in a shocked breath. Fred blows breath out angrily. Sarah giggles. Michael pushes Simon hard with his shoulder. Simon resists his brother's physical aggression for once and doesn't fall over toward his mother.

Instead, Simon turns his head to glare deep into Michael's eyes: "Well, don't you?"

"Simon, dear," Phyllis says calmly, drawing his attention away from Michael. "Of course we do. We buried him only this morning in a very nice service. I thought the Reverend gave the service a very nice touch, and the cremation went off flawlessly. Don't you think so, Fred?"

"Yes, it did." He pauses. "Right to your specifications, m'dear. As usual. I rather liked Dan's speech about his old friend. And you, Simon, spoke for the whole family. Quite right, too."

"Too bad he kept bawling," Sarah snickers.

"Sarah!" Phyllis admonishes her.

"Well, he did. I mean, the man was old. He was bound to die."

"He was not old," Simon retorts. "He was only in his seventies. He wasn't old!" he shouts. Sarah leans back, her mouth agape, her eyes widening. "Okay, okay, he wasn't old. Geeze. Take a pill."

"He wasn't old," Simon repeats at normal volume. "Did you know his heart was weak, Mommy?"

"Mommy?" Fred's sharp voice swings Simon's head toward the opposite end of the table. Fred lifts his left eyebrow lifted in judgement. Simon flushes. He'd reverted to his childhood name for Phyllis unconsciously. Fred straightens his brows and states, "Cardiac arrest is common in men his age if they don't exercise and eat well. And your grandfather unfortunately liked his cream."

"And his butter, dear. Don't forget his butter and eggs. He had two boiled eggs in the morning, every morning. He said they made him strong," Phyllis adds without sarcasm.

"It's true eggs are good for you. But he had too many for a man his age. The research shows," says Fred as he launches into a discussion of the latest nutritional science. For once Simon hates that his father specializes in nutrition and anatomy—when he's not consumed with his administrative duties, which is rare. His title of . . . Simon draws his brows together. He can't remember Fred's official title at the hospital, a title his father had made them memorize when he'd first been promoted to ensure everyone knew who he was. Simon's mind this Sunday evening has emptied itself out, like his heart has hollowed itself out, and there's nothing left to retrieve. Days and days of unwanted tears have drained him. He can't get the phone call out of his mind. Phyllis had been the one to call him, to tell him in her passionless voice, as if she was passing along the latest church news, that her father had had a heart attack and that he would be cremated at Burn & Burns, the crematorium the Smiths had used, as if the Smith's opinion was what made it right.

Only five days ago.

Before Phyllis had called Simon, earlier that morning, Gramps had called him, his chipper voice asking him how he was doing. He'd clucked at Simon to take up running. Don't be like me, boy, he'd said. You gotta get into the good habits now. Simon had laughed and said he had plenty of time. "Don't think like that,"

Gramps had said. "You never know when your time is up, eh? Never know," he'd chuckled. Simon had agreed with him good-naturedly to get along with his grandfather but hadn't intended to take up running, never thinking that hours later he'd hear that his so-alive grandfather was dead.

A sob hiccups out of him. His family drops silent and stares at him. Head down, Simon excuses himself. He runs up the stairs, two at a time, to the family bathroom. He slams the door shut and sits down on the closed toilet seat because that seat lid always has to be down, his mother will have it no other way, and in this they all obey her. She rules the family. Or maybe it's really Fred. He doesn't know. But one thing he does know: Gramps loves him. Had loved him. Wholly loved him.

Simon sinks his face into his bony hands with their delicate, tapering fingers. He resists the tears. He clutches his short, sticking-out straw-coloured hair and pulls the dead-straight strands hard, pulling his scalp forward, yearning for the physical pain to override the black hole that consumes his entire body. Even his legs hurt from the memory of seeing the coffin holding Gramps being rumbled slowly along metal rollers through the discreet black curtain into the fires beyond. Gramps couldn't be hurt by those flames, he'd assured himself as he'd watched, as he'd cried inside at the agony burns cause.

He'd visited Michael once when Michael was interning on the burn unit and had seen the searing pain etched over all the burn victims' faces despite the massive pain killers they were on. Michael had said matter-of-factly that burn pain was the worst.

And now today, only hours earlier, he'd seen Gramps being carried relentlessly into the flames. Hell had flames. People immolated themselves to protest. Others set their wives on fire in rage and hate. But Gramps was a good man. He'd worked with his hands. He should've been buried alongside his dead wife. Gramps had loved Simon and had always called him. Always. Five days now and no call. It had all been so fast, and here they are around the dinner table, talking as if it's just another Sunday. Only last

Sunday Gramps had been with them, and this Sunday he's not. It makes no sense. How can that not be strange and awful to everybody?

With his long fingers, he pulls harder on his hair, but his hair slips out of his grasp. Tears dribble out of the corners of his eyes until he can resist no longer. For the umpteenth time in three days, he weeps as silently as he can. The first two days after he'd heard those dreadful words, he'd walked around like an automaton, unblinking, unseeing. Then in the middle of the second night, a sob had erupted, convulsing his body on top of his bed, focussing his vision on his ceiling before tears had blurred the view. He'd cried until the dawn. And had continued on and off ever since.

Time ticks on.

At last Simon, after a deep shuddering breath in, lets his whole body slump into his outgoing breath. He sits there for a moment. Then stiffly, reluctantly he stands up, walks over to the lustrous sink, studiously avoids his image in the gilt-framed mirror, turns on the tap, and bathes his face, particularly his eyes, over and over with the cold water gushing out of the faucet. He twists the tap shut, dries his face off with a thickly piled cream towel, and with another sigh opens the door and trudges down the stairs back to his place at the table.

"Good, Simon. You're back in time for dessert. Melanie has cleared your place. We assumed you had finished."

"Yes," Simon mumbles, looking at the tablecloth, his blank place, his dessert silverware, his wine glass still full with his father's best red wine.

"As I thought. I hope you won't make a hash of your dessert like you did with your beef and potatoes."

"No."

"It's trifle."

Simon catches his breath. Gramps's favourite dessert. His cheeks quiver under the strain, but he controls the tears from making a reappearance. Melanie places a cut crystal bowl filled with soaked fruit and cake, rich custard, and pure white swirls of cream in front of him, pats his shoulder, and whispers in his right ear, "For your grandfather. I miss him, too."

Simon looks up sharply, but she's already walking out of the room.

"Simon," Fred says, demanding his attention. "Is your grief leave over?"

"We get a week, Fred," he replies softly.

"A week to contemplate death," Sarah giggles as Phyllis, in a voice that overlays Sarah's, asks astonished, "A week? Whatever will you do with yourself?"

"I don't know," Simon replies, realizing from her words that everyone else would be back at work, back at their volunteering and hobbies, while he'd be at home. He looks uncertainly into the days ahead, alone by himself.

2

RUSTLING DEAD LEAVES

Grief pain flows like a neverending river of needles through Simon's arteries as he leaves his parents' home, shutting the door on his family's voices. The sun has set. The streetlights are throwing pools of white light into the night that spill into nearby windows. Around his neck, Simon wraps the scarf his grandfather had given him on his first day of university. "You are a poet in my eyes, Simon," Gramps had said. "Here. This scarf will keep your voice warm. Wrap it around your neck. Poets need to be kept warm by those of us who don't have your gift."

"I'm not a poet, Gramps," Simon had retorted.

"Never mind that, Simon. Take it. Put it on."

Simon had lifted his right hand to take the folded scarf reluctantly from Gramps's gnarled and spotted hands. He'd unfolded the tightly woven scarf and scanned its indeterminate colour. He'd repressed a sigh and bowed his head slightly to raise the scarf over his head and slip it down behind his neck. He'd pulled one end down until it was much longer than the other end, lifted it to wrap around his neck, and then grasped both ends to even them up a bit. He'd looked down at the muddy-coloured scarf dangling on either side of his lean body, the fringes gently tapping at his hip bones as he'd moved. He'd been surprised at how soft it felt. He'd lifted one of the ends up to frown at the simple fringe in the same colour and weave as the scarf: a reddish-brownish-beige. He still hadn't known what colour it was, and somehow it had seemed important at the time. He'd looked up to say tritely, "Thanks," and was stopped by the proud smile wreathing Gramps's face, and in that moment, he'd decided he'd wear it, though he felt foolish.

It had become a habit, wearing the scarf.

He lifts up the left end of that same scarf and stares at the fringe in the dying light. It's ragged; some of the twisted yarns of the fringe are lost; the weave is worn here and there. Yet it feels softer. He rubs his hand on the familiar fabric back and forth, back and forth.

His chest spasms.

He drops his scarf end and starts striding along the sidewalk, letting his feet guide him as they rustle the dead autumn leaves. No dried-up leaves soil the expansive lawns he passes, but they flutter along the sidewalk and are flattened in slick piles on the edges of the road. He empties his mind and tries to empty his heart as he walks. But his heart swells up with unpleasant things, like maggots multiplying in a dead raccoon until they burst out of the corpse under the pressure of their numbers. He rubs his chest and drops his head. He tries to think of work, but it slips away from him. He tries to think of Priscilla, but though his feet change course to lead him to her house, he cannot conjure her in his mind. He loves her. He knows that. But what is love but an invitation to loss, to this awful loneliness of being left behind?

Abandoned.

It is foolish for him to think that way, but he feels abandoned. It's like Gramps had deliberately died and left him to fend for himself. Oh sure, he, Simon, has his own apartment, his own job. He's able to support himself and needs no money from his mother. Phyllis. Funny, how he's reverted to his childish conception of her. He blinks rapidly. He feels so completely on his own.

He shoves his hands into his pockets and shrugs his shoulders up to his ears, ducking his head down between them. Gramps had been a rock, a strong foundation. He knew no matter what mistakes he made, what bad choices he followed, Gramps would hold him up. Someone cared enough for him to have his back.

No longer.

Already, he yearns for someone to be that kind of person for him. But Priscilla isn't. And how could he ask her, anyway? Isn't he supposed to be the man?

He stumbles off the curb, his hands caught in his pockets, and takes two jerky steps into the intersection. Tires squeal. A man swears at the top of his voice, "You stupid fuck. Watch where you're going. Do you want to die?"

Horrified, Simon steps back, and his heels trip backward on the curb. His hands free themselves suddenly and fly up in supplication as he falls down backward onto his tailbone. The raging driver speeds off. Simon stays in position on the curb. Slowly, thoughts return. He doesn't want to die. He just doesn't want to be alone.

Simon stands up gingerly, rubbing dead leaves off his backside. He forces his mind onto the streets in the diminishing light and, ignoring the tailbone pain, hurries to Priscilla's.

Simon runs up Priscilla's walk to her front door and bangs on it with the side of his fist. He steps back. Through the door's fanlight, he sees distant lights come on. He leans leftward to follow her progress through the side window from the back of the house to the front door. She looks up as she approaches the front door and sees his face. Seeing her face, the face that loves him, dulls the needles pricking his arteries. He hears the deadbolt clunk.

"Simon!" she exclaims. She looks around him as if expecting to see somebody else, "What're you doing here?"

"Come for a walk?"

"Uh, sure."

Simon turns away to stride back down the front walk.

"Hey, wait," Priscilla yells after him. "I hafta put my coat on."

Simon stops and mumbles, "Oh sorry," to the concrete brick walk. When he feels Priscilla brush his side, he begins walking again, head down.

"Slow down, Simon," Priscilla pants.

"Oh sorry," Simon again mutters, this time to the broken sidewalk with its ribbons of tar imperfectly sealing its cracks. He slows down to a stroll. Priscilla seeks out his hand. Their hands clasp; their fingers entwine. They stroll like this as time stretches and slows. It pulls the air around them like hardening taffy being pulled long and longer until Priscilla pipes up, "So what's happening, Simon?"

"Nothing."

"Oh. Well, the funeral for your grandfather was very nice. I told Beezie all about it when I got home. She stayed late special today so she could hear all the details. I told her about the flowers—she wanted to know what kind and thought the lilies were a nice touch, that's what she said, a nice touch. Anyway, I told her about your speech—and, uh, well, it was real nice."

Uneasy quiet descends upon them, only the rustle of the leaves on the sidewalk as their feet disturb them and the distant hum of traffic on the nearby main road, intrude on the silence. They follow the sidewalk right, right, right, and right again. They are approaching her house for the third time when Priscilla, trying to quell her impatience, asks again, "So what's up, Simon?"

Simon picks up the end of his scarf with his free hand and flaps it. He drops it and rubs his chest. Priscilla purses her lips. She inhales and opens her mouth to speak when Simon suddenly spits out: "They don't miss him."

Priscilla asks cautiously, "Who don't miss who . . . Oh."

Simon stops and turns to her. His light brown lashes shadow his eyes underneath the streetlights as he plaints, "How could they, how could you forget?"

"I didn't Simon. I just . . . I mean, I didn't know who you were talking about. I'm not as quick as you, you know."

"Yes, you are."

Priscilla stifles a sigh. "You took me by surprise, Simon, that's all. I'm sorry."

"I don't understand it Priss. They don't miss him."

"I dunno . . ."

"I know."

They walk to the end of her block and turn right, staying on the sidewalk, not crossing the road. Priscilla un-entwines her fingers from his, and he tightens his hold around her palm. She winces, the streetlights her only witness to her pain.

"It hurts, Priss."

"Oh. I'm sure it's only temporary, Simon. You got closure, that's what's important, you know. You'll move on cause, well, life goes on."

"How can life go on?" he yells, disturbing the peaceful neighbourhood.

Priscilla cringes and moves a little apart from him. He pulls her back close until they are walking hip to hip. They turn the corner and the next one.

Priscilla inhales bravely before saying, "I know it's hard. I lost Papa—"

Simon stops abruptly and sweeps Priscilla into a crushing embrace, "Oh, I'm sorry Priss. I'd forgotten. Forgive me."

"There's nothing to forgive, Simon," she says into his woolly chest. "It was a long time ago, you know. I'm just saying."

Simon lets go and stares into her shadowed eyes. They stand near a massive chestnut hanging on to much of its leaves and filtering the nearest white mercury streetlight. He cannot see her clearly, and he feels her fall away from his touch ever so slightly. He tries to hold on to her, but somehow her hand squeezes out of his grasp and she is ahead of him and walking back to her front walk and her front door. "Priss?" he calls after her. She turns and waits; when he jogs up to her, she reaches back and wraps her fingers around the outside of his hand. She whispers, "You'll see, Simon. You'll move on. We all do. I gotta go in. Ma will be wondering where I am."

She lets go of his hand, runs up her walk, yanks the front door open, and slams it shut behind her.

Simon sticks his hands in the pockets of his pea jacket. He frowns down at the concrete underneath his feet, glaring at it, daring the tears to come.

Anger works.

He strides off.

And finds himself at the cemetery gates. They face the long-set sun. He hesitates. The black iron gates in their imposing varicoloured brick gothic arches stand open silently in the dark. One wide set of gates inside the main arch that rises into two turrets on either side of the calligraphic stone name, are for cars. On either side squat two shorter arches, each with their own turret on their far sides, each with their own smaller set of gates. These are for pedestrians. Simon stands in front of the south-side gates. He wonders at the fact that they are still open, that the cemetery bosses would allow people into the realm of the dead this late on a Sunday.

A neat lawn, still green, still alive, sweeps to the right up to a wide walkway. Behind bushes and cedars, at the end of the walkway, sits a parish-church like building, attached to the gates by iron fencing. It's shut up tight. He wonders what it's for. He digs his hands deep into his jacket pockets and scuffs his right shoe on the neat concrete pavers. Phyllis would be annoyed at his common behaviour. Fred would say something . . . Simon stares down at his polished black shoe with concrete dust marring its toe. Phyllis had taught them how to tie their laces; Fred had taught them how to polish their shoes right after they'd learnt to tie their laces. Simon barely remembers a time when he didn't polish his shoes every Sunday morning. Fred always snags a quick glance at all their shoes when he and his brother and sister arrive separately but within seconds of each other for Sunday dinner, and Phyllis takes a good look too. A glare is her only comment when the shoe shine is off while Fred chuckles and says, as his charcoal eyes gleam, "Still practicing, eh, Simon?"

Simon's mouth pulls to the side as he notices that here he is roughing up the toe of one of his highly polished shoes. He doesn't care. He rubs it harder on the unforgiving concrete, and the grey turns to white on the shiny black.

Suddenly, he launches himself off on that foot and shoots himself forward through the open pedestrian gate.

The cemetery is huge. He'd never been in it before until this morning. He jogs across the road that veers to the right of the gates and onto the lawn where grave stones and monuments live among the trees. His jog slows down to a brisk walk and then into a saunter over the browning grass and odd gold or burnt-red leaf that the cemetery keepers had missed in their raking up of the lawns. As his feet tread the grass, the rough scent of mould rises into his nostrils. His nose twitches. He lifts his right hand automatically and pinches his nostrils hard. The irritation leaves, and he drops his hand as he wanders between the stones, not knowing where he is, where he's going, seeking his grandfather's name on one of the stones yet being unable to read anything in the dark. The car traffic on Yonge Street fades away until there is nothing left but him and the preserved corpses in their resting places. He steps off the lawn, crosses the road, and keeps going deeper and deeper into the dead quiet of this place. The trees murmur overhead. A few leaves skitter past him in a spurt of wind.

The damned, he thinks.

Are they all damned to die and never be again? Is there nothing to be left but stones and dirt and mouldering bones? Is his grandfather rotting already, despite the embalming? He wonders: does embalming keep you looking as preserved and at peace as Gramps had looked in the viewing room? Why can he not find Gramps? Where have they put him in this grievous place?

Into his mind, into his memory, flames leap.

He halts so suddenly and so hard, he tips forward. But he doesn't notice as his body automatically rebalances itself. His hands fall out of his pockets and drop to his sides. His mouth slackens. He shuts it with a click as he swallows hard.

Gramps isn't buried.

He had been burned.

This morning.

Why had he thought he was looking for a plot with a stone on it? Why had he forgotten Phyllis had insisted on a cremation, though Fred had said the decent thing to do was embalm and bury. They'd settled their argument by both getting their way and lubricating their wishes with money: the funeral home had embalmed him, and the crematorium had burned him.

Is he getting addled that he'd forgotten their argument, forgotten the wretched service this morning, forgotten watching the coffin with Gramps in it disappearing behind the black curtain? He'd heard whispers of Fred's mother going senile early. The only grandparent he'd ever met was Gramps; the others had died before he was born or too young to remember them. Is he, too, going senile already? Is this what grief does? Is it genetic?

He pulls on his hair until the ache encircles his scalp and drives down into his mind.

He lets go and swivels on his toes and runs toward the cemetery gates, his scarf ends flapping under his arms, the fringes reaching back toward the corpses.

3

THE GROUND

Simon's mind emerges from the cocoon of sleep into the lightlessness of the early morning hour, a week after that Sunday night with his family and Priscilla. His eyes remain shut, and his mind is in that blissful state between awareness and—

He groans within himself. Memories rush in: Phyllis's phone call, the funeral home, the viewing, the service, the final . . .

Gramps is gone.

The river of needles surges and plunges into his heart.

He twists his neck and buries his face into his pillow, clutching its edges hard, bringing the pillow up around his head, almost suffocating himself in his desire to shove those memories back down the black hole of unawareness. For a moment, he cannot breathe; tendrils of ghastly night creep into the edges of his consciousness. He welcomes them.

With a sharp inhalation, he throws his pillow down to the end of his bed, horrified at what he is doing. He gasps for air. His chest heaves the worn quilt that covers him up and down. As his body recovers, his grey-green eyes focus on the silent ceiling. But he doesn't want to see. He doesn't want to see his room, his ceiling, the curtains that hide the bustling morning, or his shut door. He doesn't want to see life rumbling on. For if he sees, then it is real. Gramps really is gone. The funeral really had happened. Two Sunday dinners really had been as usual as if Gramps had never been.

He shutters his eyes and breathes. The silence buzzes with air molecules shifting in the room's coolness. Tires rushing along the road outside penetrate his consciousness. But he remains in himself, by himself. And he thinks: is that all there is? Here today, gone tomorrow, missed by no one?

He slumps into the mattress and pulls his quilt up over his head. He stills himself, trying to stop thoughts from expressing themselves, trying to pretend his stomach isn't a hollow of sorrow. But he fails. He turns slowly to the right, the effort almost too much, and collapses half on his side, half on his stomach, his right arm uncomfortably wedged beneath himself. After a while, he pulls his right arm free and his left arm out from under the quilt. He pushes the quilt down to let the cold air rush over his shoulder, his neck, his head. But it makes no difference to his inertia.

"Traffic is heavy on the 401 this morning. There is a truck rollover on the exit ramp to the—"

"Oh God!" Simon explodes. He reaches to his nightstand and grabs up his iPhone. He hurls it at his wall. It thuds resentfully onto the pine floorboards and continues channelling the radio station he'd tuned it to as his wake-up call. He groans and flattens his face into his bed. Older memories surface.

"What are you listening to there Simon? That sounds like claptrap," Simon remembers Gramps saying to him one time.

He'd replied: "It's not Gramps. It's real music, not that old stuff you listen to."

Simon rolls over onto his back as he drags his long hand over his eyes in shame at the memory. He'd been a smart fifteen-year-old, a time when, like all youths, he knew everything and old people nothing. He'd gone on to lecture Gramps about his music and how it was cool and how everybody listened to it.

"The crowd doesn't always know best, Simon," Gramps had admonished him. That's when Melanie had come into his bedroom and told him he was going to be late for school. Again. Gramps had chuckled softly, saying a chip off the old block down to the second generation, before shuffling out of his bedroom, still in his bathrobe. Gramps had come to stay with them for six months while he recuperated from his heart attack, his first heart attack, and he'd taken to coming in to Simon's room when Simon was supposed to be getting up. Gramps had been his second alarm clock, he realizes now.

A harsh cry rends from his throat as Simon remembers that Gramps is gone. A heart attack has taken him. They had all congratulated themselves on his good recovery, on him sticking to the cardiac rehab program and keeping up with his exercises for years afterward with no need to lean on anyone to remind him or help him—tough for a man his age, Phyllis had said with a hint of proud condescension at the time—but he'd begun to lapse, and none of them had noticed enough to chuff him back into it. His early enthusiasm had given him only a scant five or six or seven—he can't remember now how many years. Why can't he remember how many it's been? He should've had many more. The surgery was supposed to have given him life, not the few years they'd had. Why did he have to die?!

Simon turns back onto his right side, twists his neck further right, his hands hiding his face from his sheet, and sobs into his bed, the emotion puffing his eyes and tearing at his throat, the tears soaking through his hands into his bottom sheet.

As suddenly as the storm arose, it subsides, and his sobs turn into soughs. He lies there quivering as he recovers, and another memory surfaces, this one more recent. He'd overheard Fred saying to the funeral director about how Gramps had not taken care of his heart, that you know how it is with people like him—

Simon's eyes snap open: why had Fred been talking to the funeral director? His parents usually don't talk to the help or people like "that," not socially anyway. They are respectful to people they consider lesser than themselves, but they expect people to know their place and not fraternize, as Phyllis puts it. That's why they're not happy with him dating Priscilla. Her Ma does well, but she isn't in the right kind of profession, whatever that is. He doesn't care. He likes his girlfriend's bubbles and froth. She always has bounce. Gramps had liked her, too.

His iPhone has continued to carry on channelling Metro Morning, the show Gramps had finally convinced him to listen to when he'd begun his first full-time job after graduating with honours from UofT. The University of Toronto, he can hear his mother correcting him in his head. He sighs deeply and flops back onto his back, letting that conversation with Gramps scroll across his mind.

"You're a real man now, Simon. An adult. Time to listen to a good morning show, not that nonsense you listen to."

"The nonsense is good, Gramps!" he'd retorted.

Gramps had bored his skeptical eyes into his until he'd dropped his own defiant ones. "Alright," he'd replied trying to inject some toughness into his voice, as if he wasn't capitulating but simply humouring Gramps. But he'd failed. He isn't tough, not like Phyllis or Gramps. Not tough at all. Look at him now, lying in bed, quivering in the barren morning air, refusing to get up and go to work. He'd had a whole week off and had stayed in bed the whole week. No one had called, not even Priss. He must've scared her off with his wanting to talk about dead people.

Gramps is dead.

His body arches in protest. No! Gramps is a living person! He is! But Simon cannot deny the truth anymore. He had been living. He's gone now.

But don't people live on in other people's minds? Isn't that immortality, in a way? Why does death have to be the end?

"The Current is coming up after the news. Today on The Current—"

Simon shoots up. It's 8:30, and he's going to be late for his first day back after grief leave. He snaps his head toward his window; the light is streaking in around his curtains. When had the sun risen?

Hastily, he throws back the old quilt Gramps had given him and the white cotton sheet underneath it, the sheet from a set Phyllis had lectured to him that he must have if he is to start life off right. And here he is going to be late for work—some good start, even if he has been working awhile at this firm. He has half an hour to make it there. He scrambles out of bed and swipes up his squawking iPhone, pressing the Home button to make sure the display still works. It flashes on brightly. Relief floods him. How stupid to throw it.

He runs through his morning ablutions and streaks out his flat and up Broadview Avenue to the main intersection with the Danforth. He jogs in place while the traffic lights cycle interminably through their sequence until finally his pedestrian cross sign flashes white. He runs across Broadview, heading west toward the Viaduct, his scarf ends flying over his left shoulder as his long legs carry him past the impatient stalled traffic, through the rude cyclists trying to beat the people walking across, past the Don Valley Parkway on-ramp, playing chicken with the cars accelerating around the corner to get onto the ramp, and onto the Viaduct's narrow sidewalk. At this hour, he is the only one running on his side of the massive bridge.

Maybe he should've taken a cab.

But he hates wasting money. Both parents ingrained that rule into him. Phyllis had talked about efficiencies, and Fred about getting the biggest bang for your buck and learning to negotiate things out of people.

He shoots his right arm out of its sleeve and looks at his Bulova, a graduation gift from Gramps. It's an old-fashioned wind-up. Simon treasures it though Phyllis had scoffed at its lack of modernity. New is better, she'd said acerbically when Simon had shown it to her, pride splitting his face in a wide grin. He'd been so happy at Gramps's gift, that her tone hadn't penetrated him as he'd kept his arm stretched out for her to admire the watch. Rebelliousness at the memory hardens his mind, and he slows down to his usual fast walking clip. He's going to be late anyway; he might as well enjoy the walk. He turns his head left to look at the view toward Lake Ontario as his legs continue to stride along to work at Con Fable Insurers. This is not the good view, he thinks. Near the great lake, the CN Tower rising high to the clouds is the anchor of Toronto south and west of the valley where the Don River disappears into its constrained barricades; train tracks travel south; the DVP with its garnish of graffiti winds at the bottom of the Don Valley's eastern side; condos sprout up raggedly along the valley sides; and in the distance, before the CN Tower, tree tops and cloud bottoms frame the wealthy gold and marble towers of the financial district.

He fixes his eyes on the CN Tower for a moment. He turns his head to the right to look past the cars speeding in both directions and over the other side of the bridge where trees dressed in their autumn colours blaze flashy reds, burgundies, golds, and old greens across the expanse and far into the distance. He usually walks on that side, but today he feels called to the bleak urbanity of this side's view.

Unknowingly, his feet slow. He comes to one of the bridge's outcrops and steps into it unthinkingly. He leans his forearms on its parapet and stares to the horizon, his mind blanking into nothingness. His eyes begin to dry and itch. He blinks. He clasps his hands and drops his head, closing his eyes, letting the misery of Gramps's death once more wash over him, soak into him, form a lead ball in his stomach. He gives himself up to it and feels comforted by the weight. The world fades away, and all he knows, all he feels, is the grief.

Will he, too, be forgotten quickly when he dies?

Where has Gramps gone?

His parents go to church but never talk about death. Death is always about Jesus hanging on the cross, not about where their own dead parents are and what they want done at their funerals or what it's like to lose someone. Gramps is the first person he knows to have died. He's never known any other death . . . not anyone close anyway. Back in high school, one or another classmate had not shown up one morning, and suddenly grief counsellors were everywhere asking, "How do you feel?" He'd never known what to say because he hadn't known those classmates well. Everywhere, people had cried, but not him, and he'd felt awkward, cold, unfeeling. He'd tried to talk to Phyllis about it, but she would have none of that kind of talk at her dinner table. That's when he'd joined Michael in stopping calling her Mommy and starting calling her Phyllis. Dad had always been Fred. He'd tried to talk to him about it and had been subjected to a bewildering rush of medicalese while feeling like he was on the receiving end of a watchful bear. He hadn't known then what he should feel. He hadn't felt like this . . . like this feeling of sinking into obsidian quick sand, screaming for help inside his head, and seeing no hand reaching toward him.

Maybe no one will care if he dies. Or will miss him. If he had still been in high school, he'd have had hundreds of mourners because everyone in school turns out for those funerals, whether you knew the dead person or not. It's like a giant group hug.

But now he is an adult, one among billions of adults, adults who seemingly don't need comfort, who have to make it on their own—because that's what real men do. He is failing at it. He is late for work, and the big boss will be mad. But he doesn't care. He doesn't care at all. So long as he doesn't have to move, he doesn't have to live, he is okay.

He opens his eyes. And sees: the ground a long way down. Autumn hasn't touched the green grass far below him or the bushes. The trees underneath him still hang on to their verdancy.

It pulls at him, the ground does. It rushes up at him to fill his eyes with beauty and hunger for him to join it. The ground wants him. It whispers in his mind that it is good. He'll feel better if only he will come down. It's easy. So easy to come down. No thinking involved even. He'll never have to think again. Come, the ground sirens. Come to me, it calls. Come and be free of the weight of your grief. Here, grief lies no more.

Simon leans forward until his arms hang over the rough parapet, its gravelly surface digging into his armpits through his jacket, pressing against his chest. He stares down, down, down.

Honk.

He blinks.

Another, angrier blare of a car horn with an accompanying squeal of tires shocks him into the present, and involuntarily, he swivels around to find the commotion. Two cars, nose to tail, rock behind him. One driver throws his arm up out of his window and thrusts his head up so high it appears above the roof of his car. He rages at the driver hiding in the car in front of him. Simon crab-walks out of his haven and past the stopped cars. The one in front lurches forward, then edges away from the angry one closer to the car stopped in front of him. Simon faces fully west, puts his back firmly to the cars and that . . . that place. He isn't going to think about it. He's only going to think about work. Yes, he'll only think about work and the tongue-lashing he is going to get. Or maybe the firing speech. They fire on a dime over there.

He begins to run again.

4

FLOWERS

Simon taps his foot on the terrazzo floor as the elevator numbers on the wall above the elevator doors climb down one by one, methodically, slowly, to the ground floor. He begins to pace back and forth, keeping his eyes on those maddening numbers, letting his head twist and turn in sync with his pacing so as not to lose sight of those numbers. It's important not to lose sight of them.

Ding.

Simon flinches.

The doors slide open at a glacial pace. A woman in stilettos and a black-and-white checked Chanel suit strides out, briefcase in hand, every strand of blonde hair sprayed in place, her blue eyes hard and competent. Simon thinks: another mediation win for the insurance company coming up. He lurches onto the elevator, wondering what opening party line she had been fed to recite ostensibly to the mediator, but really to the claimant, to pressure him (or her, Simon amends in his head), to make him feel like he should take the money and run before he loses any more and to seal the deal with the subtle idea that Con Fable's offer is found spending money, not a contracted payment for lost income and for necessary health care not covered by medicare. Simon steps onto the empty elevator and jabs at the button for his floor over and over and over until the doors huff closed. It'll be a win-win either way for Con Fable, he thinks. If the claimant refuses, Con Fable will ratchet up the pressure until the claimant capitulates. If the claimant accepts, Con Fable will have once again saved mega bucks to give to investments and shareholders. Win-win.

Mega bucks. Win-win. Phrases Phyllis hates. Maybe Con Fable wouldn't like mega bucks either, although they sure like win-win.

He shifts back and forth as the elevator rides up toward his floor. Shifting isn't enough; he recommences pacing in the tiny cubicle, looking up at the numbers every time he reaches a wall. He must remember to talk professionally when he sees his boss, as he will, being so very late to work. He'd had good practice keeping words Phyllis didn't like locked up in his head. He'd learnt to do so as a boy when Fred had told him little boys don't cry like girls. They suck it in like real men. Gramps had overheard one of those exchanges when Simon had tried to stop his sniffling over a stolen toy in the face of his father's approbation, and Gramps had said, "Leave him alone Fred. He's a boy for Chrissake. He's allowed to cry, to show real emotion. You should try it sometime."

Fred had ignored him and from his great height had continued to lecture Simon on worthy male values.

Ding.

Simon blinks and looks around and up. Where is he? He lowers his searching gaze. The elevator doors are standing open. Suddenly remembering what time it is and where he's going, he hastens out. He strides through the imposing glass double entrance doors and along to his cubicle, head tucked down, stripping off his pea jacket, hoping no one will notice him.

"Simon," calls out Elaine.

No such luck. Trust Elaine to see him come in. That woman has eyes all around her head.

He stops and backtracks to her cubicle, following the heavy fragrant path of the floral perfume she favours. He looks over its wall down at her. She smiles up uncertainly at him. "How you doing?"

"Fine."

"That was a nice funeral for your Gramps."

Tears prickle at the edges of his eyes. Simon is mortified. Can she see? He digs into his jean's pockets to find a Kleenex and busily blows his nose while mumbling, "Allergies. They're lingering longer this year."

"Yeah. Tell me about it."

"Those were nice flowers the office sent."

"Only the best for you, Simon. We wanted you to know how bad we feel for you."

The edges of Simon's lips suck in then rebound back into their straight line. "Thanks," he mumbles. He clears his throat. "Um, Gramps would've liked them." He stops, but Elaine continues to look up at him expectantly. He continues all in a rush: "He, Gramps, always said carnations were the best flower because they lasted so long. They had life in them, he'd boom every time he and Phyllis argued over what flowers to get for our Sunday dinner table." He laughs uncertainly.

"Yeah?" Elaine asks, staring up at him.

"Yeah. He liked red, too. He used to say he didn't have a favourite colour. He liked all colours. So the rainbow was his favourite colour. But he liked how red yelled at you. He said red yells life, and everyone should have red in their life."

"Yeah?" Elaine replies, staring fixedly up at him.

"Gramps would've been chuffed—"

"Chuffed?" Elaine asks.

"Oh. Yes. Sorry. Chuffed, it means, well, Phyllis uses it all the time and so did Gramps. I think it means excited or pleased or something like that."

"Your Mom is British, isn't she? So it's like a British thing?"

"No, she isn't British, but Gramps immigrated from Lincolnshire."

"Where's that?"

"It's in England, on the east coast. Gramps was very British when he came here, he used to tell me. It took him awhile to see how nice a place Canada was. He came over here because his wife wanted to live with her family."

"Was she there?"

"Where?"

"At the funeral?"

"Phyllis?"

"No, I mean your grandmother."

"Oh!" Simon pauses, trying to gather his wits. "Sorry. I . . . I never met her."

Elaine creases her brow in concern, "You all right, Simon?"

"Yes. It's just . . . it's strange not to have Gramps call me every morning."

"Yeah." Elaine pauses. Silence stretches between them. "He called you every morning?"

"Yes. Every morning," Simon smiles. "Last week, he called a little earlier because he was so excited to think the Argos would be in the Grey Cup this year, though nothing topped their win on the 100th anniversary in Toronto. Raved about it for weeks. He was a fan. He used to be football mad, he told me, but then—"

Elaine replies rotely, not correcting him on his time error, "That's like soccer, isn't—"

"Hey Simon. There you are, man!" Isaac yells at him from five cubicles over. He's standing in his own next to Simon's.

Elaine scoots her chair backward into the aisle and yells back, "Don't yell from over there, Isaac. He's talking to me."

"Why would he want to do that?"

"Because he would. I sent him the office flowers. Did you do anything?"

"How could I, Elaine? You jump on those things so fast no one has time to do nothing."

"Ha!"

"Um," Simon tries to interrupt this loud exchange. "Maybe I should . . ."

All of a sudden, a crowd surrounds Simon and Elaine's cubicle.

"How you doing?"

A hand grasps Simon's left shoulder.

"Are you all right, Simon?"

Another hand slaps his back on his right side.

"It's only his grandfather, dude."

"Wait till you lose yours."

"I don't know mine."

"Whatchya talking about? You visit every New Year's in Florida."

"Yeah. We visit but doesn't mean I know him."

"Well, Simon knew his so shut up and show some respect."

The sound of a door opening at the end of the massive room penetrates the gossiping bunch around Simon. They flee back to their desks in a rapid walk, leaving Simon standing alone. He opens his mouth to say something to Elaine, but she's already typing furiously on her keyboard, her eyes glued to the large flat screen in front of her, her chair tight up to her desk, her back to him.

Simon sighs and slouches to his desk. He was so late he doesn't care that the big boss has opened his door.

"Simon!"

Simon's head shoots up; his heart quivers. Now he cares. A little.

Still holding his pea jacket, he walks to the boss's office, where his boss stands in the doorway, an immense figure in his rumpled white shirt, slightly askew tie, and grey suit pants belted tight to his towering frame.

"You're late."

"Yes," Simon says. "I apologize, sir."

"I told you to knock off that sir stuff. You private school boys are all the same."

"Sorry, s—. Sorry."

Mr. Confabulate nods once and ushers him into his office. "Sit down, Simon. And close the door."

Simon obeys, pulling up his jeans neatly from force of habit as he sits. He pulls emotional detachment on over himself like a familiar sweater first acquired at school and his parents' dinner table before Gramps had had his first heart attack. He lays his jacket tidily across his knees and looks up to see his boss watching him. Mr. Confabulate leans back in his chair and steeples his fingers. He ponders their tips for a long moment. Then he aims his brown eyes over them at Simon. Mr. Confabulate drops his hands and sits upright suddenly. He leans forward on his arms on his desk. "Look, Simon, I know you just lost your grandfather. Con Fable showed its concern by giving you a full week off. We hope you and your family appreciated our generosity."

"Of course, s—. Of course Mr. Confabulate. We did, particularly my father. He said that showed what an ethical business you are."

Mr. Confabulate allows a small smile to appear then turns serious again. "We understand and respect your grief. But you're back at work now. We expect you to turn up on time. We cannot show any more special favours. It's bad for morale. And morale is the foundation of our business. Understand?"

"Yes," Simon nods with the right amount of gravitas that he'd learnt to display at home and at school.

"We want to show the others you work as hard as them, we don't give special favours around here."

"No, s—"

"You'll stay late today."

"Of course, s—"

"Good." Mr. Confabulate straightens up in his chair and begins pulling forward some papers to sign. Simon remains seated, slow to take the hint. Mr. Confabulate pauses and looks up at him from under his unkempt brows. A a hint of impatience darkens his eyes. Simon's eyes widen as he suddenly understands that he's being dismissed. He stands up quickly, almost dropping his jacket, as he says, "Thanks. I mean, thank you Mr. Confabulate. I won't be late again." He hurries to the door, opens it, and exits like a shotput launched. He almost slams the door shut behind him in his haste but halts his hand just in time and closes it softly.

Simon walks to his cubicle, sits down in his chair, drapes his jacket across his knees, and stares at his monitor. It's off. Con Fable believes in energy reduction and green policies. Staff must turn off their computers every night, unplug any chargers, and put away their headsets tidily so as to extend their usable life. His computer has been off a whole week. And a day. He wonders if it will work again. He becomes aware of the life around him as if he is emerging out of mummy wrappings. Louder and louder rises the sound of incoherent voices, feet padding on industrial carpet, drawers sliding along their metal runners, fingers tapping keys rapidly, keys clicking and clacking, the space bar emoting its own echoing sound. He wants to run from the cacophony of sedentary work. He doesn't want to be here. He wants to be anywhere but here.

But where?

He doesn't know. Everywhere feels unpleasant. Everywhere, everyone repulses him like a sulphurous skunk. The coldness of Sunday dinners, the puzzling distance of Priscilla at her place, his own stale bedroom—they all repel him as much as this fluorescent-lit place. Restlessness overtakes him, and he jiggles his right leg faster and faster as he stares unseeingly at his blank monitor.

"Hey, man, you gonna sit there and get your ass canned? Or you gonna work?"

Simon jumps at the sudden intrusion and sends his chair back a few centimetres. He looks up to see Isaac glaring at him from over their shared cubicle wall. His restlessness vanishes under the intensity of Isaac's brown eyes.

"Well?" Isaac demands. "They fire you, they sure gonna fire me."

Simon frowns at him as he fingers dig into his jacket. "Why would they do that?"

"You got a whole week, man! You the golden boy." He gestures with his head at Simon's hair. Simon reaches up with his right hand to feel his hair. His straw-coloured hair is sticking up at all angles. Horror suffuses him as he realizes he hadn't gelled his hair into the usual neat stick-out spikes. His hair is so straight and so resistant to being lain flat that the best he can do is gel the sticking-out bits into some semblance of style. But not today. Today they're spiking every which way like a crown of thorns blown by a windmill.

Isaac's eyes relax into crinkles as he chuckles at Simon's expression. "You mean you didn't notice, man? I can't believe Mr. Con-Fab-U-Late didn't say nothing. Course, he dresses like a slob."

"Shhh," Simon hushes him. "He won't like hearing that."

"Nah," Isaac waves his hand at Simon. "He can't hear me. He's got his door closed. I checked."

"I think they monitor us through the computers."

"Sure they do. But they don't have microphones. Yet." Isaac falls silent. He looks back over his shoulder down at his desk. He turns his head back, his face a serious mask. "I don't think they do. . . . You know anything?"

Simon shakes his head.

"Well, get back to work, man. And hang up your jacket like a normal person. You can't let him see you moping around like that. While you're at work, you gotta pretend, man. Gotta pretend."

"I miss him. Gramps was—"

"Yeah, yeah. I know. Your grandfather was special to you. I wish I had one like that. I had a grandmother who baked me cookies every Sunday to take to school every week. I miss that, you know. We all miss our families. But we're at work now. Work," Isaac emphasizes with a stab of his finger at Simon. "Work!" He points at the black monitor until Simon raises himself up off the chair with a hollow stomach and knees that feel like stiff, un-oiled hinges of an old door in a tired old house and takes two steps over to the end of his cubicle. He hooks his coat on the coat-hook at the left outside corner of his assigned walls. He sits back down.

He doesn't move.

He senses impatient energy sparking toward him. He slowly turns his eyes then his head in the direction from where it's coming from. Isaac is staring hard down at him, again, his finger pointing once more at Simon's monitor. With his feet, Simon rolls his chair forward toward his desk. He leans toward the back of his desk and clicks the on/off switch on the power bar behind his wide monitor. "Better?" he asks Isaac, looking sideways up at his workmate, his grey-green eyes a mask.

"About time," Isaac replies as he disappears down out of sight.

5

THE SUICIDES

With relief, Simon closes his front door behind him and tosses his coat onto the rubbed-smooth velvet arm of his couch. All his furniture came from his parents' discards, the ones they had disposed of in the basement for their teen kids to rough up and he was allowed to pick from to furnish his own apartment. He turns the switch on his stained-glass lamp, and it throws a circle of light onto the near arm of the couch and shadows the far side of it. He wanders over to the beaten-up pine bookshelf and turns on the light that sits on the top to splash its brightness down the spines of the books. But it's fruitless; his eyes cannot focus on any of the titles. He wanders over to the flat-screen TV that dominates the wall next to the living room door and stands in front of it. Simon stares at the blurred shadow of himself on its black surface. He considers switching it on, but watching some inane show doesn't appeal to him. He turns away from it and wanders into his kitchen and sees: crusted plates and dirty flatware littering the small stretch of counter. He remembers telling Phyllis, rather arrogantly in what seems like another life, that she should give him her old silverware set as he was the cook in the family. She hadn't bought his rationalization and had told him his older brother would get it in the will and that was final. He picks up a knife smeared with dried-up peanut butter. He gazes at it sightlessly for several minutes. He tosses it into the stainless steel sink. It clinks against a pot then clanks onto the bottom of the sink.

Like a dancer in a slow-motion twirl, he surveys his kitchen: the short run of cupboards against the far wall, the old fridge directly across from the sink, the oven next to the sink, and only ten centimetres of counter space in between. Spatters of old tomato sauce coat the stove top and, over top of the dried-up sauce, a splash of . . . he peers closer. What is that? He doesn't remember cooking anything since he made the sauce, not since Phyllis had called him about Gramps dying. He leans back, back, back onto his heels until the fridge catches his back. He closes his eyes for one minute, two minutes, his shoulder blades balancing him against the humming appliance. A car's engine roaring to life on the other side of his kitchen wall wakes him. And like a picture coming into sharp focus, the filth lying all around him enters his consciousness.

Simon contracts his abdominal muscles. He shoots up, takes one sharp step to the sink, flings all the pots and flatware out of it, grabs a half-empty bottle of white cleanser and a clean cloth from the pile on the window sill, and begins scrubbing the stainless steel vigorously, his biceps contracting and relaxing as he sands away the dried-on food and cleanses the stains of his coffee that he chucked down the drain day after day. He scrubs harder and leans right down into the sink, gritting his teeth, setting his jaw in the process, his hand pushing the cloth round and round in little circles, toward himself and away, round and round. He gasps and stops. White splotches the steel, reddish where the tomato sauce had been, brown where water had evaporated from the discarded coffee. He shoves the tap handle up, and water gushes out, its reflected splash wetting his chest. He moves the handle to the hot side. He lets the water run as hot as it can get, almost scalding his skin as he runs his hand underneath the gusher. He welcomes the pain. He rinses the old food and drink and white cleanser down the drain. Satisfied at the resultant shininess, he pushes the drain catcher down into its place and fills the sink with hot water. He squirts in a generous stream of liquid detergent, hating its cheery yellow colour. Like unhealthy piss from an old man, he thinks. And shuts his eyes against the memory sidling in, the memory of seeing Gramps when Gramps had had the flu and Simon had been tasked to care for him. He flips opens his eyes and grabs the knives and forks scattered everywhere and flings them into the sink of water, not heeding the splash that covers the counter and the front of his navy blue sweater with suds.

Simon sweeps all the dishes in, splashing more and more water and suds out of the sink as he goes, watching the dishes slow as they enter the water and angle back and forth down through the suds to the bottom. He keeps the tap running until the sink is refilled; he squirts in more detergent. He snatches open the cupboard door under the sink and yanks out of it the dish rack and a rubber bucket. He fills the bucket with hot water, placing it on the narrow counter, and bangs the rack down on top of the sauce-spattered stove. He rummages around in a container in that same cupboard until he finds a scrubber suitable for non-stick surfaces. He squeezes it and squeezes it as he stares at the mound of dishes waiting for him under the popping suds.

He releases the scrubber.

He plunges his hands into the hot water and begins to wash, heedless of his hands reddening.

He scours the dishes and knives hard until, under his unyielding fingers, the stuck-on food disappears. He raises up the cleaned dishes out of the suds and dunks them into the hot water in the bucket, forcing himself to be gentle. He places the rinsed dishes into the rack. By the time he's done, dishes and flatware and pots and mugs and glasses teeter on the rack.

Exhaustion crumples him.

He stumbles backward against the fridge and folds in on himself, his arms hugging his stomach. After a while, he straightens and wanders back into the living room and flops onto the couch's soft, sagging cushions that are from a bygone day. He stretches his arms along its purple velvet with its faded streak across its back and its fuzzy black braided trim along its seam edges. He leans his head back, back, back until his neck is as arched as it can be. He stares up at the ceiling and slowly slips down until his neck has straightened and is no longer screaming in protest. He studies the tiny table for four that sits at the far end of his tiny living room. He squeezes his eyes shut then sighs. He opens his eyes and lets them roam; they come to rest on his bookshelf. The books sit there, silent, inert.

They pull at him.

He drops his arms and shoves himself up with his fists against the cushions and shambles over to the bookshelf. He raises his right hand, and his long fingers walk along the spines of all his books, beginning from the top shelf. His fingers lead his eyes from one book to the next. Thackeray. Voltaire. Dickens. Hemingway. Eliot. Austen. Leacock. He pauses. No, he doesn't want to laugh, doesn't want to be reminded of Gramps, of this gift from him. His fingers continue to step through his collection. He drops his grey-green eyes and his fingers down to the next shelf, and the next shelf, until finally when crouched down on his haunches in front of the bottom shelf, he espies a book he doesn't remember reading before. *The Suicides*. There is no author name.

Frowning, he pries it out of its position and studies its cover. He has no memory of buying this slim volume. He doesn't even know what it's about. He flips the book over in his hand and reads a list of testimonials. He snorts in disgust. Why do publishers do that? It's about as useful to a reader as the blackest of nights with no flashlight available with which to read their favourite book by. None of these testimonials tells him what the book is about, only that he should read it.

Why? Why should he read it?

He reads more testimonials. One says it's must-read poetry, another that it's about the poignancy of life. That means nothing to him. He couldn't have bought such a thing . . . although the cover is a beautiful painting of swirls of intense colour, light shining through them, and a black foundation erupting into the colours, melting the edges of the swirls it comes into contact with. As his eyes sink into the swirls, his soul shifts as if disturbed. The spine is the cacophony of colours as if it dares not show the black morass waiting at the bottom.

So who gave him this book? He flips the book back over and opens the front cover with his left hand while he cradles the volume in his right. An inscription leaps out at him.

"Simon, I missed my Papa so much that when I saw this, I had to buy it. But then I met you, and I no longer needed it. If you think you don't mean much, look at this and remember you mean a lot more to me than any book. And anyway, it'll perk up your collection. Love Priscilla."

He puzzles over that last part, about perking up his collection. He closes it and regards the cover and the title. Enlightenment lifts his brow. Typical Priss, he smiles. She was thinking of the artwork, the lively colours. He bets she'd never opened it and read it. Now intrigued, he opens it himself and begins to flip through the pages.

He walks backward to the couch until it catches him behind his knees. He sinks into it without taking his eyes off the printed word.

Many, many minutes pass.

He snaps closed the book. He stretches and yawns while his mind crackles. His mouth feels dry. He strokes his tongue over his teeth and sucks in his cheeks to try and moisten his mouth. He lets the book fall out of his hand onto the couch next to him and, raising himself up, ambles over to the kitchen. He carefully fishes a glass out of the pile on the dish rack and fills it with water. The water is room temperature, but he's too thirsty to care. What time is it? He shoots his wrist out of his sleeve and stares disbelievingly at his watch. He is a fast reader. How could so much time have passed? He's filled with an urgent desire to call Mommy, but it's too late.

Yet his mind is alive with thoughts, thoughts that that book have engendered in him, that need to be expressed.

He hunts for his iPhone until he locates it in the left pocket of his pants—why the left pocket, he wonders idly. He's always meticulous about where he puts his phone, his keys, and his wallet—but not since Gramps has died, he realizes now. He hits the speed dial button for Mommy. He blinks. There he goes again, he frowns at himself. Why the reversion? He shakes his head free of his childish name for Phyllis.

"Hello," a resentful voice answers.

He ignores her tone. "Hi, Phyllis."

"I told you not to use that common word Simon to me. Hello is perfectly proper and acceptable. And you know better than to call me after nine pm."

"I know M—. Phyllis. I'm sorry. But I had to call you."

"What was so urgent that you must call me after hours?"

"I was reading . . ."

"A book? You are calling me about a book? Simon, I know you're mad about books, but books can wait."

Simon hears her draw the phone away from her mouth and he shouts, "No. Wait!"

"Well?"

"Wait. It isn't the book, it's . . . It . . . made me think about Gramps."

An impatient sigh breathes down the line. "Did you finish your week of mourning, Simon?"

"Yes. I told you that on Sunday."

"You hardly talked on Sunday, Simon. You were like a mausoleum."

"Yes. I . . . I didn't have much to say."

"But you do now?"

"Yes."

"Well, get on with it. What about your grandfather?"

His voice drops as he asks, "Do you miss him?"

"What a question Simon! Of course, I miss him. We all do. You are not the only one in grief. But we get on with our lives. We don't indulge in endless maudlin speculation."

"I'm not speculating. I'm remembering. Don't you want to remember? Don't you want to talk about him?"

"He's dead, Simon. I loved him. But he's gone now."

Simon falls silent over the past tense. He doesn't think of Gramps existing only in the past, of loving him only in the past. He still loves him. He whispers, "I love him. Gramps can't be gone."

"What was that, Simon. Speak up."

"I said . . . I said . . . ," Simon's voice fails. He cannot get himself to repeat what he'd said. The first time, it had come out unbidden, but now that he knows Phyllis is listening, is waiting, and will absolutely hear him, he cannot say those words. He searches his mind for something else, but his mind refuses to think of anything but how much he still loves Gramps, how it's not in the past but so strongly in the present, that it dominates him more than any other thought.

"Well, if that's it, Simon, I must go. It's late, and you know how I dislike having my night-time rituals interrupted."

A sudden vision of Phyllis and her creams and her emerging from her bedroom in her lounging clothes, flashes into his internal vision. "Yes. Sorry. I . . . I just wanted to talk about Gramps with you. I thought I had a question. But . . . I was wondering . . . ," Simon falters at speaking out the newer thought that's been lurking in his mind as well.

"What were you wondering, Simon?"

"I was wondering if he was at peace? He looked at peace. Did he welcome death?"

"This is morbid, Simon. You can't be thinking along those lines. No one welcomes death. Why would any sane person welcome death? What a thing to say. Now I really must go. And no more talk like this, you understand Simon, especially not after nine."

He says, "Sorry, Phyllis," to blank air.

He depresses his iPhone's power button. Light leaves the iPhone's screen. He stands still, all feelings and thoughts vanishing from his mind and disappearing down a rabbit hole into his heart, which promptly shuts and locks the gates after them. He doesn't hear the iPhone slip out of his lax fingers and fall onto the rug beneath his feet.

6

THE VIADUCT

"Bye slacker," Isaac calls out from his cubicle. It's been a gruesome day at work, and Simon has tried to subsume himself in the form filling, the computer busy-work, the phone calls his job entails, anything to keep his mind from wandering into places hungry for his grief. Isaac's voice startles him. Simon looks up and around as Isaac peeks into his cubicle from the aisle between their cubicles and the ones opposite. Isaac is grasping a briefcase under his arm and is barely holding onto a sheaf of papers with that hand as he dangles a wrinkled leather jacket from his other hand. He pops the papers between his teeth, and his briefcase falls down.

"Mm . . . Hmm," Isaac mumbles.

"Might be easier to talk without those papers in your mouth. What do you have there?" Simon asks as he removes his headset and lays it on his desk. He rubs his ear, the one the headset was attached to all day. He hadn't realized before now how sore it had been becoming. With a final hard rub at the offended ear, he swivels his chair around to have a better gander at Isaac's load.

Isaac stoops down to pick up his briefcase, and his brown jacket leaps from his grasp onto the floor. Forgetting the papers, he opens his mouth in reflex to swear at his errant jacket and watches the stapled papers drop and splay in a fan on the tightly woven grey carpet. Letting out a grunt of frustration as he snatches up his jacket, he belatedly answers Simon's question: "Oh, just some papers." He hurriedly picks up the papers.

"Are we allowed to take those home?" Simon asks curiously as he points at Isaac's stash.

Isaac straightens up, coat and briefcase in one hand, the collected-up papers in the other, and says off-handedly, "Sure."

Simon frowns and asks, "Are you sure?"

"Don't worry about it," Isaac snaps.

Simon raises his hands in surrender. "I'm just curious. I'm the new guy, remember?" he smiles. "I just want to know the rules. That's all."

Isaac scrutinizes Simon's face for a minute or two, and Simon cannot tell what he, Isaac, is thinking behind his schooled visage. All of a sudden, Isaac grins, "Hey, no problem, man. You're a good guy, Simon. Well, see you later."

Simon gazes after Isaac as he disappears. Soon, other heads pop up over their cubicle tops and bob toward the exit as well. Simon watches them go, but his thoughts begin to wander, to leave his present and to enter the past.

"Hey Simon!"

Simon jumps.

"Startle you?"

"Oh. Hi, Elaine," Simon says, releasing his breath.

"The boss got you working late? Some of us are going out for a beer. Wanna join us?"

"I can't, sorry . . . Yes. I'm working late." Simon shrugs and smiles apologetically.

"Well, if it's not too late when you're done, come 'n join us, okay?"

"Yes. Thanks, Elaine."

"Just leave the sad face here where it belongs, you know." She pauses as if she wants to say more, but then her lips stretch wide, flashing her straight white teeth, and she leaves, her floral perfume lingering behind her. The sounds of computers turning off, of voices calling out in relieved goodbyes, of doors opening, of one of the elevators dinging as one load of happy workers after another gets on, fade after only five minutes. The constantly discreetly ringing phones silence, too, with everyone gone.

The stillness is oppressive.

Simon remains where he'd been when Elaine had startled him: sitting on his chair facing the aisle between his cubicle and the one opposite. Time slides by, and Simon doesn't notice. He hears a door click open and the blinds tapping against the door's window in concert with it opening. Voices muffled by the distance between them and him and by the multiple cubicle walls in between him and them, talk for a few minutes. They cease. He hears soft footfalls heading toward him, and he suddenly realizes he's supposed to be working. He scoots his chair back and around toward his desk and moves his mouse to stop the screen saver.

"Simon. I'm leaving, but you won't use that as an excuse to slack, right?"

Moved the mouse just in time, Simon thinks in relief as he turns toward Mr. Confabulate. "No. No, Mr. Confabulate. I'm catching up on treatment plan applications from last week," he says as simultaneously he hopes the spreadsheet on the screen behind him is the right one. He shifts slightly to cover the monitor with his slim torso as best he can.

Mr. Confabulate regards him for a moment as a snake does a mouse. Simon's heart speeds up, yet he holds still and keeps the look of a hard worker on his face. His boss nods sharply, says, "Good, good," and tramps off. Simon listens to his footfalls fade toward the exit. Another set joins him near the office's entrance, and he hears the low tones of two male voices. The elevator dings, the doors hush open, footfalls echo on the hard elevator floor as the two men walk onto it, and then the doors slide closed. Simon stretches his ears to listen to the sudden quiet to see if anyone else is left in his area.

He doesn't hear a sound.

He swivels back around and picks up the handset from his office desk phone. He is tired of the headset. Tired of work. Tired of . . .

He punches in the familiar numbers and listens to one ring, two rings, three rings . . . Just as he is about to hang up, Priscilla gasps into the phone, "Hello?"

"Hi, Priss. It's me."

"Simon! Listen, I'm heading out to Bikram yoga."

"Right. Yes. Sorry. I forgot. It's Monday."

"No, Simon, it's Tuesday. But you're right, I normally like to start the week off right. But she postponed it till today. Really puts me off, you know. I hate when she does that."

"Oh. Sorry about that, Priss."

"No prob," she replies airily. But then asks accusingly: "Where were you on Friday, anyway? We waited for you, you know."

"Sorry, Priss. I forgot. I guess I . . . well, I was on grief leave. Gramps was on my mind a lot last week."

"I know, Simon. We all miss him," she sighs.

"It's so unreal, Priss. I can't believe he's gone. It's been over a week . . . no . . . more . . . I haven't heard from him. I keep expecting the phone to ring. I find myself staring at it, wondering why it won't ring, why it's staying silent, like it's mad at me or something. It won't let me speak to him."

"Whoa, Simon. It's just a phone." Priscilla laughs uneasily.

"I know that. But it feels like it's blocking him. I really miss him. I want to talk to him, Priss. Like today, for instance, like I'd be telling him how it went today, and he'd be telling me how to schmooze the boss better, go for that promotion. He always gives me . . . I mean . . . gave me different advice from Fred. But they both taught me the same thing, you know, just in different ways: how to give the boss what he wants so that I'll get a promotion. I've barely been in this job a month."

"Has it been that long?" Priscilla interrupts.

Simon blinks at the grey wall of his cubicle as he loses his train of thought. He replies automatically as he tries to recall where he'd been going with all his talking. "Yes. Fred got me in for an interview with the company director. But it took awhile to find me a place. They wanted me to start at the bottom rung but not too bottom."

"It's nice to have connected parents. Listen—"

"He only got me an interview, Priss. Gramps said the same thing too, lectured me on how he had to work from the ground up when he arrived in Canada. No connections for him, he said. He seemed to think I'd never make anything of myself if I got a hand up. Not a real worker, he joked once, yet he did mean it, you know. I told him that I worked hard. I remember how he stared at me, making me feel like I was one of those green grasshoppers I used to collect as a kid in jars then watch them to see what they'd do. Gramps is tough like that. And then he said the—"

"I remember. You told me, Simon. At the time. Listen—"

"I was so startled, Priss. I don't know why he said it. I hadn't even—"

"I know, Simon. I know. But listen, I gotta go. Yoga won't wait for me. The instructor is real strict about being punctual."

Simon feels the stab of her words. "Sorry, Priss. I didn't mean—"

"Yeah, no prob," Priscilla interrupts again. And then he's listening to a dial tone.

Simon removes the phone from his ear and stares at the handset as if it can tell him what just happened. Priss never hangs up on him abruptly like that.

He sighs and cradles the handset gently. He turns toward his computer. Its screen saver flashes patterns of neon-green lines into his eyes, deepening the faint green in his grey eyes. He follows the moving lines with his eyes, mesmerized. He shakes his head to release his gaze and inches up to his desk. He grabs the mouse and jerks it into action. The screen saver stops, and the spreadsheet reappears. He stares at it, trying to take in what client it's about, what the numbers are saying. At last, his mind focuses, and he's able to comprehend the figures. He releases the mouse to pull his chair closer by pulling on the edge of his desk with both of his hands. He straightens his back. He releases the edge of the desk and raises his hands. He hovers his fingers over his keyboard. And freezes in that position. His hands may be ready for action, but he is not.

A bang startles him. His fingertips drop onto the keys. He begins typing furiously. A cart rolls toward him, the bottles and mops in it thudding against each other, one wheel squeaking rhythmically. Simon keeps on typing.

The squeaking cart stops and starts and stops and starts. After a while, the cleaner pokes her nose into his cubicle and asks if she can clean. He shakes his head no, keeping his back to her, not stopping his typing, and she moves on to Isaac's cubicle. The sounds of fluids being sprayed onto surfaces and garbage cans being emptied recede from his consciousness as he drowns himself in the work at hand. He keeps typing and making decisions on claimant files, referring to Con Fable's rules in their manuals on how to reject claims as he does so, long after the cleaner has left his area and gone to the other side of the building and then onto the elevator to clean another floor. When half the lights go out automatically, leaving him in a half-light that makes it impossible to read the manuals on his desk without bending down and sticking his nose an inch from the type, he stops. He clicks off the powerbar. He rolls up the wire of his headset neatly and places the headset in its designated location. He stands and stretches. He unhooks his pea jacket from its place and shoves his arms into it. He wraps the scarf his Gramps had given him around his neck, and with hands deep in his jeans pockets, he shuffles off to the elevator.

The cold of the night air slices his face. Simon hunches into his open jacket and wanders the city streets according to where his feet take him. He finds himself at the Necropolis. Another cemetery. He stares in through its wrought-iron fence and wonders what all those corpses thought about when they were alive and not buried under cheek-by-jowl stones among leaning trees and unruly large bushes. They are so quiet in there. His mind empties of all thought as he leans against the fence's rusting painted spikes; he sinks into the quietude of the graveyard.

His muscles stiffen. Yet he remains in place, fixed on the tombstones with their engraved words and names blurred by time, ignoring the cars accelerating behind him. Slowly, slowly, the lack of movement in the place before him creeps up on his awareness and prickles the back of his neck.

He hastily pushes himself off the fence. He buttons up his jacket in a defensive gesture and hurries down the street toward the great lake that anchors the city. Abruptly he jaywalks across the road, a horn telling him off, and heads toward the densely packed apartment towers of St. James Town, its rotting white buildings looming over him, casting shadows into the no-mans land of open spaces in between them. He doesn't care that his senses are screaming danger, that the voice inside his head is telling him to get out of here. He welcomes the danger, welcomes the life of those alarm bells going off in his mind.

A shadow flits before him.

A menacing voice speaks suddenly next to him, "Hey pal, you want some?"

Simon rears back, shakes his head swiftly.

"Then whatchya doing here? Spying?"

Simon shakes his head harder at the shadow he's trying not to see and the thoughts he's trying not to think.

"What's the matter with you? You can't talk to me? You dissing me or what?"

Simon opens his mouth, but all that comes out is a croak. His legs tighten, his stomach hollows, his eyes sharpen, his heart hammers. A metallic glint gleams briefly in the dissipated photons from a far-off streetlight. *Run! Run! Run!* scream the thoughts in his head, so loudly that this time Simon obeys. Simon runs like the cross-country racer he used to be. He stops only when he finds himself at the corner leading toward the Viaduct.

He bends over, panting and grabbing his knees for support. The traffic beside him is stalled. It's the second Danforth rush hour, the one for people wanting to dine out in Greektown, to linger over drinks until midnight. The few times he's driven his parents' car, he doesn't come along here at this hour. It's better to walk or take the subway. But the TTC is not for him. Not for us, Phyllis would intone often. He and his brother and sister only took the TTC during that time of high school when they didn't have their driver's licences yet. He hadn't used public transit since then. He'd rather walk.

He straightens up haltingly, dragging his hands up his legs as he does so, until they dangle freely when he stands tall. He sighs and shrugs back into himself, shoving his hands into his jacket pockets. He ambles around the corner and onto the bridge. He'd long since grown used to the narrowness of the sidewalk, how close the cyclists zip by and how close the fast-moving cars feel. Still, he is glad that he is moving faster than anyone else right now. Gramps had encouraged him to walk. One of the nice things about living in the city, he used to say, is that you can walk anywhere. Or take the TTC, he'd whisper behind his hand, a wary eye on whichever one of Simon's parents was close by. Simon would grin at him and tell him his family didn't take the TTC. Gramps hated that attitude, but Simon couldn't see why. He'd said that they didn't have to sit on a grubby subway or jostle with the smelly hordes when they could drive. That was one of those few times that Gramps had been so angry, he'd said not a word more to him and had ignored him for the rest of that Sunday dinner evening. Simon had shrugged off Gramps's disapprobation yet had chewed over what Gramps had said about walking. He liked to stretch his legs. He'd been on the cross-country team in school and then later he'd chosen the location of his new apartment so that he could walk to where he needed to go. Whether home or the library or the store, he could walk it. The next week he'd told Gramps he'd begun walking. He wasn't borrowing his parents' 1991 Mercedes anymore. Gramps had clapped him on the back, all his animosity over Simon preferring to drive over taking the TTC gone. Simon was back in his good graces.

Honk!

Simon jumps. He looks around, blinking rapidly. Where is he? He steps to his right and bumps into the rough railings of the Viaduct's parapet. He looks down at his offended arm and, while beginning to rub it, raises his head again. He is in one of those outcroppings near the DVP, the city's exasperated name for the Don Valley Parkway. The view captures his eye, and he steps closer to the square-sculpted rail with its particles of red granite. He leans his arms on the rail's hardness and stares down and to his left, toward the white stream of headlights that stop and start on the DVP's northbound lanes. The stream of red lights heading south flow along faster. He turns his head to look to his right at the dark expanse of trees with the glittering skyscrapers rising above them. The CN Tower's sides are washed in LED pink. He drops his head and lets gravity pull it around and down to hang between his shoulders as he stares unseeingly at the ground.

The ground seems to rise up toward him. He blinks his eyes into focus. Dark shapes appear among darker shapes, all seeming to wave at him. They tug at him to join them. He sinks into their pleasant pull and moves imperceptibly toward them.

He lunges backward.

He is safe nowhere.

He takes another step backward and slips off the sidewalk and onto the bicycle path.

Angry bicycle bells ring at him. Simon stumbles and weaves. A bicycle grazes his backside and pushes him onto his hands and knees back onto the sidewalk.

"Watch where you're going!" the cyclist shouts as she pedals away.

Simon pushes himself up carefully to a standing position. He brushes off his knees and wipes his hands together to get all the grit off. Once more, he is facing that lake-side view and that treacherous ground that calls to him, that waits for him. He thinks about it.

Suddenly, in horror, he swivels on the balls of his feet and propels himself away. He speeds up into a jog. He jogs faster and faster until he hits a run. He runs and runs and runs toward home.

7

CLUBBING

“Priss! Guess what I found?”

"What?"

"The Suicides."

"The what?"

"The Suicides."

"What's that? Is it like a grisly murder series?" Priscilla asks.

"No, no. You gave it to me."

"I did?"

"Yes."

The wireless connection's soundlessness is her puzzled answer. Simon worries she's gone. He speaks anxiously, hoping her voice will answer him, "You don't remember?"

"Nooo," she says, her voice telling him she's trying to remember. "No, I don't. When did I do that?"

"I think when we first met. There's no date on it. But listen, this is what you wrote: Dearest Simon, I missed my Papa so much that when I saw this, I had to buy it. But then I met you, and I no longer needed it. But it'll perk up your collection. Love Priscilla."

"Oh."

"Do you remember that?"

"Um, I guess," she replies.

"I . . . I hadn't realized I meant that much to you, Priss."

"Well, you do, Simon. I mean, we've been going out forever. I don't go out forever with just any guy, you know," she giggles.

Simon blushes and stammers, "I . . . I . . . I'm sorry, Priss. I didn't know. And . . . and I feel badly that I haven't read it yet. I mean, I have now . . . well, that is . . . ," Simon trails off. Then he says all in a rush, "I will read it all again, I promise."

"That's okay, Simon. You should forget about it. Throw it out."

"No!" he replies horrified. "No! It's a book—"

"Meh," Priscilla interrupts. "Poetry from the past." Priscilla trills, "Forget the past, Simon. Throw it out."

Simon frowns at his bookcase. He says, "I thought you didn't remember it."

"I do. Now, I mean. Well, thinking about it, it's come back, like, you know?"

Simon nods as if Priss can see him. "But I can't throw it out, Priss. You gave it to me. It meant something to you. I want to treasure it. For you."

"No, not for me. Don't do it for me."

"Why not?"

"You want to do something for me, throw it out," she says tersely. "It's not a good book Simon. I gave it to you because I . . . well . . . it doesn't matter. Throw it out."

Simon purses his lips at the phone. He can't throw it out. He won't throw it out. Her high-pitched voice startles him. "Are you going to throw it out, Simon?"

"No."

"Please, Simon? Please? For me? I wish you'd forget all about it."

"How can I, Priss? You hardly talked about your Papa. This is my way to get to know you better and honour your gift. What was he like?"

"How should I know, Simon? I was four when he died, remember? Don't you remember? You forgot about the book, and you even forgot how old I was?" she shouts.

Simon swallows guiltily. "No, no, I didn't forget. It just . . . it just escaped my mind, Priss." Shame suffuses his face, and he wants to pull the iPhone away from his ear, wants to hide, anything to escape the wheel of guilt spinning in his head. He doesn't know how he can make amends; it feels so awful forgetting that she'd been only four. How could she remember anything about her Papa? Yet he feels this vague sense swimming up into his consciousness that she does remember something. An urgency to know her father fills him. The need to hear what she remembers about him, drives him. He wants to hit his head with the iPhone over and over for his self-centredness, but he also wants to keep the rectangular device glued to his ear to hear anything she remembers about Papa. He beseeches, "I knew you were four. Really, I did, Priss. I'm sorry I never asked you about him before and thought today . . . that . . . maybe . . . you could tell me about him? I know, Priss, I shouldn't ask with you not remembering . . . ," his voice trails off.

"It's okay, Simon. Really. It's not like you don't have a dad. I guess it's kind of strange for you with having a dad and all, not knowing what it's like not having one. I mean, how would you know what it's like?" Priscilla ends lightly.

"I hadn't thought of it like that. Fred is so present in my life. He's always there."

"There you go."

"And I cannot imagine a life without him dominating the dining room table, telling us what to do and where we're going wrong, him and Phyllis sparring . . ."

"Yeah. My friends talk about their parents fighting all the time. It's normal, eh?"

"I had this vision of your Papa being this nice guy who loved your Ma and you and didn't want to leave. And how devastating that must've been losing him."

"Uh, yeah. Hey, about tonight—"

"What was he like?"

Priscilla sighs heavily into his ear hot against the phone. Simon can almost feel her breath. He swallows and quavers, "I'm sorry, Priss. I gather you don't want to talk about him? But I just . . . I thought my silence must've seemed to you like I didn't want to know, that I didn't care, that he didn't matter to me because he was dead and gone, when it should've mattered because he was your Papa. And even though he's dead, his life matters to you and so it should to me. He doesn't have to die in our memories and lives."

"He is dead," Priscilla says with finality in her voice. "I don't even remember him. Not really. So yeah, he no longer matters. Not to me, anyway."

"But he does, Priss. He does! He was your Papa. You said you missed him."

"Yeah. I did. Then. I don't now. Forget him, Simon. Forget the book. Forget you read that. I was out of my mind, really out of my mind, when I wrote that."

"How can I forget when you wrote how much I meant to you, that you no longer needed this book because you had me?"

"It was a stupid book to get. I shouldn't have bought it," she says in a flat voice. "And I shouldn't have given it to you." She suddenly inhales angrily, "I don't know what I was thinking! I told you to throw it out. If I mean that much to you, you'll do what I say!"

"Tell me the little you remember about your Papa first. Please?"

"There's nothing to tell. I don't want to talk about him. Let's talk—"

"Why not? You must remember him since you said you missed him. How can you not still miss him?"

"Easy. I work. I have other friends. Ma is still alive. I have cousins and Aunts and Uncles. I don't need him to be alive. I don't have to pretend he's alive anymore. Why won't you listen to me? I thought you were different from my other boyfriends. Hey," she lilts, "Why don't you tell me about your father?"

Simon sidesteps her question and says: "Remembering isn't pretending, Priss."

"It is to me. And you need to stop it with your grandfather."

"We're not talking about him. We're talking about your Papa."

"Oh yeah? We're talking about your Gramps. All this sudden interest in Papa isn't cause you care, Simon. You're just like my other boyfriends. It's all about you, you, you! It's all about you and Gramps and you pretending he's still alive. How's that for pretending, eh?" Priscilla triumphs. Her pitch drops. She says flatly, "This is boring. He's dead. Move on."

Simon's heart slams against his ribs, bang, bang, bang. His breathing shallows as spears of pain assault his lungs.

"C'mon Simon," Priscilla wheedles. "You need to get back into life. That's what I learned after I met you. Thinking about him is only going to keep you stuck in the past. He's dead. I got over Papa dying. You can, too. And you know, it's not like he was your dad; he was just your grandfather."

Simon chokes.

Priscilla hurries on, "I know you guys were close. But, really Simon, it isn't the same as losing one of your parents. You'll see."

Simon's head swims. His legs lose strength. His body drops, and his tailbone sinks into the edge of the couch's sagging cushions and slides forward into space. His back rubs against the facing edges of the cushions, against the couch's frame. He lands on the floor with a thump.

Priscilla doesn't hear his fall through the phone. She switches gears abruptly and asks chirpily: "Hey, are you coming clubbing tonight? The whole gang's been asking where you are. It's getting hard making excuses for you, you know. C'mon, Simon, you gotta get out, join us, have fun. I know you miss your Gramps and all. But life goes on. You gotta get back into it, not be such a downer. The longer you stay in the past, the worse you'll be."

"Right," Simon croaks.

Priscilla sighs in relief. "Super. We'll see you tonight?"

Simon replies, "Yes," as his thoughts and feelings flee into an abyss of nothingness.

She hangs up.

Simon depresses his iPhone's power button. His fingers release, and the black rectangular device falls out of his slack hand onto the floor. Simon sags. He can no longer resist the pain that's like a river of needles speeding through his arteries and breaking through their walls. His hands slide off his legs; his knees drop until his legs lie straight. His feet rotate outwards. He sits for long empty minutes. Finally, like an automaton, he stands up and walks into his bedroom to pull out his clubbing clothes. He doesn't see them, only knows where they are from habit. He dresses and leaves, picking up his iPhone from the floor automatically on the way out.

He walks out of his quiet neighbourhood and downhill to Queen Street until he spots a taxi. He hails it. He gets in, gives the driver the location, and stares unseeingly at the passing urban-scape of Queen Street's old brick buildings then the modernity of the Eaton Centre then the imperious tall buildings around University Avenue and then the buzzing retail ones on the Queen West strip. The driver's voice lands him back into the present, into awareness, with a whump.

"Pardon?"

"I'm letting you off here. Or you can pay me to sit in traffic until we get to The Alligator. It's your money. Your choice, sir."

"No, no, it's okay," Simon says as he digs into first one then the other of his shiny, tight black pants' pockets and pulls out his money clip. He peels out two tens and a five, puts them in the hand of the driver, and leaps out. He strides south to Adelaide, the noise of cars and people and pumping music rising to greet him as he approaches the Entertainment District. He weaves in and out of the drunk-happy partiers in their tight, short skirts and tight, ankle-skimming pants, with their too-skimpy tops in the cold November air, until he reaches The Alligator. He smiles briefly when he spots Priscilla at the same time that she sees him. She waves. Her reddened lips part, revealing her white teeth shining in the artificially lit night. Somehow she persuades everyone to move out of his way and the bouncer to let them both inside. His heart syncopates to her delight in seeing him, each beat pulsing through his arteries, melting the needling pain into wanted warmth.

She shouts in his ear as they enter the darkness scissored by lasers and ear-fracturing music: "The rest are here already. I said I'd wait for you." She threads her arm through his and smiles widely up at him, her red lips an invitation to party. "I'm glad you're here."

Simon cringes against the high volume, once so familiar, now an alien sound. But when he looks down into his girlfriend's face upturned to his, he feels lighter and smiles back. All that matters is the here and now, he tells himself.

The here and now.

Priscilla pulls him toward the bar of pulsing blues and reds that chase each other along its length. It's separated from the main floor by a floor-to-ceiling glass wall. The wall muffles some of the beating sound, to Simon's relief; still Priscilla must yell their order: a Manhattan for her and a Coffee Vodka Martini for him. He doesn't stop her. He hasn't drunk any alcohol since Gramps died. Vodka tonic is his drink, like it had been for Gramps.

He drifts into the memory of the first time Gramps had made him that libation.

Gramps had given him precise instructions as Simon had mixed the tonic. Gramps had made him repeat every one of those instructions back before allowing him to follow it and then listen to the next instruction. When finished, Simon had handed the tonic to him, and Gramps had sipped it and thrown it down the sink. Try again, he'd instructed Simon. Over and over, Simon had tried. On the fifth time, he'd slowed down his movements, pausing his hands to listen to each instruction with his eyes on his Gramps's eyes and his ears attuned to his grandfather's every tone. That attempt had satisfied Gramps that Simon knew how to make a decent vodka tonic. After nodding and smiling at the pleasure of sipping Simon's decent vodka tonic, Gramps had handed him the glass filled with the innocuous-looking clear liquid. Simon had taken his first sip. For a moment, nothing. And then it hit. His eyes had sprung open. Then they'd squeezed shut as he grimaced and shaken his head in pain that had burned his mind and tongue and esophagus while Gramps had thrown his head back and roared. Simon had put the glass back on the drinks cart and waited for Gramps to settle down. When he had, Simon had declared, "I don't like it. I'm not drinking it."

Gramps had chuckled and picked up the glass. He handed it back to Simon, who had reluctantly taken it again. Gramps had said, "That was exactly my reaction when I had my first one. But you'll see, you'll like it."

"I doubt it," Simon had retorted acerbically.

Gramps had chuckled. He'd flung his head up in a tiny movement toward Simon. "Take a small sip."

Gramps had been more stubborn than he and under those amused eyes, Simon had obeyed. He'd taken a smaller sip, and to his surprise, the pain was less. He'd tasted another few drops and had liked the feel of the liquid going down. Since then, as Gramps had said, he'd been hooked.

"Hey!" Priscilla jostles his arm. "Where are you? Your drink is almost ready."

Simon focusses his eyes on the bartender who is holding up his fat fluted stemmed glass filled with a clear liquid and in his other hand is holding a small, frosted glass pitcher filled with a concoction of coffee and coffee syrup. Whisps rising up from the pitcher testify to its freezing temperature. He pours the thick black coffee mixture lazily into the fluted glass in a figure-eight motion. The black turns brown at its edges and creates twisted streams that snake lazily through the clear liquid down to the bottom of the flute, where the streams gather themselves into a glistening pool of brew underneath clarity.

The bartender sets the glass down gently in front of him as the last of the coffee tendrils are joining the pool. Simon stares at it mesmerized. He hears Priscilla call out, "C'mon Simon," as she clicks away in her jaunty stiletto heels. He reaches out for his glass and delicately takes the stem between his thumb and two of his fingers. He raises it and holds it up to the light. It has been a long time since he'd drunk this deceptively powerful concoction. Priss's favourite for him, he recalls. He carries it over to the glass panel that separates the bar area from the dance floor and watches the gyrating bodies on the other side. He glances down at his glass and, almost against his will, raises it to his lips and sips. First the smoothness comes, then the sharp bite of coffee and the compromise of the syrup, and last the burn. He closes his eyes in surrender. He shudders. He opens his eyes and seeks out Priscilla as he sips again at his drink, allowing the Coffee Vodka Martini to slither its magic down his throat, before sipping again. The martini sluices the remaining needles of pain in his blood.

Simon relaxes and finally finds Priscilla with his eyes. She has made her way unerringly to their group, not far from the glass wall that separates them. He flings back his head to drain the last drop from his fluted glass and turns back to the bar. Barely has he set the glass down then a bartender comes by and swipes it off the counter. Oblivious, Simon heads to the end of the bar and circles around the glass wall. The full volume of the DJ's beat hits his ears. This is his life, he reminds himself. He stretches his lips. He welcomes the beating, overwhelming electronics that push their way rhythmically into his heart.

Simon wends through the thrusting, jerking crowd toward Priscilla, shots of red and blue blinding him on every thump of the dance music. She and their group are huddled close together so that they can hear each other's bellows over the cacophony of the club. The phony happiness creeps around Simon as he approaches them; it pokes at him to join in. He does. Priscilla threads her arm through his and pulls him close. Someone hollers, "Let's dance!" Priscilla immediately lets go of his arm and grabs his hand. She leads him to the middle of the dance floor. She lets go and thrusts her arms upward, eyes closed in ecstasy, her hips jerking side to side. But Simon feels no desire, no contagion of beat moving his feet. Where did the warmth go? He forces his mind into the beat away from the needles of pain streaming back into his blood. His body obeys the music in the accustomed Friday-night way, and he is soon gyrating at Priscilla lost in her own dance.

The electronic drums thumping through the people, the sweaty, perfumed bodies bumping into him yet staying apart, the shooting lights, the obsidian floor swallowing up his feet—they batter at him in their insistence on being happy. They overtake him. He loses himself into the demand to revel in the adrenaline rush, into the belief that this is the best part of the week.

The martini has vanished the sharp pain.

One dance version of a popular song morphs into another and another. The pairs in the group coalesce. The dance goes on and on. And then without thinking about it, without realizing what he's doing, gradually Simon spirals away in time to the beat until he is on the outside of the circle.

No one has noticed as each dances in their own self.

He keeps spiralling away, throwing his arms up and down and to the side in tune with his feet, until he finds himself at the exit.

He drops his arms and stumbles out of the club into the damp November air. He bumps blindly into a drunk man.

"Hey, watch where you're going!" The man tries to swing at him and misses. A burly policeman grabs the man's arm and wrenches it behind his back, while Simon disappears quickly into the crowd that's looking for pizza, for different cocktails, for another club. Reaching John Street, he turns left and jogs away from The Alligator, away from the Friday night clubbing to . . . he doesn't know where. He decelerates to a fast walk. He walks and walks until he can no longer hear the hard beats, the drunken shouts, the clip clop of towering police horses, or even the honks of impatient cars. He doesn't slow down until he reaches the quiet residential streets with their narrow three-story brick houses with their front porch lights here and there lit up and their occasional window glowing blue.

He halts and leans against a gate. He closes his eyes and lets his mind rest in the neighbourhood peace of Toronto. After a while, he sets off again but at an unhurried pace, not sure where he's going, but knowing he cannot return.

8

REMEMBRANCE

Dressed in his best black suit, his only black suit, underneath his little-worn nightshade coat, Simon walks behind his parents, his brother, and his sister in the stream of people entering the imposing church his parents attend. A sidesperson welcomes them in in hushed tones and hands them each a thin bulletin made of azure folded paper. Clutching the bulletin in his right hand, he follows his parents and brother and sister to his parents' pew, one near the front but not too near and on the left side of the centre aisle. It has been a long time since Simon and his siblings have attended church regularly, though Phyllis and Fred rarely miss a Sunday. Phyllis slides into the pew first while Fred stands beside it waiting for his children to file in, eldest first, youngest last.

Gramps hated this day.

That memory jumps into Simon's head, of Gramps's almost ritualistic mutterings about being forced to attend, being forced to fall into line with his daughter's wishes. The memory's sudden appearance vacuums out his breath. The pain churns his blood. He stumbles. Sarah looks back at him.

"What's the matter with you?" she hisses. She grabs Simon's arm and pulls him into the pew. He falls into his seat and slaps the back of the hard mahogany bench. The hand holding the bulletin spasms. His cashmere blend suit and merino wool coat muffle the shock. Sarah rolls her eyes, and Fred slides in to sit next to him, effectively hemming him in. After a moment of sitting stock still, Simon creaks forward to slip the crinkled bulletin into the half-empty prayer book holder screwed to the back of the pew in front of him. He doesn't need the bulletin. He never looks at it; it holds no interest for him with its announcements and rote ritual hymns and prayers. He strips off his supple leather gloves and folds them in half and then half again, the leather giving way easily to his movements. After a while, he realizes that he's folded them into such a tiny package, they've become akin to a hard ball. He stuffs them hurriedly into his left pocket.

"Hey!" Sarah protests as he elbows her accidentally.

"Sorry," he mumbles.

She glares at him.

Fred growls, "The trouble with you two is you don't behave like adults."

Simon bows his head and shuts his eyes. He closes himself off from his family and from this place, this place of meaningless words and obedient bowing and standing and sitting for no reason that he has ever been able to see.

Fred's commanding hand under his elbow, pushing him up, springs open his eyelids. Before his knees straighten, Fred lets go, and Simon drops then lurches forward into the pew back in front of him. He rocks the pew, and the woman in front of him twists her head around to give him a stern look. He smiles a weak apology and straightens himself up carefully. Fred remains impassive beside him, and Simon dares not look at his face. He knows the tiny smile is there.

By this time, the congregation is well into warbling the first hymn. The organ's deep notes vibrate off the echoing walls and sing into Simon's heart. The organ's power holds his body in thrall. The organist is skilled, Simon notes somewhere in his head, as he always does. The church has held fast onto their organist for the last twenty-five years, through three changes of ministers—each change led by his mother, who would fill their Sunday dinners in those days with the politicking of choosing a new minister to lead the church.

Gramps's voice charges into his head: "That organist is the only good thing about this blasted service." Gramps had said that every year.

Simon quivers at the memory as the short opening hymn ends in the organ's fading notes. The congregation sits down with a chorus of groaning pews and muffled coughs. The minister strides to the front of the nave, his flowing cassock billowing out as he leaps up the three shallow steps that lead to the altar. Simon blinks. Shouldn't he have been in the procession? He shoots a sidelong glance at Fred, whose lips are twitching. He sends his eyes left to Phyllis, whose rigid profile tells him that the minister had breached protocol. Simon returns his attention to the man with the unlined face and thick, brown hair standing atop the steps with the altar behind him. The young minister clears his throat as he faces the people and waits a beat. He begins the service.

"We are gathered here today to remember those who sacrificed their lives . . ."

Simon hears Gramps's acerbic voice roaring into his inner ear, drowning out the real-in-the-flesh minister's voice: "Not just those who served. There is us civilians who sacrificed, too. But do they remember us? No sirree."

One time, when he had still been a brash boy with no fear, Simon had dared to ask, "What sacrifice?" Gramps had shot him a fierce look that had quailed his heart, but he had squeaked out how could he know if he didn't ask. Gramps had glowered at him.

Simon had held his breath, and then Gramps had nodded slowly, thoughtfully.

"Please stand for the singing of O Canada."

The congregation rises up with a united whoosh of air and a harmony of feet shifting on the floor to support their collective obeisance. Simon lags behind by only a second. Fred touches him shoulder to shoulder, a small but hard touch. Simon keeps his eyes forward facing. And that's when Simon notices that three of the Sunday School regulars have taken the flags off the wall and have marched them to the front centre of the church. Somehow he had missed that procession. The two girls and one boy are standing as straight as can be, holding the flags, keeping them off the floor. The minister watches them intently from his perch at the top of the steps.

The organ bellows the opening stanza of the national anthem as the congregation listens. The organist pauses. Expectancy tenses the air. The organist crashes through the waiting breaths with the opening notes of the first verse. The minister begins to sing with gusto. The congregation joins in, Simon along with them. The music resounds through his body, and his voice magnifies the power of his emotions. Gramps had always had a tear in his eye during the singing of the national anthem. Simon had never known why until the day he'd visited him in the hospital after his heart attack.

"I'm so proud to be Canadian," Gramps had declared in his newly raspy voice. It was like the heart attack had snuffed the energy out of his vocal cords to compensate for it not having snuffed out his body. Gramps sounding feeble and next to death had scared Simon. After each and every visit, as soon as he'd left the hospital, he'd suck in a deep breath of air and push that fear out into the city where it belonged. Fear was death, and death didn't belong in him. He wanted no part of it, and he didn't want to think about it. Back then.

Simon had laughed at Gramps's declaration of pride, and Gramps had glowered at him.

"We came here to get away from the war and privation of England, you pampered boy, and Canada welcomed us with open arms. Don't laugh."

Simon had swallowed and hastily apologized. He'd fallen silent, had shuffled his feet as he tried to figure out where to look, what to say, until finally he'd shifted his gaze back to the bed. Gramps was lying sunken into the pillows with his eyes closed.

A pause in the anthem brings Simon back to the present. The congregation's confident, united singing of the first verse falters as the organist and minister lead them into the second verse. They all must refer to the bulletin for the words. Reluctantly, Simon retrieves his bulletin from where he'd stuck it, flips it open, and finds the second verse. Fred says underneath the singing voices, "A little slow today, eh, Simon? I don't think Phyllis would like that. But I won't tell." Simon joins in hastily:

"Ruler supreme, who hearest humble prayer,
Hold our Dominion in thy loving care;
Help us to find, O God, in thee
A lasting, rich reward,
As waiting for the better Day,
We ever stand on guard.
God keep our land glorious and free!
O Canada, we stand on guard for thee.
O Canada, we stand on guard for thee."

The first time he'd seen that verse, he was a teen. He'd rolled his eyes and smirked at Sarah. Gramps had elbowed him hard in the ribs. He'd never disrespected those words of the national anthem again, not in front of Gramps, anyway. And even though Gramps is not beside him, he can still feel Gramps's sharp elbow stabbing his side, still experience that sense of a bigger, wiser man telling him wordlessly to show respect, to always show respect.

The organ stops; the congregation remains standing. The church falls into a hush.

The girl holding the Canadian flag leads the other two holding the neighbouring flags in lowering them to the ground. The minister looks apprehensive as he watches the children. But the girl takes hold of the far edge of the flag and pulls it toward the staff so that it doesn't touch the carpeted floor. She whispers to the boy on her left to do the same. The other girl has copied her already.

From the back of the church, a tenor voice carries through the assembled people and on to the minister and children as it recites the names of the fallen, the men who had died serving King and country during the two world wars. The voice pauses infinitesimally between the reading of each name. The voice falls silent; its last echoes die away. The minister closes his eyes and bows his head. They stand for two minutes. Old memories, new respect tense the still air.

In the silence, Simon remembers.

One night Gramps had gotten drunk. He'd graduated from cardiac rehab and had decided to celebrate with a glass of his vodka tonic. He'd slipped away from the family talking in the living room after dinner. No one had noticed except Simon. Simon had followed him to the basement where Gramps had had his lair, as he called it. The old and the young had sunk into the two club chairs, a table between them holding the vodka and tonic bottles. Gramps had declared defiantly that one glass was not going to do him any harm and had mixed each of them their accustomed drink. Simon hadn't protested, even when Gramps had mixed a second one. It was on his third drink that Gramps had let loose.

"It was a ghastly bright day when Mummy decided we had to move. We lived in the country, away from all the fighting, or so we thought. So we thought . . ."

Simon didn't say a word and sipped his drink as quietly as he could.

Gramps suddenly roused himself and spoke again as if he hadn't petered out: "Oh sure, we billeted the Canadian boys in our home. Mummy had put three to a room in our tall High Street house. They didn't mind the cramped quarters. Oh no, we didn't in those days. We were used to small spaces. Not like today. Yes, not like today . . ."

Gramps tossed back a large mouthful of his drink, swilled the alcohol around his tongue, and swallowed. Hard. "They were always cheerful those boys, teasing Mummy over the breakfast table, flirting with Pat, my older sister. Mummy finally had enough of that. She told off those boys good. She told them that if they didn't stop flirting with her daughter, they'd be out on their you-know-whats. They behaved after that," Gramps chuckled. "But when Mummy wasn't looking, one of them would slip my sister a wink. He was sweet on Pat."

Gramps smiled in remembrance. He made himself another drink, sipped contentedly, and settled down further into his black leather chair.

"And Pat was sweet on him. But neither dared tell Mummy. Pat was only sixteen then, you see."

Simon wasn't particularly interested, but somehow it was pleasant sitting there listening to the old man drone on, and he'd found himself wanting to ask Gramps how old he'd been but not wanting to interrupt.

Gramps had laid his head back on his chair and gazed up at the ceiling. "Yup. They were sweet on each other."

He fell silent for a long time. Simon thought he'd fallen asleep when Gramps startled him with the words: "It was ghastly."

"What was?" Simon blurted out.

"The sun."

"The sun?"

"It was the sun that made it worse. We weren't used to the sun, you see. England is a bit greyer than here, you know. Well, you wouldn't know, would you? But it was always cloudy and rainy. And that day the sun came out. Not even a whiff of a cloud disturbed the blue sky. It had perked us right up. It had rained and rained and rained, even longer than usual in our bit of the country. We had chattered about the day, and Pat and her fellow had gone off to work together. I don't know how she did it, but she'd convinced Mummy to let her work at the air force base where the Canadians were stationed. They'd fly in and out of there and repair the tattered planes when they came in from a sortie across the channel. It was safer where we were to do that than right at the south coast. They also did some training . . . I think." Gramps squinted, trying to retrieve an uncertain memory. He shook his head, "doesn't matter," he muttered and sipped his tonic. He shifted down further into his chair and continued: "So you see, we were happy that day. It was a Friday. A good day. We were all looking forward to the weekly dance, even me. It would be the first time I was allowed to go, even though Mummy said I was too young. But Pat had persuaded Mummy. Oh, she had worked on her for months, had Pat. And finally Mummy seeing the sun come out had relented that very morning.

"I was doing the chores when it happened. It came out of the sky with a scream. We all heard it in the house; through those damn thick brick walls we heard it. The earth shook as it thumped into the ground. It was like the very air went still. And then whoosh. The explosion rattled the old windows. I remember a glass fell over on the table and rolled off it. It shattered, and I ran over it, hearing it crunch into little pieces under my boots. I was running after Mummy, you see. She'd looked out the living room window when we heard that damn thump. She somehow knew what had happened. She ran out of the house, leaving the front door wide open. She never left that door open. I chased after her.

"Other doors opened all along the High Street, and women and old men and us boys too young to fight, we all ran out. We were all running for the base. I saw the last of the fireball disappear into the thick black smoke as we ran toward it, not thinking what we were doing, only thinking about our loved ones." Gramps looked into his glass balefully. "That damn fireball. It billowed up higher and fatter like some great evil thing. Mummy ran so fast, I couldn't keep up. I pumped my arms as hard as I could. But it was like she had wings on her feet, and she outpaced everyone, even the men. I couldn't keep up. I couldn't. My heart was pounding so hard," Gramps pounded the arm of his chair as he said each word: "Pounding, pounding, pounding because I suddenly cottoned on to where the plane had crashed. You see, Pat was there. Her fellow was due to fly out that morning.

"Everything slowed down. Then Mummy began screaming. God, it was awful." Gramps's hand shook as he raised his glass to his mouth. He lowered it again and slashed at his eyes with the back of his free hand. "Mummy screamed Pat's name. Over and over, she screamed it. Her scream stretched out and got lower as it reached me. The fire engine bells began to clang, and a siren went off at the base. I think it was already screaming, but I hadn't heard it over the pounding of my heart and boots. The siren, the bells, they echoed in my head like terrifying harmonies. I wanted to shut my ears. The crackle of grass sounded unnaturally loud as a plane on fire shot off little fires that flickered outward across the field toward the running men. Their far-away shouts came on the wind toward me along with the smell of burning flesh. I'd never smelled it before. I knew what it was though. It was horrid. And ghastly. And I didn't want to go there. But I had to. Mummy was going, and I had to be with her. I was the man of the house. Father had said so when he'd left. I was afraid, so afraid. I tried to run faster. I thought my lungs were going to burst. Fear made my boots so heavy, and they thudded like that plane had every time one of my feet hit the pavement. I wanted to stop. I didn't want to see. I wanted to catch up to Mummy more though. I couldn't be alone. I feared being alone."

Gramps paused and wiped both of his eyes with the fingers of his left hand, like he was trying to pinch out that memory of his day, while he tightened his hold on his drinks glass. Simon's heart was thumping; he had unconsciously moved to the edge of his seat and was hanging on to his glass between his legs, hardly daring to breathe.

"That's when Pat staggered out of the field of smoke. She looked stunned. I wiped my eyes because I thought I was hallucinating, and my hands turned black. I couldn't figure out at all why they were black. Suddenly, Mummy was there in the field holding Pat as Pat stared sightlessly over her shoulder, soot patching her face, her arms, everywhere. Her hair stuck out like someone had taken a shredder to it. She was a mess. But she was alive. Time suddenly sped up to normal again, and I was there too. We hugged and hugged. Under that blasted sun, we hugged, we were so glad to be alive. And then Pat said: he's gone."

Gramps had gulped the dregs of his vodka tonic then. Simon hadn't been able to speak. A lump the size of a baseball had stuck in his throat. His chest had burned, and his eyes had flamed in unshed tears. Gramps had laid his head back, closed his eyes, and shortly after, a soft snore had emanated from him. Simon had grabbed Gramps's empty glass from his relaxing hand before it fell to the floor. Along with the almost empty bottles, he'd placed it carefully on the drinks cart so as not to wake his grandfather. Simon had shifted back into his chair slowly, soundlessly and laid his own head back. He'd sat there wide awake for hours, keeping vigil over his Gramps.

A tug on his sleeve and a warning stare from Sarah, yanks Simon back into the present. The entire congregation is sitting but him. The minister is studiously ignoring him, which makes it all the more obvious he is the only one left standing. The Remembrance Day part of the service is over, and the minister is moving on.

Simon sits down and folds the nightshade tails of his coat over his knees. He gloms on to the stained glass window behind the altar with its hard-edged depiction of the crucified Jesus and blinks hard.

9

MELANIE IS GONE

Simon slips off his pea jacket and hangs it up on the solid wooden hanger in the hall closet. Remembrance Day has faded away along with November. The air is chillier now. Simon grasps his scarf to unwind it from around his neck then pauses. He looks down at his hand holding the part of the scarf that dangles down his right side. He lifts that end toward his face and stares at the uneven fringe. He drops it and leaves his scarf on. It makes him feel secure, like he is not alone.

He follows the murmur of voices as they lead him from the hallway in to the living room and saunters in. He spots his mother a hair after she spots him and his togs. He braces himself.

"What on earth are you wearing, Simon?"

"Jeans," he replies, hooking his thumbs into his pockets.

His mother's eyes roam up from the offending denim encasing his legs, up over his well-worn scarf, and up into his grey-green irises. He stares back, not caring of her disapproval. A lot of things suddenly don't matter to him anymore in his new detached state. He'd stopped clubbing every Friday night with Priscilla after that night he'd left abruptly. And he doesn't miss it. He misses her though . . . a bit. He wants to be with her, yet he wants to be with nobody. He still attends Sunday dinners because he has always gone to his parents' house on Sundays; but today he hadn't had the energy to change into the obligatory suit for Phyllis. Why does it matter?

Phyllis clamps her lips tight. He remains standing as nonchalantly as he can under her disapprobation; but her disapproval begins to penetrate his shut-down shell. He shifts his weight from one foot to the other. Maybe he should have changed into his suit, put the energy into ironing his white shirt's cuffs, and inserted the silver cufflinks with their discreet plaid pattern. Yet he can't back down now: he is aware in the periphery of his sight that his entire family is watching him. Fred is studiously focussing on the fire, yet a small smile belies his seemingly total focus on the flames that dance over the logs. Michael and Sarah are openly grinning, like spectators at a gladiator circus, the winner already chosen and known.

"I'll allow you this once, Simon. But if you show up in jeans again, you can leave."

"Yes, Phyllis."

Fred says, "Now that you've heard your mother, go get your drink." Simon dutifully walks over to the drinks cart. He stops. He stares down at the crystal decanters brimming with jewel tones of whisky and red wine and the clarity of vodka. A wire-bound spritzer bottle stands ready nearby. Crystal whisky glasses nestle next to the crystal goblets for red wine, waiting to be filled up. They all gleam clean in the low lights of evening at his parents'. At the far end of the cart, little white plates offer wedges of lime and lemon, every wedge the exact same size and cut.

"C'mon, Simon. What are you waiting for? Get your drink and join us already. Michael has some delicious gossip," Sarah enjoins.

"I do not," Michael retorts.

"Yes, you do. I ran into Penelope who told me all about it. But I want to hear from your mouth, Michael, the horse's mouth."

"Haha."

As he listens to their back-and-forth drama, Simon continues to contemplate and reject every drink before him. He doesn't even feel like plain seltzer. He shrugs, and sliding his hands deep into his cotton pockets, he ambles back to his bickering siblings. Sarah is relentless in her badgering of Michael "to spill."

"Why do you want to listen to gossip, Sarah?" Simon interrupts her as he approaches them.

"What other kind of conversation is interesting?"

"Lots of things."

"Like what?"

Simon shrugs.

Sarah turns full toward him and contemplates his still visage for a moment. She says: "You've gotten to be so serious, Simon. Priss tells me you don't go clubbing with her anymore. She's wondering if you're losing interest."

"That's between me and her," he replies without emotion.

"Well, you're no fun. I can't even get you to tell all," Sarah pouts. "I told Priss I'd find out what was up. So what's up?"

"Nothing."

"Of course there's something. You don't have a drink in your hand. Trying to be the odd duck, are you, Simon? Trying to make us feel like lushes?"

"He doesn't have to try hard to do that with you Sarah," Michael retorts dryly. "What drink number are you on?" He waves his right hand toward the drinks cart, stained ice cubes tinkling against the inside walls of his crystal tumbler. "Melanie had to refill the decanters after your foray through them."

Sarah slaps Michael playfully on the shoulder, "You should talk. I think that's your second whisky, isn't it?"

Michael grins in reply.

Simon turns his head away to see what his parents are up to. Phyllis has joined Fred by the fire, and their heads lean in toward each other. He frowns. He hasn't seen them look like a couple fond of each other in . . . he frowns harder as he strives to recall and fails. Shrugging to himself, he returns his attention to his sibling group and gesturing with his head toward their parents, asks sotto voce, "What's up with them?"

"Who's gossiping now?" Sarah leers.

"I'm not gossiping."

"Sure. That's cause you're a man."

Simon opens his mouth to retort and then shuts it. Maybe his question is gossip. But they're his parents, and something is up. That could affect him. Is that gossip? He doesn't know what to think. He shakes his head at all his heavy thinking. And suddenly he doesn't want to know.

Michael growls, "I think it's something to do with Melanie."

"Melanie?"

Michael drains his whisky tumbler in one final gulp. He lowers it as he says: "C'mon. Phyllis will be calling us to the table shortly."

"Melanie isn't here to call us in for dinner," Phyllis speaks across the room to the three of them, her children, as she pulls away from Fred. "But it's time we went in. Sarah, help me bring in the dishes. You boys will clear up when we've finished eating. Go sit down."

The three men obey as the two women vanish from the living room, Phyllis's heels clicking down the hallway to the kitchen. Fred, Michael, and Simon walk through the connecting door into the dining room and sit in their accustomed places. The table has already been set. They pick up their napkins where they lie on the table, shake them out, and place them on their laps. They wait. And speak not a word to each other. They each stare into the distance, communing privately with their own thoughts. But Simon doesn't like his. He jumps up, grabs the full water jug, and fills everyone's water glasses with the icy liquid. The heavy jug is considerably lighter when he is done. He doesn't bother going in to the kitchen to refill it because he knows his family is light on water, heavy on wine. Simon sits back down. Seconds tick by, tick, tick, tick. The dining room's nineteenth-century wall clock loudens in Simon's ears.

Whoosh. Phyllis and Sarah steam into the dining room carrying trays bearing the serving dishes. They lay the platter and serving bowls heaped with food on the table and then put the empty trays on the buffet at the end of the room.

"Start serving yourselves. We will have to make do in what I understand is called family-style dining until Melanie returns," Phyllis instructs them all.

Fred picks up the platter of fried chicken and, using the tongs, helps himself to two thighs. He passes the platter on to Michael, who takes a breast for himself and then passes the platter on to Simon, who helps himself to a couple of wings.

"Is that all you're going to have, Simon?" Phyllis questions him, her thin grey eyebrows drawing in toward each other.

"Yes," he replies as he passes the platter over to her. Meanwhile, Sarah has helped herself to mashed potatoes, and Fred and Michael have filled their plates with peas. Phyllis hands the bread basket around and points out the butter dishes. Fred gets up to fill their wine glasses.

"I found this at the Summerhill LCBO the other day," Fred intones as he picks up a bottle by its neck and angles it toward Michael with its label facing his older son. "Tell me what you think, Michael," he says. He'd already uncorked it so it could breathe the requisite amount of time before serving. He fills his son's glass with the ruby liquid.

Michael raises his glass, sniffs it delicately, sips, swirls the wine around in his mouth, and smiles beatifically as he swallows. "Excellent, Fred. I hope you bought more than one bottle?"

Fred smiles smugly. "I did." With a sideways glance at Simon, he continues: "I'm glad you, Michael, understand good wine."

Fred sets the bottle down near his place and sits himself back down. The family commences eating.

Simon chews slowly. He finishes one wing and decides a sufficient amount of time has passed that it is now safe to ask: "What happened to Melanie?"

"Nothing."

Simon looks at Phyllis puzzled.

"It's a personal matter," she allows in a way that tells him firmly the subject is closed.

"I don't ever remember her not being here before. She's always here. It's strange not to see her."

"Don't whine, Simon. We'll all have to cope while she's away."

"Yes," Simon replies shortly. But though his mouth says nothing, his mind worries away at what could pull her away from them. Melanie is always happy; she's a trooper; she doesn't even let colds slow her down—although she is careful not to infect anyone else, sometimes wearing a mask and gloves to keep them, the family, safe from catching her bug, whatever bug she has.

For Melanie not to be here must be serious.

He suddenly wonders if she's had a heart attack. She's close to his parents' age. He examines Phyllis and Fred surreptitiously. They're both solidly built; neither are fat. Some would even say they're skinny, like him. Phyllis's hair is iron grey, while Fred's is a distinguished blonde. He knows his dad has a lot of white hair, but he can hardly see it in the midst of his pale blonde that waves attractively over the top of his head and is the precise length behind his ears for a distinguished professional. His parents don't look like they're prone to having a heart attack. But how old was Gramps when he had his first one? Wasn't he their age? Maybe Melanie did have a heart attack. People die from those. Is she really going to come back? Maybe Phyllis is protecting them all or being optimistic.

"What is going on in that head of yours, Simon?" Sarah startles him. "You look like you're about to have a panic attack!" She laughs uproariously.

Phyllis halts mid-knifing up a knob of mashed potatoes onto her fork. "You do look wretched, Simon. Whatever is the matter with you?"

"Did . . . did Melanie have a heart attack?" The words come out of Simon's mouth strangled.

"No, of course not," Fred replies. "Your mother is being overly dramatic."

"I am not, Fred. We've had enough drama in this house for the year."

"Gramps is enough drama?" Simon gasps. "Gramps was your dad! He wasn't drama. He didn't want to die! He wanted to live! How can you call his death drama as if it was som-som-something that rose up and accosted you. He is your dad!"

"Was Simon, was," Phyllis replies quietly but firmly. "Don't you think it's time to get on with your life?"

Simon stares at her, his mouth hanging open, unable to reply. His fork slips out of his hand and clanks onto his plate.

"Oh, c'mon, Simon. Don't be such a drama queen," Sarah chides.

He turns his head and stares at her.

Fred clears his throat, and Simon looks at him. Fred drives his own mind into Simon's eyes. He says not a word for a long, long moment. Then he states: "Look son." He stops but continues to hold Simon's pupil-filled grey-green irises with his own penetrating charcoal eyes. Simon cannot blink. Fred addresses him again: "We all miss Gramps. He was the life of the party. It's been tough going these past few Sunday dinners without him. He knew how to keep a conversation going and when to chuff someone along when they were in a foul mood." He glances meaningfully down the length of the table at Phyllis. "Or to keep the tone light. He told great stories, and I know how close you were to him. But your mood is putting a pall over our weekly dinners, son, and your mother is feeling it. I tell her, give him time. You're our sensitive boy. We've always known that. But it's time to focus on the people who are here now, even that girlfriend of yours, what is her name, ah yes, Priscilla." A quiet choke from the other end of the table emphasizes his point. "Melanie has not had a heart attack. But her grandmother has died. She was over a hundred, but your mother and I thought it would upset you even more, send you in to an even deeper gloom than you've already sunk yourself into. But I see that your own thoughts are conjuring worse stories than that. That is your way," Fred shakes his head sorrowfully while continuing to pin Simon's eyes to his. "She will be away for some indefinite time because she is the Executor and must wrap up the estate. As you know, she has a large family."

Simon nods. He cannot speak or turn his gaze away from Fred's scrutiny.

"Now that we have that out of the way, I want you to eat, Simon. You've gnawed at one wing long enough. You have a second one to chew on. I won't have you wasting food in my house."

Simon nods. Fred breaks the connection by looking down at what is left of dinner on his plate. Simon turns his attention to the plump wing left on his. With surgical precision, he cuts the meat from the tiny bones of his second wing and nibbles at it as the conversation between Fred and Michael about Michael's next rotation washes over him. Phyllis interrupts the medical talk to say that they have to start planning for Christmas. With Melanie gone this year, each of them will have to chip in.

Simon's heart plummets into his stomach. Christmas without Gramps and now without Melanie shepherding them through this fraught holiday—the thought is unbearable. How can they celebrate? But Sarah's eyes shine as she holds forth on the round of parties she's going to attend, and Michael, ignoring his sister's talk, speculates about when he'll have free moments in his schedule, reminding Phyllis that in this part of his career, he isn't sure exactly when he'll have time to help out. But Phyllis is having none of Michael's excuses. She informs him that she's spoken to the hospital chief about intern and residency schedules and knows when he'll be off. She expects him to contribute, and if he's tired, well, they all worked extra hard when she and Fred were young. It is the penalty of youth. Before she can turn on him, Simon slides his knife and fork together on his plate, pushing the little chicken bones to one side. He shoves his chair back and says, "I'll clear the dishes, Phyllis." He gathers their dirty plates up rapidly, piling on their knives and forks, and pounds out to the kitchen. He lays the pile down carefully on the marble-topped island near the dishwasher, cloaked in its cupboard-matching veneer of polished walnut in its place underneath the counter.

But he doesn't put the dishes into the machine to be washed.

Instead, Simon slips up the back stairs and treads softly to his parents' bedroom. He shuts the door quietly and tip-toes to their bathroom. As he does so, he pulls a small round metal box out from his pocket. He'd found it in Gramps's things when he'd gone through them on Phyllis's command last week. Gramps had used it to store his nitroglycerin medication, tiny white pills he'd slip under his tongue when he'd have one of his attacks. Simon had not paid much attention to those attacks because his grandfather had made such light of them. But now he knew they'd been warning signs. They'd all missed them. Or he had missed them, and the medical people in his family had known but denied their severity. If they'd heeded them, maybe . . . no, no maybe. Gramps would be alive today and celebrating Christmas with them. So would Melanie. No, no, her grandmother was old. She would've still died. But at least Gramps would still have been with them.

Angry gloom envelops him. Simon opens his mother's medicine cabinet and takes in its clutter without registering what he's seeing. He focuses. He scans the myriad contents rapidly. He reaches a hand in and searches through the pill bottles carefully but expeditiously. He finds the one he's looking for. He lifts it toward himself with care, pushes down and twists off the cap quickly, shakes out one pill, puts the pill in Gramps's little metal box, stuffs the box in the tiny pocket above his right front pocket, snaps the lid of the pill bottle back on, and replaces the bottle exactly where he'd found it. He carefully closes the medicine cabinet door and tip-toes out and down, back down to his family.

10

POETRY BLIZZARD

"It's flying out there, man," Isaac yells as he stretches up onto his tippy toes in his cubicle and looks toward the far-off windows. Simon wants to warn Isaac not to yell. Mr. Confabulate has a habit of looking out his office window or opening his door and spotting all the slackers in their cubicles then reprimanding them. But curiosity wins out, and he raises himself out of his chair and stretches his neck so that he can just see over the cubicle wall as he looks toward the windows over other cubicle walls, filing cabinets, and people walking between them and the windows. One known to report to their boss who isn't working, turns their head in their direction. Simon dips back down quickly. He hopes he wasn't seen.

Isaac doesn't seem to care.

Every half hour, Isaac pushes his chair back so that it almost wheels out into the aisle between the cubicles, stands up, and stretches his arms and back with an exaggerated yawn. "Not going to get a kink in my back cause of this job," he'd declare every time. Simon envies his insouciance. He would never dare be so obvious in the flouting of break rules—one break in mid-morning, one lunch break, and one break in mid-afternoon only. Simon conscientiously sticks to the break rules and to reviewing every treatment plan carefully while Isaac breezes through his work, declining treatment plans at a rate Simon dares not. Yet Mr. Confabulate notices approvingly Isaac's productivity and seems oblivious to Isaac's flouting of office rules. How can that be? Simon once hissed at Isaac to be careful, but Issac had laughed at him, told him to lighten up.

Simon can't laugh.

Ever since the day he was late, he's become extra careful, keeping his rear end in his chair and his nose turned toward the computer screen. Hearing Mr. Confabulate's heavy footfalls on the carpet coming toward him, feeling those never-miss eyes on his back, keeps him at least looking like he's working. His mind may wander, but Mr. Confabulate can't see that from his office window, and Isaac will warn him if he espies the boss coming and thinks Simon has zoned out. He isn't sure how Isaac can perceive that through the cubicle walls.

Isaac's penetrating voice brings Simon back to the present. Cautiously, Simon raises his head and eyes again above the cubicle wall and sees: snow flying horizontally from east to west across their windows. "It's backward!" he exclaims.

"Yeah, man. I thought there was something wrong with that snow."

"What? You mean other than it's falling," Elaine says from behind Simon, her voice like a cat landing on his shoulders, claws outstretched. He jumps, rotates, and lands to stare at Elaine.

She arches her eyebrows. "What? I'm not allowed to walk around? You heard the new office rule; we're not supposed to email or phone people with simple requests; we have to get up and go talk. So. I'm getting up and going talking."

"About what?" Simon asks.

"Yeah, about what, Elaine?" Isaac parrots, glancing at her over his shoulder.

"Snow," she says, grinning at them.

Simon scrutinizes her face. Is she joshing them, or is she serious? He can never tell. Isaac's shout of laughter hits the back of his head. "Aw, man, you believe her? Nah, she's just trying to find out more about your love life. We've heard nothing from you about Priscilla. It used to be all Priss this and Priss that. But now, nothing. You're starving her, man."

"Don't be silly, Isaac. I'm here on serious business," Elaine shoots back while sliding her eyes toward Simon, her eyebrows arching a silent query.

"Yeah, sure," Isaac says, chuckling and turning to step over to the cubicle wall he shares with Simon.

Elaine replies haughtily, "Well, I'll have you know, I've come to tell you it's quitting time. Our esteemed boss emailed me, but he forgot to email everyone else. You know how he is with email. He—"

The two men join her, "—hits Reply All to his boss, and the wrong name to everyone else."

They shake their heads. They settle into their own thoughts for a moment over why bosses don't know how to use email or computers. Then Isaac lays his arms on top of the shared wall of his cubicle, tilting it dangerously toward Simon.

"Hey!" Simon warns.

"Oh, sorry, man," Isaac says, taking his weight and arms off the wall. "So are you for real, Elaine?"

"I thought you wouldn't believe me, so I brought the proof right here," she says flapping a letter-sized sheet of paper at them.

Simon takes it as he is closer and scans it quickly. He looks up toward Isaac. "She's right. Due to the blizzard, Mr Confabulate has commanded us to leave," he rotates his left wrist to check his watch, "now."

Simon hands back the sheet of paper to Elaine while Isaac vanishes from view as he swoops down to his computer to log off. Simon outpaces him in logging off and shutting down all his equipment. By the time they've shoved their arms into their jackets, Elaine has informed the rest of the cubicle row and moved on to the next row, picking up gossip as she goes.

Simon and Isaac hustle side by competitive side to the elevator. Isaac hits the down button first. The elevator dings ten seconds later; its doors open; and they are almost launched into it by their oncoming colleagues thundering into them from behind. They fill the elevator shoulder to shoulder, chest to back. Humid anticipation breathes into the air. The elevator closes its doors slowly, beeping an ear-wrenching alarm until the doors mercifully touch. The elevator lurches down, jostling the insurance workers eager to leave their office for the blizzard. It picks up speed as it approaches the ground floor. It stops with a soft bounce; the doors open; and the workers explode out into the hallway and through the revolving exit doors into the howling snowy gale. One by one as they are hurtled into the blizzard by the rotating door, they hunch their heads into their shoulders and head-butt the snow and wind as they struggle toward the closest TTC subway station. Snowflakes thick in the air like a swirling fog of midges builds up puffy blankets on their hair and coats, on sidewalk and cars. It bites Simon's eyes, fills his lashes. He blindly tramps after the herd and finds himself underground in the station. He shakes off the snow with the rest of them. Relief at being out of that roaring whiteness flows through his muscles, dropping his shoulders, yet he feels like an alien in an unknown land. It's been many years since he'd last used the TTC. Noticing Simon's discomfiture, Isaac laughs at him and claps him on the back. He reaches into one of his jacket pockets, digging deep into it. With an "ah-ha" he pulls out a small bicoloured coin. Isaac puts the token in Simon's gloved hand. "Here, man, use one of these."

Simon stares at it.

"It's called a token, man. It'll pay for your ride." Simon glances up at Isaac then frowns down at the token, not remembering what to do with it. In fact, he's sure he's never seen one of them before. He was a student the last time he'd been on the subway, and he remembered using a student pass. But not this small round silver and dirty-gold coloured thing.

Isaac full out laughs at him. He grabs his elbow. "C'mon man, follow me." Isaac pulls him to join the throng heading through plastic gates set between metal stanchions. Simon doesn't resist. Isaac lets go of him as they reach one of the gates. He taps a black card against a faded green bump on the corner of the right stanchion and pushes himself through the slow-moving gate. From the other side, he turns around and indicates to Simon to go to the booth. Simon frowns at the booth with its line of shivering people, standing in melting snow as they wait to get past the booth and through its gate. He looks back at Isaac.

Isaac nods as he shouts, "Yeah. Drop it in the thing there."

"Hey, pay or move!" someone yells from behind Simon, as a shoulder shoves into him to move him to the side. Simon staggers. "Sorry," Simon says.

Isaac laughs, "Move or get out of the way is the TTC motto." He shakes his head, chuckling, and walks toward the booth's gate to wait for Simon.

Simon joins the line and when he reaches the front of the booth, he looks at Isaac. Isaac lifts his left hand, pinching his forefinger and thumb together then letting go. Simon mimics his actions over the fare box, letting the token drop in. Isaac motions toward himself, and Simon walks through the open gate. Isaac chuckles, "Man, it's like teaching a kid." He smiles good-naturedly. Simon is pushed forward into Isaac by the person behind him. "Sorry," Simon blushes as he straightens up and steps to his right out of the way of the people streaming through the booth's gate. Isaac follows him.

"Where you headed, man?" Isaac asks Simon.

"Home."

Isaac rolls his eyes.

"I mean," Simon pauses then stares in confusion at Issac and says, "I don't know what stop."

"Yeah, right, okay, where you live?"

"Near Broadview."

"That's easy then. Take the eastbound subway to Broadview and get off there. You can hop on a streetcar going your way, if you want. Get a transfer for that." Isaac looks around and points to a waist-high red machine like standing like a soldier on duty. "Grab one from there." Isaac eyes him. "Here, follow me." Simon follows him to a red machine standing against the tiled wall. Isaac pushes a worn silver button on the front of it. It clicks. Isaac reaches through a small plastic door and retrieves a small rectangular piece of paper. He hands it to Simon. "Keep hold of that. It's your," he lowers his tone and slows his voice, "proof of payment." Isaac grins as Simon blinks at him, holding the transfer in the air like a signal flag. "I'm going west. See you later." And Isaac is gone.

Simon looks for the signs and follows their direction as people weave around him at a rapid pace. He jogs down the steps, trying to keep pace with the others, and finds himself jammed in the thawing crowd on the platform. He digs his hands into his pockets and hunches his shoulders, tucking his chin into his chest. He doesn't like it here. He wants to get out, but the thought of that blizzard . . .

A rumble and growing clatter of metal wheels on track herald the arrival of the train. The crowd moves forward as one. The subway train stops, and the doors slide open. A few people manoeuvre their way out of the doors, trying not to get trampled on by the platform crowd who are pushing themselves on board, sweeping Simon into the train along with them. He finds himself in the middle, as far away from the doors as he can possibly be. He sends his eyes this way and that, searching for a handhold. A chime sounds, and the doors glide closed. The train jerks forward, and Simon lurches into a woman next to him who gives him a dirty stay-away-from-me-pervert look. He blushes and smiles apologetically. He spots a handle hanging down from an overhead rail and attempts to latch on to it as the train sways him back and forth. He grasps it at last and hangs on for dear life.

Simon breathes.

After a while, he swivels his head this way and that, vaguely remembering there were maps in the train. He'd forgotten to look for where Broadview is on the subway line while he was waiting on the platform. In fact, he can't remember seeing a map out there. At last, he spots a map over a door in among the line of lit-up ads, but it's too much on an angle from where he's standing for him to see it clearly and the crowd contains several people taller than him standing between him and the map. He sighs and closes his eyes against the press of moist coats, hot air, and chatter.

The train rumbles on, swaying rhythmically in the tunnels, stopping and starting with predictable suddenness as it screeches into every station and groans out a minute later. He dozes. He awakes all of a sudden when the train jerks his hand off the overhead handle. He stumbles and catches one of the vertical poles to prevent himself from falling. He looks around. No one looks back. The train is half full, and they are stopped in a tunnel. He is the only one left standing. He hurries down the car to look at the map. He finds Broadview. The train spasms then trundles into a station. Simon peers through the window in the subway train doors underneath the map to see what station they're pulling into. He doesn't recognize the name on the wall. As the doors slide apart, he cranes his neck to look at the map over his head and realizes he is far east of where he's supposed to be. Simon leaps out the open doors as the chime sounds and amber lights above him flash. The doors snap closed on his back.

He should take the westbound train back, Simon tells himself, as he sprints up the tiled stairs toward the station exit. He stops upon seeing a map at the top. He was on the westbound platform.

Simon blinks and looks back down from whence he came. He shrugs, not caring how he began eastbound and ended up westbound, for he cannot stand the thought of being on this system one more moment. He has to get out—even the blizzard is preferable. He strides toward the second set of stairs to the top and outside.

Ten seconds of leaning into flying snow, then leaning against the powerful wind as he turns the corner onto the Danforth, Simon regrets his decision. He squints down the street through the tiny, hurtling snowflakes that sting his cheeks and eyes, burrow into his hair. He blinks against the cold vortex, seeking sight of a warm coffee shop. A Starbucks even. Or a Tim Hortons. It would be a . . . what do they call them? . . . a Timmies out here, he thinks. This is Timmies territory, isn't it? A door opens just ahead of him; a man exits and immediately hunches against the keening wind. Before the door slams closed behind him, Simon hears a voice breaking through the constant caterwauling of the blizzard. The voice's rhythmic tones attract him. The man disappears rapidly into the tearing snow while Simon turns instinctively toward that rhythmic voice and the warmth that the briefly opened door had promised.

He reaches out a snow-covered arm and pulls the door toward himself. He enters the unknown place. It's crowded. And it's humid from the warmth of many bodies and snow-soaked coats. He scans the crowd in the steamy room for a space and sees one against a wall. He mumbles, "excuse me, excuse me," as he wends his way toward that space. In between two people, he leans against the wall in relief. The snow blanketing him begins to melt. It drips from his hair into his eyes. He brushes his hand backward across his hair several times. The spikes of his straw-coloured hair have softened under the snowy onslaught. He brushes snow off the shoulders of his jacket before it all melts and seeps into him. He unbuttons his jacket against the heat of the coffee house and begins to observe where he finds himself.

Simon follows the lines of everyone's eyes toward the back of this quaint, dark coffee shop with its fantasy murals decorating its walls and its burnished wooden counter covered in glass jars filled with various kinds of biscotti. A lone man stands at the back in a cleared patch with a microphone sitting angled upward in a mic stand before him. In his shaking hand, he holds a much-creased sheet of paper. He finishes speaking, and everyone applauds lightly. A burly, English-looking man saunters up to the mic as the man leaves it.

"Thank you, Emory. We now have Jill with her haiku. Give Jill a round of applause." He leaves, and a thin thing with straggling blonde hair sidles up to the mic, head down, eyes on her sheet of paper. She stands not too close to it. She glances up swiftly, smiles swiftly, leans into the mic, breathes out hello, then leans back. The crowd waits. Simon can feel the crowd's anticipation and examines the faces, perplexed. He returns his gaze to her face. She doesn't look like much. But he waits with the others.

Inhaling slowly, deeply, she leans back toward the mic and exhales out soft words, the microphone picking up her breath, broadcasting her voice all the way to the front of the shop.

"I come to her as

One alone with no one but

Me and my life."

She leans back.

"You're missing a syllable," someone shouts from near Simon. Simon looks around for the owner of the voice, puzzled.

"She's allowed to miss a syllable," another voice shouts back. "This isn't the nationals."

"You're supposed to adhere to the rules."

"Don't be so literal."

"I can be literal if I want to. She should be, too."

"Poetry's not literal. It's metaphorical."

"Like the rules!"

As the crowd laughs, Simon catches sight of the person outraged at the violation of haiku rules: five, seven, five syllables.

He looks toward the back again, but the blonde girl has vanished. The burly man has taken her place. "Rules are made to be symbolic," he states baldly in his deep voice.

"You mean, broken," calls out the original offended voice.

The burly man grins in reply. He must be the owner of this coffee shop, Simon surmises. Near to the shop owner stands a tall redhead. "Oh good," she says in a carrying voice while her lips stretch wide to reveal happy teeth. "I like breaking rules." Confidence oozes from her.

The shop owner's eyes alight on her, his hand on the mic stand, and growls, "It's not your turn yet."

"That's okay, I can wait," she retorts.

Simon smiles at her spirit.

The shop owner gestures to someone out of Simon's sight as he lets go of the stand and steps toward the redhead, forcing her to move back. Another man with long black hair appears out of the crowd. He strides to the back. He doesn't take even a second before leaning down and barking into the mic:

"The noose awaits me.

But so does the bridge over

The river. I jump."

Shocked silence greets this offering as the man strides toward the wall opposite Simon and disappears into the dimness there.

Clearing his throat, the shop owner returns to the mic and says, "Jackie. I believe it's your turn."

"It is," the redhead chirps. It's as if the man with the long black hair had never spoken, thinks Simon, yet he cannot get the stark words out of his mind. Did he mean it? Is he going to jump? The thought attracts him. He shakes his head at himself, suddenly repulsed. He isn't going to jump. Where did that inane idea come from? The man's words were said for shock value. Only shock value, he reassures himself. After all, the man left the mic as abruptly as he went up to it. Shock value, that's all.

The redhead is speaking. He's missed her intro and the title. She looks pleased with herself, like a cat who's filched the tuna. He straightens up from the wall. He suddenly remembers how she approved the breaking of the haiku rules. He's eager to hear her words. He feels she is going to break the rules in a big way.

Jackie clears her throat and reads:

"I gaze upon the stars
At night, their rays like tears
Of joy, of wonder that explode
Into grief upon seeing Leviathan
Roam upon the earth, that creature the demons cheer,
That God created for our misery.
We, who inhabit this place of misery,
Look to the heavens, to the stars
For their cheer
To dry our tears
That the great Leviathan
Did gloat to see in us explode.
And now our anger roils, it explodes,
Cloaking our misery
That he feeds on, that fat Leviathan.
But our fury reflects off him to feed the stars,
Who shed drops and drops of fiery tears
Upon us to bring back in us a spark of cheer.
Oh, so much angst in us does need cheer
To succor, else our hearts explode
Into crimson gushers flooding the land, drowning our tears.
Oh, such misery
They do see, the stars
When they look upon the proud work of Leviathan."

Jackie pauses to smile lasciviously before continuing:

"He curls his tail, he purses his mouth, he squeezes his body round his happy prey, does Leviathan.

He feasts on complacent pride and cheers

To see from their mighty fortresses, the constellations' impotent fury in his starring

Role on earth, his domain of rock formed when God the universe did explode.

He looks fondly on the banquet his happy prey creates from our misery,

He and them slaking their thirst with our tears.

From the heavens, drop by drop, claret and choler tears

Fizzle and burn the armour of the fearless Leviathan.

But he heeds nothing but what he wants: misery.

His enemy is cheer,

And he quickly explodes

It back up to the stars.

But the stars dry their tears

As God, as Ahura Mazda, explodes the vain Leviathan.

And all we who suffer cheer to see the end of our misery."

Jackie stops speaking. That was no haiku, Simon marvels as he waits to hear the breaking-rules critic. But nary a voice speaks out.

Jackie's silence holds the crowd silent for long moments. She stands patiently at the mic as the crowd processes her words. The shop owner has his beefy arms crossed over his barrel chest and looks ruefully at her but admiringly, too.

No one speaks.

Simon waits for her to continue, for someone in the crowd to speak, for the shop owner to take the mic back.

But nobody moves. Is this part of her persona, Simon wonders, to make the crowd wait, and they know it?

As the long seconds tick by, uncertainty crosses her face. And then Simon begins clapping, not knowing why, but wanting to hear more, more of her poetry, more of her voice, more about . . . he shies away from thinking about what. Deep inside him, his mind and physical being resonate with her words and with the idea that this is truly a haven from the bluster outside. It brings clarity and strength into his mind, his thoughts, his memory. With each clap, he remembers each person in his life, who they are to him: Fred, Phyllis, Michael, Sarah, Melanie, Priscilla.

Priscilla.

His thoughts pause.

Priscilla.

She'd been such a part of his life, and he's been empty since he left her at the nightclub. Lost. Maybe he shouldn't have ignored her. His life had had a map. Work. Marriage. Children. Family. A map like Gramps, like Fred's. He'd been well on his way to following that map when he'd blown it with his grief over Gramps and walking away from Priscilla. He needs to rectify that. Immediately the sound of the others joining him in his applause fills his ears, and the coffee shop comes alive to his senses again. His eyes focus on the back of the intimate place. The redhead smiles in relief and gratitude.

11

THE LORD SPEAKS

"I'm in the kitchen," Simon calls out as he hears his front door open and shut. Priscilla whips off her knitted cap, shrugs out of her long wool coat, and unhooks her boots with her feet, letting them fly off and land on the wooden floor where they fall sideways. She trots into the kitchen in her stockinged feet and right up to Simon, who smiles down at her. She lifts up her heels to stand on tippy toe and reaches up with her lips, and he joins his to hers.

She smiles coyly up at him from the corners of her eyes as she retreats back down. She sniffs the air appreciably and looks around. "You're cooking!"

"Yes," Simon smiles, his eyes on the half-hidden profile of her face.

Priscilla tilts her head toward him and returns his smile with a flirtatious gleam. "It's great to see you cooking. So what are we having?"

"It's a cold night so I thought we'd have something warm and comforting."

Priscilla jumps up and down, clapping her hands, exclaiming, "Oh goody! My fave!"

Simon grins, "Yes. For you. And I thought we'd start with oyster mushroom Parmesan."

The stove timer dings right on cue. Simon steps past Priscilla, slips on a faded, slightly charred oven glove, and pulls open the squeaky oven door. Priscilla peers over his bent shoulder as he reaches in and pulls out a scallop dish with oyster mushrooms fanned out to fit the dish's shape. The beigy-grey mushrooms with their wide caps and thinly curled edges are covered in golden Parmesan crumbs.

Priscilla inhales with gusto. "Mmmm. They smell so good."

Simon carries the dish to the small dining table in the next room and places it on a round brass pot holder. The table is already set with flatware for each course. The claret wine already poured. Priscilla slides quickly into her seat. Simon returns to the kitchen to remove his oven glove. He tosses it on his counter. In mere seconds and steps, he's sitting and serving Priscilla a wide spoonful of cheesy mushrooms. Next, he serves himself, the same amount as he'd given Priscilla. The two eat in delighted silence.

They have second helpings.

Simon removes the empty scallop dish to the kitchen, while Priscilla refills her wine glass and gulps from her full glass. "Simon," she calls out. "You're awesomesauce!"

Simon pokes his head out from the kitchen, "What?"

"Awesomesauce! Like the best cook a girl can ask for."

Simon blushes and ducks his head back in the kitchen.

"You know, most boyfriends can't cook. I'm sooo envied. They, like, drool, every time I tell them what you cooked for me. It's about time you cooked again!"

"Here we are," Simon announces as he reappears, carrying a big blue dish and trying not to blush. The lid has already been removed. "Vegetarian Shepherd's Pie," he declares as he sets it down. Mashed potatoes rising and falling in golden-topped waves greet Priscilla's eyes. She grins at the potatoes and at Simon's pink face.

"It's the heat from the oven," he says, fanning his face as he sits down.

"Sure, Simon, sure," Priscilla teases him.

Simon clears his throat, shyly, and sinks a large serving spoon into the potatoes, down, down into the vegetables and lentils underneath. He heaps a generous portion onto a plate for her. He suddenly stands up and disappears into the kitchen and returns with a polished maple-wood bowl filled with a light salad of greens, tiny cherry tomatoes, cubes of avocado, and slivers of red onion. He picks up a glass jar that had been sitting on the table, shakes it, twists off its cap, and drizzles his lemon juice-olive oil dressing over the salad. He tosses the raw vegetables with the bowl's matching salad servers. He carefully scoops up a large portion between the two servers and with great care moves the servers over the table, over to Priscilla's plate. He opens up the servers like a giant claw widening, and the portion of greens and tomatoes tumble down onto her plate next to the Shepherd's Pie. He repeats the move for himself, except this time, an errant cherry tomato escapes the grip of the servers. It rolls across the table until it hits his dinner fork. After he puts the servers back into their bowl, he snatches up the tomato and pops it into his mouth. Priscilla doesn't notice because she is already forking up her first bite of the Shepherd's Pie.

They nosh together for several minutes. Simon leans back to take a break. Priscilla slows down.

"I found this place, Priss," Simon says.

"Oh yeah," she says through a mouthful.

"I found it that day we had the blizzard."

She nods and keeps on chewing.

"It's this coffee shop. You'd like it. It's small and quaint. It's got real wood, and I think I saw one of those old coffee urns like they have in Italy."

Priscilla slants her eyes up at him as her jaws slow down their gustatory activity. "Oh?" she asks.

"I'm not sure exactly where it is. It's east of here. But I can find it again. I noted down its name," he finishes, tapping his head.

Priscilla returns her gaze to her plate and, with great attentiveness, uses her knife to push a tomato into the bowl of her fork and then a small chunk of avocado. She stares at the tomato sitting in her fork for a moment. But before she lifts up the fork to engulf its contents with her mouth, she asks, "What's it called?" And she lifts her head to look straight into his eyes.

Simon squints in an effort of memory. "The Coffee Place? The Solo?"

Priscilla laughs, "I thought so. You never remember names of places that aren't important to you." She bites down on her fork and sucks the tomato and avocado into her mouth.

Simon blushes, the pink soaking into his straw-coloured hair and white scalp.

Priscilla hastily puts her hand in front of her mouth, the edges of her upturned lips showing on either side of her fingers. Simon's blush deepens into red. "It is important to me Priss," he says, stressing the word is as he struggles to regain his composure. "I thought I remembered it. Anyway," he rushes on. "I'll know it when I see it."

Priscilla contemplates his face, which is now fading back to his normal fairness. She grins with her lips, her eyes contemplative. She says, "I know. You're good at the visual." She pauses and then speaks all at once: "So when d'you want to show me this place?"

Simon hesitates then plunges in, "I thought on its next poetry night."

"It's what?" she splutters, dropping her fork with a clatter onto her almost empty plate.

"It's . . . it's next poetry night." Simon looks into her shocked eyes with his own, trying hard not to look away.

"Poetry?" she repeats, unable to hide her disgust.

"Yes. Poetry. It's good to listen to," he replies defensively. "Gramps liked poetry. You gave me poetry!"

Priscilla groans. "That was a mistake, Simon. I thought I told you."

Simon frowns, and she hurriedly sits up and puts on a careless expression. She shrugs. "Well, I suppose old folks would. I mean, they're into it. But . . . I mean, people our age . . . ," she trails off as she lowers her eyes back to her plate. She shoves the last bite of potatoes round and round until they finally comply and allow her to push her fork underneath them so that she can raise them up to her lips and eager tongue.

"I didn't think I was. But you gave me *The Suicides*—"

"Oh!" Priscilla flashes up at him. "Not that thing again. I thought you got rid of it. Didn't I tell you to get rid of it? It's bad news."

"No. It's not. It's good poetry. Listen, I'll get it and read you one." He begins to rise from his chair.

"No," she shakes her head hard. "I don't want to hear it."

Simon sinks back down. He falters, "It's good poetry. I don't remember reading those in school, but—"

"We didn't read them in school because they're morbid. Those dudes must've been delusional."

"But don't you think about death?"

"No. I. Do. Not. And neither should you. It's not normal."

"Death is part of life."

"We don't have to think about it. Now stop it, Simon. Stop it! I thought this was supposed to be us getting back together again. You were making . . . what's that thing called, your Gramps used to say . . ."

"Making amends?" Simon replies desultorily.

"Yes, that!" She smiles. "This dinner is to make amends for ignoring me, isn't it?" She lowers her eyelids and chin and peeps up at him.

Simon breathes, his heart loud in his ears. He asks: "Do you want dessert?"

"Chocolate?" she asks, raising her head and looking full into his eyes with her gleeful ones.

"Well, not chocolate, per se," he drags out in reply.

"Don't be so literal, Simon," she says playfully slapping him across the table. "It has chocolate, though, right?" she asks hopefully.

Simon nods as Priscilla beams. He pushes his chair back to fetch the sweet stuff.

A few days later, Simon still feels Priscilla's hard words ringing in his head as he trudges along the Danforth looking for the coffee shop in the cold black of a winter night. After he'd dropped the subject and served up the chocolate and strawberry mousse, with its swirling hat of whipped cream, they had gone on to talk about some gossip from her work he wasn't interested in and cannot remember now. The whole time he'd listened to Priss prattle on, he'd ached to share that coffee house experience with her, to read her the poem he'd read earlier in the day during the pause between putting the Shepherd's Pie in the oven and preparing the mushrooms.

A riot of colour on one of the storefronts he's approaching captures his attention. It's a coffee shop. It looks familiar. That must be it, he decides. He pushes open the door. The room is half filled this time. Everyone is out shopping or recovering from overwork, he thinks. It's that time of year. This is one evening he's glad Con Fable has precise working hours. No one at his level is to put in overtime unless they're late; they wouldn't acknowledge overtime if you did it for any other reason. He's feeling released that, as of yesterday, he's caught up from his being late that seemingly long ago day.

He walks over to the bar and orders an espresso from the burly shop owner who's wiping the well-worn wood counter. The man rumbles out the price, and Simon pays. While he waits for his coffee, he unbuttons his pea jacket and scans the room.

"Didn't I see you here last week?"

Startled, Simon whips his head toward the voice. The redhead is standing near him.

"Uh," he drags out incoherently.

She smiles mischievously and lilts, "I have that effect on men. Yeah, I'm sure I saw you. You were standing over there against the wall." She points with a pale finger across from the near wall and door. He looks over in the direction of her finger then turns back to her. "Yes."

"Not talkative are you? I'm not surprised. You have that look. And your hair," she lifts her eyelids up high to get a better view of his sticking-out hair.

Simon blushes. She laughs, a deep-throated, good-natured laugh. "Stick around after your coffee. You might like what I read. It's not an original. But it's good."

Simon nods automatically. At that moment, the burly man says, "Your coffee." Simon turns back to the counter. He picks up the espresso cup and turns around to speak to the redhead, but she's gone. He carries his espresso to an empty table, its round flatness hardly large enough to hold his espresso cup and a plate if he'd had one. Simon sips the bitter brew slowly. He lets himself sink into the warmth of the space, and time passes.

An ear-piercing squeal heralds the mic at the back of the room being switched on. The shop owner taps it a few times, reciting, "Testing, testing." Simon smiles at the familiar refrain. Satisfied, the owner steps back and gestures with his head to someone out of view. Simon sits up.

The redhead saunters up to the microphone. Simon shifts forward in his seat. He crosses his arms halfway across the table and leans on them. Her eyes flit from table to table; when she finds him, her lips curve up slightly and then straighten so quickly, Simon isn't sure if he saw right. She clears her throat. "This is a poem by Lord Byron, the most romantic of the romantic poets," she pronounces with drama and flair.

"*A Fragment*,[1] by George Gordon Byron, sixth Baron Byron, or Lord Byron," she intones, deepening the timbre of her voice.

She pauses.

She begins to read in deep, warning tones that rise and fall as in the rhythm of a heart that is slowing down, that is speeding up, that is moving from life to sleep awhile eternal:

"Could I remount the river of my years

To the first fountain of our smiles and tears,

I would not trace again the stream of hours

Between their outworn banks of withered flowers,

But bid it flow as now—until it glides

Into the number of the nameless tides."

She stops.

She says nothing as she keeps her eyes downcast on the sheets clutched in her two hands.

She lets the silence stretch like a rubber band being pulled and pulled to its utmost limits until Simon feels that he must call out to her to continue. And that's when she resumes speaking the verse in a voice like a soft rustling autumn leaf in the evening grass:

"What is this Death?—a quiet of the heart?"

She stops again. Simon holds his breath. Lord Byron has caught his feelings exactly. It is a quiet of Gramps's heart, but his, too, as it beats on in sync and against all the lives that live around him yet yearns to once again beat alongside Gramps's.

---

1   *A Fragment*, by Lord Byron, from *The Works of Lord Byron*, Vol. 4, downloaded from Project Gutenberg, in the public domain. It was written in 1816, first published in 1830.

But that is not to be.

Simon blinks rapidly and holds himself still in case the moisture rimming his eyelids spills.

The redhead parts her lips, inhales gently, and on the exhale, says:

"The whole of that of which we are a part?"

The redhead's voice has risen into the questions of grief and doubt, and now it plunges into the cadence of death.

"For Life is but a vision—"

A vision, yes, thinks Simon. Is life real? Is death real? How does one tell?

"—what I see
Of all which lives alone is Life to me,
And being so—the absent are the dead,
Who haunt us from tranquillity, and spread
A dreary shroud around us, and invest
With sad remembrancers our hours of rest."

It is a dreary shroud that has enveloped him since the day Gramps died, Simon admits to himself. And no one sees the shroud. They see him carrying an assumed dreariness, as him haunting their complacent assumption that they are alive and always will be. They have no sad remembrances. But Lord Byron does. He knows. Simon releases himself into the redheads's voice, into the words of the long-dead poet.

"The absent are the dead—for they are cold,
And ne'er can be what once we did behold;
And they are changed, and cheerless,—or if yet
The unforgotten do not all forget,"

Simon's eyes swim. His vision of the redhead blurs.

"Since thus divided—equal must it be
If the deep barrier be of earth, or sea;
It may be both—but one day end it must
In the dark union of insensate dust."

Is the dust insensate, Simon wonders, or humans? The granules of dust or snow he kicks down the sidewalk in his treading to and from work, seem more alive to the vagaries of life.

"The under-earth inhabitants—are they
But mingled millions decomposed to clay?
The ashes of a thousand ages spread
Wherever Man has trodden or shall tread?
Or do they in their silent cities dwell
Each in his incommunicative cell?"

We do not need to be dead, Simon reflects, to each be in an incommunicative cell. Stop it, Priss had remonstrated him. And so he had. He'd served her her chocolate, and they'd talked of inconsequential things that had the veneer of communication but was just talking with no meaning. Simon sighs bitterly and straightens his back.

"Or have they their own language?—"

Simon leans forward, putting his elbows on the table. He rests his chin on his curled fists. He stares intently at the redhead. "Their own language": the words echo in his head.

"—and a sense
Of breathless being?—darkened and intense
As Midnight in her solitude?—Oh Earth!
Where are the past?—and wherefore had they birth?
The dead are thy inheritors—and we
But bubbles on thy surface; and the key
Of thy profundity is in the Grave,
The ebon portal of thy peopled cave,
Where I would walk in spirit, and behold
Our elements resolved to things untold,
And fathom hidden wonders, and explore
The essence of great bosoms now no more."

The redhead stops speaking and steps back from the microphone

Simon expires his held breath and slumps back in his chair.

12

WORDS

"Hey, what poems did Gramps like?" Simon blurts into the middle of the conversation around the dinner table.

Forks and voices fall silent at this strange non sequitur. They had been talking about the to-Michael long hours (and to-Fred short hours) medical residents are required to work.

"I mean," Simon says, suddenly remembering his mother doesn't like the familiar "Hey" and not feeling at all guilty about it but wanting to distract her before she can gripe. "Gramps told me once that I had an affinity for English. He believed I should pursue English literature. That's what he said: 'Simon, pursue studies in English,'" Simon mimics his grandfather, deepening his voice to the older man's timbre. Even after all this time, he can still recall the sound of his grandfather's voice. The pleasure at remembering his Gramps's voice splits his mouth into a smile. He continues happily, "He thought it was 'my thing.' But that's all he said, aside from repeating that back in his day they had to learn and memorize such things, verse and prose. Not like today, he'd say, where your memory is neglected by these new-fangled teachers. 'We were tough back then, had to use our noggin or else,' he'd say. But he never recited any of his favourite poems to me nor told me about his favourite authors, just that that sort of thing made him the man he was." Simon looks over at Phyllis hopefully as he finishes speaking, releasing his breath.

"He knew his poetry," she says shortly and resumes eating.

Simon forges on gallantly, "I know. But I was wondering if he liked it. If he had . . . appreciated it . . . if he had favourites?"

"Appreciate it?" Phyllis frowns at Simon. "Of course he appreciated it. We all appreciate a good turn of phrase. I hope we brought you up to respect the English language and to use it the way it ought to be used."

"Yes, you did, Phyllis," Simon replies with a disarming smile while straining to persevere against his heart drumming on his ribs. "But I was trying to remember last night if I'd heard him recite a favourite line or stanza. And I couldn't."

Phyllis fixes her eyes on him as if to say there is nothing more to be said.

"I remember him reciting one," Sarah pipes up.

"Yes?" Simon whips his head toward her.

"Yup," she replies. She sucks in air to puff out her chest and cheeks and then commences reciting in the imitation of a gruff voice:

"There once was a man named Odd,

He was a very odd man indeed,

He kept on about memory

Bugged his famil-y

And wouldn't shut up like Maude."

Sarah falls back against her chair, clutching her stomach, her mouth wide, her breath spasming laughter through her throat. Simon's face darkens red. Michael says dryly, "I see you're watching those old 1970s' shows again. And you're as bad at limericking as ever."

Sarah sits up and pouts, "Well, at least I try. And it got Simon to shut up already."

"Sarah! I will not have that vulgar language used at my dinner table," Phyllis reprimands.

Sarah grins unrepentantly. Then she meets Phyllis's hawk stare. She swallows and murmurs, "Yes, Mom. I'm sorry, Mom."

Phyllis nods sharply once while Fred chuckles under his breath. He says only so that Sarah can hear, although Simon catches it too with his hyper-vigilant ears: "You know better than to think you can best your mother, Sarah. Why do you even try?" He shakes his head sadly. "You know you're not up to her standard." He smiles sideways at her; Sarah suddenly finds her plate fascinating.

Deflated, Simon stares down at his plate, too, with its mournful island of mashed potatoes in its withering creek of gravy; a gristle from his slice of roast beef lies flabbily at the side of his plate, and one errant pea rolls laggardly toward the creek of gravy. It has been the same meal every Sunday since Melanie had gone away. They had used to have this roast beef dinner once a month, mostly on Melanie's Sundays off, as this is the only meal his mother knows how to do well—and that she is willing to do. But Simon is heartily weary of it. It was bad enough to have such a heavy dinner weekly in the winter before Christmas. But December has ticked into the new year. The snows have melted in a winter thaw; the cold air has slipped away up north to hide for a few days; and a heavy roast beef dinner is not suiting his stomach.

For a few weeks now . . . he pauses in his thoughts as he tries to recall how long it's been . . . but he cannot. Time shifts, sometimes lengthening till a recent event seems much in the past, sometimes shortening so that two months ago feels like yesterday. But he's sure it's been at least a few weeks that he has deliberately avoided talking about Gramps. But the urge to bring his grandfather back into his life is intense. He had reasoned with himself that it would be okay for him to ask about Gramps's likes; that should be innocuous enough, he'd assured himself. Talking about a dead man as if he's talking about a distant relative he wants to know better cannot be construed as morbid or living in the past, he'd reasoned within his own head.

But his sub-conscious must have known he was wrong because he'd delayed speaking about it, didn't open his mouth to say the words since he'd arrived two hours earlier. And what has that worrying and rehearsing gotten him? Words blurted out in a way he hadn't meant to say, and a slap back. And he remains without an answer.

What were Gramps's favourite poems?

He wonders if Gramps would have accompanied him to the coffee shop. He had been so certain Priss would enjoy it and would accompany him that he hadn't conceived that she would say no. In the nights before he'd told her about the coffee shop, he had dreamt of scenarios wherein the two of them would walk hand-in-hand together to the coffee shop; would huddle close at one of the tiny tables; would lean on each other, shoulder to shoulder, while listening to the poets; would maybe discuss the poetry with the poets afterwards; and would then walk home arm-in-arm in the cold, chatting about what the poets had meant when they'd said this line or that haiku. Despite his inherent nervousness, his fantasy had led him to believe she'd leap at the idea when he'd asked her that evening. He tastes his disappointment once more, feels again like a dog chastised hiding his tail between his legs. He sighs and returns in his mind to that last time in the coffee shop when he'd sat enraptured by those words of Lord Byron's as spoken by Jackie, as he'd learnt her name was. He understood from Jackie, the redhead—

Her red hair flames into his retrospection, cutting off all conscious thought. He sinks into the memory of her welcome.

A clink of glass against ring from somewhere beside him restarts his brain. He could not have guessed her name from the vibrancy of her hair. Yet it suits her, he thinks, a smile alighting briefly on his lips before disappearing as the memory of her hair reasserts itself. Unlike Priss's hair, her hair entices.

He sits up and drops his fork. Priscilla is his girlfriend, he scolds himself.

"Whatever is the matter with you?" Phyllis asks.

"He's probably realized he's about to get a promotion," Sarah mocks.

"What?" Fred responds. "Simon, a promotion?" He barks out one disbelieving shout and stabs at the last piece of meat on his plate, sticks it in his mouth, and chews dramatically.

"I heard you talking to Mom," Sarah announces.

Phyllis ignores her husband and her daughter and scolds Simon over Fred's half-formed denial: "Really Simon. I have taught you better."

"Sorry, Phyllis. I mean, pardon?"

"Put your knife and fork together if you're finished. Don't just drop your fork noisily like that. You startled us all."

"Oh, don't worry about that, Phyllis, he has more important things to think about. Simon is making his mark at Con Fable."

"I told you," Sarah mutters under her breath to her plate.

Simon gapes at Fred, trying to keep up with his father's sudden one-eighty. He should be used to that, he reprimands himself as Fred keeps on talking: ". . . hear you're doing good work, Simon, and saving Con Fable a lot of money. They like how you handle the claimants. Apparently, you don't get much flack back."

"No," Simon says, striving to keep up.

"You just might get a promotion if you play your cards right. You can do that, can't you, son?"

Simon stammers, "A . . . a promotion?"

"Yes. I know it's early. Too soon. But the company always likes to spot an up-and-comer. They keep an eye on all new employees to see who has good mettle, who will become a benefit to the company. I hear they seem to think it's you."

"I'm not surprised," Michael drawls.

"He's such a good company boy," Sarah hoots.

Simon's face flames.

"Don't mock him, Sarah," Fred commands. "You should be so good. He's a better worker than you will ever be. In fact, Simon, I think we should have a celebratory whisky. I was just given a bottle of Macallan I think you'll appreciate—"

"It's premature, dear," Phyllis interrupts.

"I work hard at what I do," Sarah protests at the same time.

"Yes," Fred bites off the word without looking at Sarah. "You work hard at what you do. And come here to the bank of parent for the rest."

"Hey, I'm your daughter. It's in your interest to keep me looking good," she retorts, her reddening eyes fixed defiantly on her father.

Michael scoffs with biting laughter. Simon sinks into himself, retreating from them all. It's as if he's seeing them falling away on the other side of a long film lens; their voices recede, becoming incoherent bickering, leaving him behind in a bubble for one. Sarah's voice is sharp in its pseudo-braveness; Fred's deep and disdainful; Michael's deriding while detached; and Phyllis's authoritarian. Their tones bang and slide against each other, and Simon sees himself receding further away from this unhappy bunch. He is the unhappiest of them all, for his voice has fallen silent under their critical onslaught.

Disconnected and disembodied, he doesn't know where he fits in. The only thing he knows is that he does not like clubbing anymore. And that after he'd left the coffee shop, Byron resounding in his ears, Jackie in his eyes, he knew he couldn't return. No, there is one other thing he knows: he likes to visit the cemetery where Gramps's ashes reside, although he still doesn't know where the urn of his courageous, elder relative is stashed. Phyllis has not told them, and he dares not ask. Yet being somewhere in the near vicinity of Gramps gives him some strange sort of comfort. He'd retreated to there after he'd let the coffee shop door close behind him.

The crisp, quiet cold of the dead had drained his mind of all thought, all emotion that had gathered up onto themselves during the long, rapidly passing hours in the overheated shop, with its poets' narcotic words fanning terrible ideas in the fathomage of his soul. As he'd walked among the soft old stones and glittering new ones, the snow deadening his footsteps, he'd felt all angst draining away. He'd arrived home so late that the early morning stirrings of the market crowd had begun. That's when he determined to himself to look only ahead to his burgeoning life of a man of work, of a man moving into a deepening relationship with the woman he loves. Work. Marriage. Family. And, he'd told himself, he would remember Gramps in his private moments but no more in public. He'd fallen asleep there, where he'd collapsed angled across his sagging couch.

A solid elbow into his ribs chokes him back through that strange long lens and into the present. Simon glowers at Michael, and Michael gestures hard with his head to Phyllis's end of the table. Simon turns his head one-eighty and encounters his mother's impatient glare. Oh, he suddenly realizes, it's his turn.

"Sorry, Phyllis," he says as he hurriedly pushes back his chair and gathers up the plates and silverware.

"You are lost too often in daydreaming, Simon." Phyllis's cutting voice halts Simon as he reaches for Sarah's plate. "Your grandfather has been gone long enough for you to join us in the present. But if you must know: his favourite line was, 'It was a long way to Tipperary.' It wasn't a poem as you may define it, but he used to say to me that that song was poetry."

Simon waits hopefully, but Phyllis has finished. He says, "Thank you, Phyllis," and shrinks back into himself. He picks up Sarah's plate, with its knife and fork neatly pushed together, and carries the pile of plates and their baggage of knives and forks into the kitchen. He fills the dishwasher in the precise way his mother prefers. They had all learnt years ago that if they didn't do it right, she'd make them redo it. And every time she'd bought a new dishwasher, she'd teach them, supervise them, and then expect them to fill it correctly.

He pops the dishwasher detergent tab into its little nook and closes the door. The dishwasher is not yet full, and so he doesn't turn it on. Phyllis will only tolerate a full dishwasher being run. It's wasteful otherwise, she used to pronounce.

He hand washes the silverware and automatically places the pieces on the rack next to the sink to dry. Turning off the water, he listens to the conversation filtering in through the closed kitchen door. Phyllis had put the coffee urn on the buffet in the dining room so that they could help themselves to coffee after the main part of the meal without having to travel all the way into the kitchen. He cocks his head and cannot hear any movement from the table to the buffet. They must've helped themselves to coffee already. And they don't seem to have noticed that he's turned off the tap or that he should be finished by now. He swivels silently on his toes and leaps up the back stairs like a cat, two steps at a time. He jogs lightly to his parents' bathroom and opens the medicine cabinet. With two fingers, he digs his grandfather's round pill box out of his right front pants' pocket and opens it.

It is almost full.

He considers its fullness and decides he can fit two more in it.

He carefully slides the pill bottle he wants out of its place in his mother's collection, noting which way the label is facing, opens it, and extracts two round pink pills. He drops them carefully into his grandfather's box, and with some gingerly manoeuvring, replaces the lid. He shoves it deep into his pants pocket and returns his mother's pill bottle to its place in the cabinet, adjusting it until the label is facing the same way around as before. He pauses before closing the medicine cabinet door. Phyllis hasn't said anything about missing some pills: will this extraction be the one to twig her to what he's doing? He shakes his head; if he's honest with himself, he knows she won't. Phyllis never talks about sickness or medications or even seeing her GP. Her husband is a doctor, yet she pretends the whole messy area of sickness doesn't exist unless circumstances force her to, like when Gramps had had his heart attack. A few missing pills will be easy enough for her to dismiss as not having happened.

He closes the cabinet door and contemplates his reflected visage.

When Gramps had had his heart attack, they, his family, had all copied her avoidance habit then: seemingly concerned but trying to keep a distance. They had dutifully visited him, tip-toeing out as soon as they'd thought he'd fallen asleep, pretending not to hear him if he said anything while they were fleeing in their polite way. They had all felt satisfied with themselves that they'd visited and been supportive in the prescribed way and in the way they felt was suitable, given their busy schedules and commitments. Phyllis had deferred to Fred in the medical aspects of Gramps's care, and that is when Michael had confirmed that medicine was for him.

Yet in all their support, all their doing the right thing, they had not listened to the sick man, had not asked Gramps how he'd felt, had not listened to what he felt he needed.

He grimaces at himself in the mirror.

Hypocrite.

He hadn't asked either.

13

RULES ARE MADE TO BE

"Summoned to the office, man," Isaac says from over the shared cubicle wall, startling Simon. "It's F Day."

Simon squirrels his eyebrows at him puzzled. Isaac shrugs and saunters off.

"Oh," Simon mouths as the meaning of Isaac's shorthand falls into his mind. He droops. He doesn't want to say goodbye to another person.

The computer blanks to his screensaver, recalling him to his work. He moves his mouse. He frowns at his login screen. He types in his password and leans forward to perceive only what is in front of him.

He has Mrs. Smothe's treatment plan up. It's her third one from her physiotherapist. Time to say no, Simon decides. Twelve weeks of physiotherapy is gilding the lily and is past Con Fable's recommended guidelines. He glances at Con Fable's hefty book of guidelines open near his right hand. He riffles through the pages to find and reread the details on physiotherapy treatment plans. He has them memorized by now, but it reassures him to reread the details and not let time blur them a little bit here, a little bit there, and lead him astray. Guidelines are comforting. Obeying them won't get him into trouble.

A crash in Isaac's cubicle jerks him upright and hastily shut the tome in one movement. He stands up gingerly till only his eyes are above the cubicle wall, looks toward Mr. Confabulate's office, sees that the door is shut and the blinds closed, and straightens up to his full height. "What happened?" he asks.

"You know, the F word, man, it failed me," Isaac humphs as he slides his keyboard viciously across his desk, his legs standing rigidly apart.

"Firing Day," Simon says sympathetically.

"Yeah, firing day. Some firing day," Isaac says as he slams his mouse toward the keyboard and begins swearing under his breath. The mouse bounces off the keyboard and slides toward the edge of the desk. Isaac stops and turns fully to face Simon. He puts his hands on his hips and sounds off: "What happened? I tell you what happened. He didn't fire me, that's what happened, man. He reprimanded me. The boss had the balls to reprimand me!" He points to himself. "He said I wasn't turning down enough treatment plans. I was being too lenient." Isaac throws his arms outward to east and west of him. "Lenient!" Isaac croaks, emphasizing each sentence with a shake of his arms. "If he believed that, he should've fired me for not following SOP. Instead, he lectures me! This is how the fraudsters get away with things, he said. This is why people stage car accidents cause people like me make it so easy to get money out of us. Fraud, he said. Fraud, my ass. It isn't them creating fraud," Isaac says as he widens his eyes, lifts his eyebrows, juts his face forward, and balls his hands into hard fists at the end of his outstretched arms. "He doesn't see these plans day after day, like we do. I've turned them down faster than anyone around here. Same deal every performance day. We all know they're legit, right, man? But, me, I do my job the Con Fable rule way, man."

"It's business," Simon replies in a neutral tone.

Isaac shoots him a baleful look and drops his arms. "You're getting promoted, ain't you, big man? Not surprised, no siree, I'm not. You're connected. You connected folk get promoted above the rest of us hard workers."

Simon objects, "I thought you wanted to be fired?" Isaac's irises deepen, his mouth sets. Simon stammers, "Maybe not?" He clears his throat, "I learnt the guidelines like everyone else. You have to follow the rules, Isaac."

"I do."

"My father taught me that."

"Why? I gotta ask why I still should?" Isaac glares his question right into Simon's grey-green-surrounded pupils. "Did he teach you the hidden rules?"

Simon opens his mouth to answer and hesitates. Isaac's second question confuses him, and he skips backward to his first. Yet answering that it's company policy, it's the way to stay employed all of a sudden seems not quite the right answer in the face of Isaac's challenge. Hidden rules? Is Isaac paranoid? Simon closes his mouth. Isaac nods, mumbles, "I thought so," and snatches his keyboard and mouse from where they had landed, slams them down in place in front of the computer screen, grabs his chair and slams into it, drags himself closer to his desk, and commences banging out letters to clients. Isaac mutters, "Time to make up new rules. Truth rules."

As he watches Isaac's angry movements, Simon wonders: isn't Con Fable right about most claimants being fraudsters? Isn't that why they have so many guidelines to ensure transparency and truth? Is Isaac right? Are the rules right? Should he always obey them? Simon lowers his head and stares unseeingly at his blank cubicle wall. He has not pinned anything up on it like the others have on their walls. He doesn't want to disturb its clean blankness.

Simon's mind wanders back to the guidelines, written and unwritten. Standard operating procedure is to mark down the claim by two-thirds. It's easier to do the markdown on claims that involve body work on dented cars because Con Fable has long since negotiated contracts with certain autobody shops and ordered their claimants in a friendly way to use those autobody shops, advising they're the most trustworthy. After Con Fable was caught trying to do that with treatment providers, they were forced to institute automatic denial as their first line of defence, or better yet to stall the claimant during their initial call from applying. Then they can deny accident benefits as being too late. Simon has become good at stalling claimants until past the seven-day cutoff deadline. In their ignorance, most make it easy for him to stall them, so easy he can let his mind perambulate into other avenues of thought, like that poem Jackie had recited or Jackie herself—he shakes his head. He mustn't go there.

He retreats to his chair and back to Mrs. Smothe's treatment plan application. He thinks of how polite a claimant she is—not like the ones who can't be fobbed off. Con Fable labels them repeaters or fraudsters. They have special guidelines on how to wear down the claimants who fight for the full value of their legitimate claims. The first step is to label them malingerers, people with somatic disorders. And they have a heavily guarded list of doctors and clinics who are willing to produce the correct label. Some of these things are not explicitly said, but Mr. Confabulate makes them understand them with his little pep chats as he circumambulates their cubicles during one of his random inspections. But as much as Simon understands company policy, part of him cannot believe that that many people deliberately hit other cars so as to make a false claim. It would hurt too much, he always thinks. Still, rules are rules.

Isaac's imprecations break through Simon's thoughts. Simon wishes he can rebel like Isaac. Isaac seems freer; Isaac doesn't care what other people think.

"You better get back to work, promotion boy, else Mr. Confabulate will notice. He watches all our computers, you know," Isaac instructs through the soft wall.

Simon pulls himself closer to his desk and returns to Mrs. Smothe's treatment plan. No, he doesn't believe she's lying about her injuries or her pain, but he cannot believe that she needs more physiotherapy. He was sympathetic when the second plan had arrived for his approval. But no more. As Fred often instructs, one cannot let people malinger. At some point, you need to throw the patient out of the nest; they must learn to fly on their own and deal with their health problems as real adults do, not depend on paid professionals to hold their hands. That's what friends are for, if they want to go that route. But Canadians are rugged. Individual. That's the mark of a man, of every member of his family: being able to soar freely, alone. Whenever he repeated that lecture, they knew he'd had a particularly needy patient that day.

Mrs. Smothe has to prove that she actually requires more physiotherapy, not just believe so. Beliefs can lead you astray, as Fred teaches. Simon considers the name of the treatment provider. The name is familiar from Mr. Confabulate's last discussion with Simon about which treatment providers to watch out for. This one has a vested interest in keeping on clients, Mr. Confabulate had asserted. The orientation teacher Simon had had when he'd first started working at Con Fable had highlighted some treatment providers as examples of difficult ones, and this one had been one of those, Simon is sure. Don't believe the providers, the orientation teacher had hammered home, when they say they are running off their feet morning, noon, and night and are unable to see new patients for weeks. They tell you that to gain your sympathy. But it's not true. They make good money off our largesse, he had instructed. And Simon had accepted unquestioningly what the teacher had said and what Mr. Confabulate reminds him when he looks over his shoulder at his work. Why would either man lie? The providers are probably like him, feeling sorry for these people injured in car crashes. But sympathy doesn't make people well. They have to get on with their lives, get on with being productive citizens, like Simon is now.

Is he really going to get a promotion? Simon sits back and gazes up at the white expanse of the office ceiling. With Isaac repeating what Sarah had blurted out, he begins to wonder if it's true. He can't rely on what Fred says; so often he talks to relax him, to feel good, to allay his defences until he lets down his guard so that the descent is sweeter for Fred when—.

Simon scoffs at his thoughts and sits forward again to consider Mrs. Smothe's treatment provider again. Yes, he knows the provider for himself. Her name is on many of the forms that come across his desk. She must have a big practice. How she sees so many injured people baffles him. He flips open Con Fable's book, searching for the applicable guidelines again. His finger stops at the right one. He nods as he reads that Con Fable requires that physiotherapists see their insured patients for a half hour minimum. With so many clients, how can this provider do that? Maybe he should send one of their auditors in. He likes Elly. She can fake an injury with the best of them, long enough to experience the full term of a typical treatment plan. He grasps his mouse and moves it to the Start button. He brings up the audit program—

"That'll teach you!"

Simon jumps and shushes Isaac through their shared cubicle wall. "Mr. Confabulate will hear you."

"Don't care, man. Don't care," Isaac calls back.

Simon stands up and takes the step over to the cubicle wall to see what Isaac is up to. "What are you doing?" he asks as he peers over the top of the wall.

Isaac grins wickedly up at him. Then resumes his furious typing.

Simon shakes his head ruefully and returns to work. Where was he? Oh, that's right. He was going to send in Elly. He fills in the audit request and adds in the notes section a request that Elly do it. He next calls up the rejection template and with two mouse clicks sends a rejection letter to the treatment provider with the standard paragraph saying that Con Fable will be requesting an IME, independent medical exam.

With Mrs. Smothe taken care of, he moves on to the next treatment plan. This one is for psychological care. Elaine loves these ones. She devours every detail of the claimant's difficulties. Submission of a psychological treatment plan heralds Con Fable's legal department getting involved. They automatically demand copies of all medical records; the opposing side usually sends them in, in dribs and drabs, as slowly as they can. He doesn't know how Con Fable gets the government's health insurance plan to send them the claimant's lifetime history of medical claims. Then Con Fable sends the records to psychologists versed in administering scales, requesting a lengthy report on the claimant. Insurance mills, Elaine calls them with relish. She likes them for the gossip fodder they provide. They follow Con Fable's formula, going through claimants like sand in the hand. Once the records and reports arrive back in their section, they make the rounds, with Elaine having the first gander at them, always immediately sussing out which ones have the juiciest tidbits in them and tying them to medicare billings. He always knows the days she finds good ones, for she looks like a lion satiated after a good kill with blood still on its lips.

Isaac crows, "There. That'll teach you. Another one done."

Simon blinks. He hears Isaac chuckle under his breath. His curiosity impels him up and out of his chair, around the shared cubicle wall, and into Isaac's cubicle to stand behind him and watch what he's doing. He doesn't notice Elaine zipping backward in her chair out of her cubicle to follow him with a considering eye. She stands and walks over. "What is he doing?" she asks from right behind Simon.

Simon whirls around. "What are you doing Elaine?" he gasps.

She returns his shocked stare calmly and replies, "What are you doing?"

"I—"

"He's watching me approve every treatment plan in my file, is what he's doing. You want to join in, Elaine? I call it liberation day for claimants. See here. This here, he had a bad whiplash in his . . . let's see, third car accident. Boy, he sure is accident prone. Oh, yeah, he needs to get himself a new car. Those old buggies, man, they're bad. Anyway, he got X-rays, even an MRI, to prove his neck is all straightened out of shape, and look at where his shoulder is at? Tsk. But guidelines say only eight weeks physiotherapy and no laser after the first denial and regimental IME. Not gonna fix him up, no way José. But guidelines must be right, right Simon? So I follow them, man. I turn down his first treatment plan and approve his second smaller one that we all know won't work like his first one would've, like a good Con Fable em-ploy-ee, right Simon?"

Simon swallows hard.

"And look where it got me? It got me into Mr. Con-Fab-U-Late's office is where it got me because I was to wait for his third before approving. And now I'm looking at his third because his eight weeks weren't enough. This boy's in bad shape. He needs his physiotherapy. He's a janitor, man. He can't work in that kind of pain with his neck not moving and all. But it's business, they tell you, just business. Well, it's his business, too, and he sends me a letter asking me why I don't want him to work no more. I send it to legal like a good em-ploy-ee."

By this time, a small crowd has gathered behind Simon and Elaine, attracted by Isaac's outraged tones. They all cram in to Isaac's cubicle, too fascinated to remember that Mr. Confabulate could see them, as Isaac's voice rises indignantly.

"So what it gets me? It gets me a reprimand, that's what. I'm trying to save this badass company some measly bucks on the neck of this poor boy, and I get reprimanded. No more, man. No more. This boy gonna get his physio. I'm gonna give him eight weeks more."

"The treatment plan says four."

"Oh, will you look at that," Isaac says. "So it does. Simon wants me to do the right thing, Elaine. Well, what is the right thing, Simon?" Isaac asks as he twists his head around to glare into Simon's eyes. "Well? I'm not asking a rhetorical question here. What is the right thing?"

Simon opens his mouth. He closes it. He knits his brows.

"You see. When you come from a big-shot family, you don't know what the right thing is anymore, money had got you so twisted around. All you think is keep the money for yourself. Well, this boy, he paid his money. You think if he'd missed one premium payment, Con Fable would've been lenient, would've said that's okay, we don't mind taking you to court to get our money, we expect to have to fight to get your premiums. No. They would've cut him off, and he wouldn't have been able to make them change their mind. But we can stop paying them, and they have to fight us. We make them fight us for every single penny, with IMEs and lawyers and mediation after mediation and pre-trials and trials, and we drag it out, oh man, do we drag it out. And then they don't get the full value of their claim, anyway. What does Con Fable say, Simon?"

"They say the best claim is one disallowed," Simon replies rotely.

"Yeah, that's what they say. But what's it mean?"

Simon furrows his brows, sends his eyes to the left then to the right, then back at Isaac. His lips part, but no words come.

"No guts," Isaac says with derision as he erases the "4" in the treatment plan on his screen and meticulously writes an "8" in with his mouse. Simon has to admire his skill, while wondering how he came by it at the same time that Elaine bursts out with astonishment, "You can do that? I didn't know you could do that."

Isaac smiles self-deprecatingly and replaces the old file with the new doctored file. He clicks approve and sends it off. He leans back in his chair and does a double fist pump.

"What is going on here?"

The entire crowd behind Isaac whips around as one. Flurried exclamations of "nothing" and "just wanted to consult" sound as the crowd swirls around Mr. Confabulate and retreats back to their respective cubicles, leaving Simon alone with Isaac and their boss.

Simon says all in one burst: "We were having a discussion on guidelines, sir." He continues talking rapidly as he walks back to his cubicle, pulling Mr. Confabulate along with the strength of his voice. "I was going over a psychological treatment plan, and I had a question about one of the requirements for denial. Isaac is good at denial. He knows the guidelines well, and I thought to consult him. Others heard our discussion, too, and wanted clarification."

"Alright, alright, Simon. Enough. Look, I came to call you into my office. But I might as well tell you here. I'm promoting you." His points his right forefinger right at Simon's chest and smiles widely.

Simon stills.

"Yes. You'll still have to work in the cubicle I'm afraid," he says as he looks around the cramped space with contempt, dropping his hand. "But you'll get a raise in your salary. We're putting you up to the next pay grade. We'll start to feed you the cases that've been denied but approved by IMEs, which we need to contest. It requires finesse and Con Fable-type thinking, which keeps Con Fable's stockholders happy. When they're satisfied with their dividend yields, we know we're doing right. But you'll need the stomach for it. Are you up for the challenge?" Mr. Confabulate doesn't pause for a reply. "These claimants' lawyers are savvy and know all the loopholes. It'll be your job to wear them down. Don't let them suck you into their stories," he says, wagging a finger in Simon's face. "They're good at that. Remember . . ."

"We're a business," Simon completes automatically.

Mr. Confabulate nods sharply, "That's right. They try to make you see differently. These people would malinger for years if we let them. But it's our duty to see that they give up their claim by . . . ," Simon's boss pauses to see what Simon will say.

"Denying them," Simon says.

Mr. Confabulate slaps him on his shoulder. "Good. You'll do Con Fable proud." He strides back to his office.

Simon falls against his desk, befuddled about his promotion and relieved that Mr. Confabulate had forgotten about Isaac.

Isaac sticks his head around the cubicle wall. "What did I tell you? You got that promotion."

Simon nods.

Isaac straightens up and enters Simon's cubicle. He has his jacket, hat, and scarf on. He buttons up his jacket as he takes a step toward Simon. He holds out his hand. Simon takes it mindlessly. Isaac's grip recalls him to his senses and lifts his eyes to Isaac's stern stare. "Congratulations, man. You got the promotion, just like someone like you should. Me, I quit."

Isaac shakes Simon's hand once and lets it go. He turns around but stops in the aisle. He looks over his shoulder at Simon, "It's a good day to quit. I made a lot of hurting people feel better by giving them the care they need for just a little while longer. What about you, Simon? Can you say the same thing?"

14

POWER AND PRISCILLA

"Can you say the same thing?" Isaac's words spin in his head like a dryer that won't turn off, tumbling his emotions round and round, stirring up cognitive dissonance, making him itch. The only solution is to hunker down in front of his computer and focus on his work. As long as he is line driving his mind into reading and deciding whether to approve or disallow treatment claims, he can keep Isaac's unsettling behaviour and disturbing ideas out of his head.

"What is the right thing?" The question pops up into Simon's consciousness like a helium balloon that won't be tied down. Simon leans so far forward his nose almost touches his screen. The work fills his vision, blinds him to the question.

But every time Simon relaxes into the comforting back of his chair and his mind relaxes its hold on his work, Isaac's words spiral back into his head. He cannot stand it. He refocuses on his work. It's a report on the injuries sustained by one of their claimants after he sped right into the back of a car, being unable to come to a full stop in time. One hundred percent his fault. He checks the police report. He nods his head; the report will note the finding of fault by the police, the increase in premiums, and Con Fable's standard reasons for cutting off the claimant's accident benefits. Simon types automatically, listing the litany of injuries sustained by the claimant that he's including in the report as being suspect and the reason for a mediation. The report will go to his boss who will then forward it on to the Con Fable representative at the mediation and include standard Con Fable arguments for ensuring the claimant agrees to a low settlement. He doesn't notice the office emptying or the shouts of goodbye. Only when the cleaner pokes her head into his cubicle and asks him if she can clean does he realize the time—and at the same moment remembers that he was supposed to have met Priss at her place so that the two of them could drive to her friend's roomy cottage for the weekend, somewhere east of Peterborough. He yanks his phone out of his pocket. Sure enough, there's a message from Priss. How had he missed hearing her ring tone, the one he'd programmed to sound after work hours? He shakes his head and connects quickly to his voice mail. He grimaces at her increasingly angry messages. He takes a breath and presses her contact number.

"Where are you, Simon?"

"At work," he grovels.

"I thought you weren't allowed overtime."

"I'm not, but . . ."

"But nothing. You know, I had to leave. I can't keep my friends waiting. I'm not rude like you."

"I'm sorry, Priss, I'm sorry."

"And I bet you'll say you can't come now, right?"

Simon had been about to say that, but he gulps down those words. He hears himself say: "I'm coming. Just tell me where it is."

"Really? I emailed you the map, you know. And how are you planning on coming?"

"Oh." They were supposed to drive up together. She has a car. He does not. "Sorry Priss."

"You should check your email, Simon. I can't be calling you and emailing you about the same thing, you know."

"I know, I know. I'm sorry."

"Okay," Priss says mollified. "But how are you coming?"

"I'll borrow my mother's car."

"Really? Not your father's? It's faster." Priss's anger cycles up again. "It's embarrassing you're not here. I wish you were here, like right now. They're whispering about our relationship, I know it."

"I'm really sorry, Priss. But I can't use Fred's car. Phyllis's is fast, I promise. It'll get me to you quickly, I promise."

"I'll hold you to that," Priscilla replies and hangs up in his ear. Prickles of pain enter him.

Her words, "It's faster," echo in his mind; he flashes to the report he'd sent off before he called her, the words he used to condemn the speeding man to a trial and inadequate medical coverage. The Con Fable way. His way. "What is the right thing, Simon?" Isaac's voice jumps into his consciousness. His hand reflexively grips his iPhone, and he buries his thoughts under the rush of grabbing his jacket. At the same time as he shrugs into it, he tries to dial Phyllis's number. But there's no answer. The needles of grief and shame churn up his blood, flinging themselves this way and that, stabbing through his artery walls into his cells, sewing excruciating agony into him.

Simon flees Con Fable's offices and races to his parents' place, dialling Phyllis every few minutes with no success, trying to keep the voices and the questions out of his head. He strides around the corner onto his parents' street and then hesitates slightly behind a soaring cedar. He peeks around its needle-heavy branches toward his parents' house, lit up by little lights along the walk and a lantern over the door. He's not sure how his parents will react to him showing up out of the blue, asking to borrow the car. Both of his parents insist on a phone call beforehand, and him not being able to reach them would not be accepted as a valid excuse. Simon swallows. He presses the icon for their home phone number again on his iPhone.

"Hello?"

Simon sighs in relief, "Hello, Mommy. It's Simon."

"I know who it is, Simon, and why are you sounding like a child? I'm in a rush. We're about to leave. Fred has made us extraordinarily late, even for him. I don't know how I'll explain this to the Wilsons. At least since their stint in Spain, they do have a habit of dining late."

"I was hoping to borrow your car."

"Well, you can't. We need it." For the second time that evening, Simon hears empty air in his ear. He stands there for long minutes, unsure what to do, until from his vantage point, he sees the rear of Phyllis's Jaguar appear from the other side of the house. She is backing down the driveway, Fred in the front passenger seat, his distinctive shadow in profile to him, the shadow that got him the job at Con Fable.

Phyllis backs her sleek car into the street, her brake lights flaring red, then dimming as she changes gear and accelerates away from him. Simon watches her taillights grow smaller and smaller then turn right at the corner and vanish.

Something clicks in his mind.

Anxiety flees, and his body hardens with determination.

Without thinking consciously about it, he finds himself walking up to the house instead of away. He sees his hand inserting his key into their lock—what is he doing, he thinks fleetingly, as he turns the key in the lock and pushes the door open. He watches himself disengage the alarm and yank off his shoes to leave no trace of his presence. He treads in his socked feet down to Fred's office, while his conscious mind says he mustn't do this, he must go home, why won't he stop? He doesn't stop; instead he looks up and down the hallway as he stands outside the shut office door. The house is silent. There is no other presence in it but for himself. Yet he feels not alone. He tries to turn himself around; instead he turns the knob of the office door and enters the room of the shadow that sent him to Con Fable and along the path to those questions he doesn't want to hear, the questions he has no answer to, questions on top of things he must not talk about. Con Fable rules, Fred rules, Phyllis rules, are absolute. He walks straight to Fred's desk. He knows where the keys are. He finds them and exits the way he came in.

He shoves his feet into his shoes and hustles to the garage, keeping close to the walls of the house and then to the garage in case anyone is watching. But in this neighbourhood, people mind their own business. That's why Fred and Phyllis like it.

He slips into the garage through the side door and raises up the heavy garage door from the inside. He pauses to scan the empty driveway in front of him before turning around to ponder the red car that sits there.

What is he doing?

He is borrowing a car. No big deal. Sarah does it all the time.

Simon frowns; well, not all the time. And he himself has never done it before. He folds into himself and stares at the keys in his hand. He must return them. "What about you, Simon? Can you say the same thing?" Isaac's repeating voice bangs around in his head.

Simon grabs his hair and pulls. But Isaac's voice grows stronger, his questions insistent.

You don't have to listen, comes the unbidden thought.

The car is waiting.

Simon straightens and takes two giant steps to the gleaming car Fred had backed into its slot. He unlocks it. He opens the door. He slides into the driver's seat. It hugs him. He inserts the key into the ignition and presses the red "Engine Start" button.

The engine growls to life, and he feels the power of its twelve pistons as they rapidly cycle up and down, up and down, thrilling into his feet, up his legs, through his pelvis, and up into his stomach. The fiery power sets a rabble of butterflies fluttering up from his stomach and into his breast. A sly grin comes over his face as a force shuts down his mind and takes over his body. He shifts into first gear and gently touches the accelerator to ease the car forward out of the garage. He brakes. He unwinds himself out of the seat, out of the car, and pulls the garage door down on its oiled wheels. He slides back in to the driver's seat, closes the door with a satisfying thunk, belts himself in, and drives into the street and then toward the country.

He impatiently tolerates the traffic laws as he drives north through the city up to Highway 7. Rush hour is long over. Night has settled over the asphalt as he drives east to Peterborough and that cottage Priss wants him to join her at. He hadn't checked his email for directions, but it doesn't matter to him.

It's east. The dawn gone. The night extending.

Though his mind is detached, his hand shifts gears up angrily as the traffic thins. He accelerates. Even this far east along the highway, the city doesn't release its clutch on the road for many kilometres. He longs to open up more the throttle of the red Ferrari. He's never felt this way before. When Fred had bought his Ferrari last year, his endless talk with Michael about its features had become a drone in his head. He doesn't even remember the model name; something that sounds Italian, of course. He utters a sound of dismissal under his breath. What does it matter what its name is as long as it can hurtle him down this snake of a road?

His thoughts and mind recede once again.

He glances down at the plethora of controls while he's still cruising at a hundred and twenty. He doesn't know what they all mean, but the Race one pops out at him. He sinks down into his seat, eyes straight ahead, hungry for the road to open up, muscles tensing, waiting, anticipating the rush.

And then there are no more buildings, no more streetlights, no more traffic. It's him and the unfurling blacktop curling left and right with its solid yellow line down the middle. He flips on the high beams and accelerates down the road as it straightens and the solid yellow becomes slashes of yellow. They flash by until they seemingly blur into one.

A turn appears.

The engine whines as he accelerates the car into the turn, forcing it to reach maximum RPMs. Tiny round red lights shoot one, two, three around the steering wheel; he shifts with his fingers at the last minute—a quick pull of the little gear on the left side of the steering wheel, and the engine rumbles its satisfaction as the turn slingshots car and Simon fast down the straight.

He howls down the highway under the melanoid night, the power and speed enthralling him, strengthening him. A car materializes into view up ahead and then a truck coming the other way further ahead, a tiny dot at first then rapidly growing as it speeds toward him. He narrows his eyes and contracts his arm muscles. The car ahead of him is moving too slowly. The centre line is solid yellow. But the truck is his. He knows it. This is the moment. He knows now why he borrowed his father's red car.

His foot depresses the pedal under his shoe, the engine pitching up and up and up. He releases it like lightening as he shifts up a gear then depresses it fast as he guides the steering wheel to move into the oncoming lane, the fire under the hood growling like a lion smelling its kill. The truck's horn sounds a low, bellowing note of warning. Simon focuses in on the front grill. The headlights brighten as they grow. Round twins of white. He keeps both hands on the wheel as his foot mashes the accelerator to the floor. A grin slashes his face as the grill fills his vision. Under his command, the gasoline-fuelled engine revs fast and long, eating up the metres toward his destination.

Simon's eyes blink.

Fear borrows his breath.

He twists the wheel to the right, sharp, fast.

The whisper as he slices between truck and car keens in his ear.

The car is behind him. The truck is behind him. And the empty road disappears in front of him beyond the reach of his beams.

His heart thumps in his chest, and he cannot hear even the roaring whine of the engine under his control. He spots an intersection up ahead, a gravel side road disappearing between trees on his right. He gears down and, as he reaches it, brakes hard to skid ninety degrees right onto it. The Ferrari's wheels squeal their fury. Gravel stones whip the shining red exterior, pinging their outrage at being disturbed. He releases his foot and crawls along the edge of the road until at last all inertia gone, the red Ferrari stops. He turns off the engine.

The quiet of a country night greets him.

He leans his arms over the top of the steering wheel and rests his forehead on his crossed wrists. The wind soughs through the ragged trees around him. His fingers tighten around the small wheel. What happened?

Simon has no answer.

Simon raises himself up and looks into his sideview mirror back at the highway. A car appears and disappears as it zooms west. What had possessed him?

He twists his head this way and that, his eyes widening, his lower jaw dropping, his breath quickening, taking in the cockpit of where he finds himself. Fred's car. This is the car that Simon has never borrowed, never used. Simon is forbidden to drive Fred's Ferraris.

He has broken a rule.

He doesn't know why.

But he knows he cannot go to Peterborough. His only saving grace will be if he arrives home before his parents. The Wilsons' are notorious partiers. Fred and Phyllis usually leave her Jaguar in their driveway, too tired to deal with parking it carefully in the garage. They may not notice the missing Ferrari until the morning. Had he closed the garage door? He cannot remember. He swallows and starts the engine. A snarl rumbles through him. This time the power scares him for what it had done and for what it may do to him again. He sends a small prayer up, like he used to when a child before he spurned the falsity of church. He retreats for home as quickly as his fear at losing control again will let him.

"Let's go to a movie," Priscilla chirps over the phone. Simon shakes his head, confused. He had successfully returned the Ferrari without either of his parents knowing what had happened. He had luckily thought to fill up the tank on the way back. And then he had gone home and flopped down on his couch, relieved to be safe, not wanting to move again, willing the memory of what had happened to flow out of him. He'd called Priss when his heart had calmed down to its normal rate and had been astounded to hear some excuse leaving his mouth as soon as she had said hello, an excuse he cannot remember now. But she had been merry in her tipsiness and had forgiven him quickly. Priss drunk was a happy girlfriend, especially when she had told him that it was best he hadn't shown because it was turning out to be a girls' weekend. None of the boys had shown up. She was relieved he hadn't either, leaving him feeling like a ping pong ball but he, too, relieved. And now she is calling him up.

Simon agrees to her plan, and he walks over to her place to pick her up. He knocks on her door, and she yanks it open eagerly. "Ma is away."

Priscilla pulls him in, and Simon neither resists nor closes the gap between them.

Priscilla hurriedly unbuttons his jacket while at the same time time pulling him toward the living room so that he must follow. She strips off his jacket without his help and lets it fall to the floor behind him. She grabs his hand and drags him over to the couch. He passively follows yet remains apart from her. She doesn't notice as she pushes him down and straddles his lap. She langurously moves in and kisses him deeply.

Simon feels her lips pressing his and nothing more. Suddenly unsure and unhappy, he pushes her up and then off his lap.

"What the hell, Simon?"

"I'm sorry," he replies, his hands twisting in his lap.

"Aren't I attractive? Do I have garlic breath or something?"

Simon glances up quickly and takes in her straight shiny hair that flows over her shoulders and covers her breasts. He takes in her dewy skin and snapping deep brown eyes. He takes in the shape of her underneath her tight sheathe of a dress. And he shakes his head. "No. Your breath is fine. And your beauty is exotic and deeply compelling," he says without a trace of emotion.

"Then what is it?" she demands.

He pauses, staring into the space in front of him, not looking at Priss. One thought after another enters and exits his mind, none he can or wants to say to her and none he understands himself. He doesn't want those thoughts. He forces them down, and he remembers his promotion. "I got a promotion."

He hears her shift into a proper sitting position. He sends his eyes right; she is staring at him. "This is bad news?" she asks in disbelief.

"No, no. The family told me it was going to happen."

"They did?" she asks. "How did he know? I mean, it must've been Fred who knew, right?"

Simon shrugs, "He did."

"You kind of feel it's not because of your own initiative?"

He looks full at her, slightly shocked at her insight and her unusual-to-her vocabulary. He says, "Yes," while at the same time thinking that simply following orders nets a person a promotion in Con Fable. And maybe the "who" is important too, as Isaac had said. The thought prickles across his back.

She narrows her eyes at him. "Is that all Simon? Cause it's not like you. You never had a problem with Fred helping you out before. Look how you got the job."

"Yes, but I had to pass the interview."

She snorts.

"I did," he protests, while hearing Isaac in his head, while seeing Fred's shadow slide by him. He rolls his shoulders as the prickles intensify into a demanding itch.

She smiles at him from under her long lashes. "Okay Simon. Whatever you say. You got the job yourself. I'm not objecting that Fred helped you out. I think you're lucky. You need connections to get ahead in this world. Look at me. I don't have connections, but at least I have you." She peeps at him.

Simon shifts uneasily and looks away from her, down at his fine hands. She leans forward and pinches his arm, shaking it. "Don't be so serious, silly. This is a good thing. You got a promotion. We should celebrate. And I know how."

"No!"

Priscilla rears back.

"I'm sorry, Priss, I . . . I'm not in the mood. I don't know why. I just feel restless. Look why don't we go to that movie?"

"Okay."

But neither of them moves. Simon continues to sit at the end of the sofa, tight up against its arm, staring at his hands as they twist around and around. Priscilla scoots to sit at the other end of the sofa, her legs curled under her, her back leaning against its arm as she contemplates him.

Like the words were being dragged out of her, she asks, "Are you still missing your grandfather?"

"Yes."

"Well, don't. He's gone, and he's not missing you."

"How do you know that?"

"Papa didn't miss me. He left. How could he have—," she chokes off the words.

Simon angles around so that he can see her. "How could he have what?" he asks curiously.

She shakes her head and bites her lip. She sucks in her breath and says, "Enough. He doesn't miss you, and you need to get on with your life. You can't live like this. I can't live with you like this. It's miserable."

"No," he replies slowly. "Grief isn't miserable."

"It makes everyone else miserable. It makes me miserable. I want to be happy, only happy. The dead don't make me happy. Life is for us."

"Life is for the living, but the dead are part of the living. Don't you see that, Priss? We forget them too quickly; we forget how they made us, shaped us, or maybe even changed us. Without them, we forget ourselves."

"Papa did nothing for me. I was four when he died."

"Those were important years, Priscilla."

"So what? They don't matter now. I had more years without him than with him. And so will you. With your grandfather, I mean."

"Will I?"

"Of course!"

"We don't know when we're going to die, do we?"

"You're too young to die, Simon. Don't be stupid. You don't mean it."

"Yes, I do. We don't know. Nobody knows. That's why death is scary. It's easier if you know, don't you think?"

"No, it isn't. It's easier if we don't think about it at all."

"Why?"

"Why? You're being grim, Simon. You bring the mood down. I don't want to kiss you now, either." She folds her arms across her chest and scowls at him, pain wrinkling her inner eyebrows up.

He furrows his brow. "I'm sorry, Priscilla. I'm sorry I can't stop thinking about Gramps. It's like a sinkhole has opened underneath my feet, and I don't know how not to fall in. I'm trying not to. I'm reaching out, but—"

"Well, talking about it doesn't help." She unfolds her arms, leans forward, and stretches her hand out to touch his arm. "You have to move on, Simon. Accept that promotion. Be grateful for Fred's help. He knows how to live as a real man. Forget your grandfather. He's gone. Thinking about him and death will only make you depressed. If you stop talking about it, stop trying to make us talk about it, you'll see, you'll stop thinking about it and be much happier. We have a future ahead of us, don't you see, Simon? A future."

He nods, yet he yearns not to be alone in his grief, to be able to share it with another. Even if they cannot feel the grief, at least be sympathetic with it and sit with him. He doesn't want to be alone.

"We've talked about marriage before. You want babies. I want babies. We can make new memories, don't you think?" Priscilla entreats, interrupting his thoughts.

Simon nods.

"But if you keep talking about death, it's kind of hard to make babies, right?"

He nods.

She removes her hand from his arm and sits up, putting her feet on the floor while keeping her head turned toward him, her eyes on his face. He drops his eyes under the scrutiny of hers. "C'mon, Simon. So you're not in the mood. It's no big deal. It's only one time. It's night, it's cloudy. Kind of dampens things, eh, when it's so grey outside. I wish the sun would come out. All we've had is cloud, cloud, cloud. It kind of gets to a person. I understand, Simon. Why don't we go to that movie?"

Simon gazes at the sofa he's sitting on, at the texture of the traditional brocade, at the soft ochre colour, at the wrinkles engendered by her now-absent weight, at the way the cushions don't meet on their surfaces but come together in their middles so that he cannot see all the way down the crack between them. He brushes his hand lightly over the fabric, feeling the coarse weave and subtle changes between the raised pattern and background. He brushes his hand back and forth, back and forth, and follows its movement with his eyes as they defocus until all he sees is a blur of chapped pink on ochre. Priscilla leans down into his view and looks up into his face. "Simon, c'mon. Let's go to a movie."

Forced back into the present, into thinking, into a decision, Simon declares, "No."

He stands up. Priscilla cranes her neck.

"We need to take a break."

"A break?" Her mouth falls open.

"Yes," he says to the space above her and then he looks down. And into the face of her shock, his sudden decision weakens. "Just a little while," he wheadles. "As you said, I'm making you miserable."

"I didn't mean—"

"I know what you meant. I just need some time to think. Yes?"

Priscilla nods reluctantly. She whispers, "At least this time you're telling me."

"I'll get in touch."

Priscilla's face whitens. Pain shines her eyes. They both know he won't, but neither wants to out the lie. He turns on his heel, gathers up his jacket where Priscilla had stripped it off him, and walks out the door.

15

THE STRANGER

"I can't do this," Simon mutters as he hits the sidewalk after leaving Priscilla. He hunches into his jacket as the unkind wind blows through the sticking up strands of his hair. The wind's cold edge burns along his scalp as it tries to flatten and raise up his hair at the same time.

He feels manipulated.

He feels alone.

He doesn't know what he feels.

He strides faster and faster away from Priscilla and her familiar home of the last five years. Up until this very moment, he'd envisioned his life with her. Suddenly, his life will be without. Up until he heard himself say "No" to her, he'd thought vaguely of marrying her. He lengthens his strides. She'd wanted marriage and children, but though he'd agreed with her whenever she broached the subject, he'd wanted, what? He slows down. He'd not talked of having children together, only that he had wanted some. She had said . . . even minutes ago Priscilla had been saying they each wanted babies. Had he? He clenches his jaw, thrusts out his chest, and powers forward with his arms swinging in step with his feet. He was the one who hadn't felt a great need for babies. He was the one who'd had a vague idea that they were included in life not that he actually wanted one or two or three. One was born, one went to school, one got a job, one got married, one had children.

One died.

He arrives at a main intersection. The red traffic light halts his steps and his thoughts. He shifts his weight from foot to foot, back and forth, side to side. He wants to cross the street in the same direction that he's been going in, but the light prohibits him from acting out his wishes. He looks quickly left to right and back again; cars zoom toward him from both directions, lanes and lanes of them vying to get ahead of all the others. Pedestrians hustle across in tandem with the cars and bunch up around him as they reach the corner and wait with him to cross in the other direction. Their collective breath frosts the night air.

His light turns green, and the crowd swarms around him as they instantly react to the light's permission. Slower than the crowd in starting, he speeds up and walks through them to beat them to the other side. He keeps walking in a straight line and drops his head to contemplate the sidewalk. The last snow has been cleared by someone, but snowflakes have drifted down since the last shovelling, and the tread of many feet has melted it down to a few wisps of slippery grey that course across the concrete.

He isn't sure where he's walking to; he knows only that he's walking away from Priscilla, away from his round-and-round thoughts, away from what he has envisioned his life to be. Envisioned? He pauses physically as he pauses in his thoughts. Has he envisioned anything? Consciously, thoughtfully envisioned? No, he forces himself to admit, he hasn't thought much about where he's headed in his life, hadn't thought he needed to with the shadow of Fred's expectations and Gramps's eventful life always guiding him. He jams his hands in his pockets and resumes walking. He did well in school because that was what was expected. One received "A"s and nothing else would do. Fred's sneering scorn upon seeing a "B" was enough to keep one motivated. His parents had sent him to a top psychologist, one recommended by others in their circle, while he was still in grade school to determine what he was interested in. They had guided his education based on the psychologist's results, and he had not protested. He'd been too young, hadn't he, to know his own self? His elite high school had mandated their own tests in his final year to see where his aptitude and potential career lay. He had neither agreed nor disagreed with the findings. His parents had studied the report intently, but he had left it on his desk unread, passively following Fred and Phyllis's lead. Why did he need to read it when they had and would tell him what to do? Gramps had encouraged him to read it, to take charge of his own destiny. It's yours to take, he'd pushed.

Simon had dismissed his words until Frosh Week.

Gramps had pulled him aside just before he had left for this introductory week to university, had taken him down to the basement for a last-night-as-a-kid drink, as Gramps had put it. Gramps had asked him point blank what he liked. He still remembers the piercing look Gramps had given him over his vodka tonic before he'd taken his first sip. He, Simon, had parrotted what Fred and Phyllis had told him, what they'd said the test results had indicated for his future.

Gramps had shaken his head sadly and said, "Don't tell me what others have told you what you're interested in. Tell me what you like."

Simon had rearranged the words.

Gramps had smiled and called him out for essentially repeating his parrotting.

Then Gramps had told him what he, Simon, liked. Only later had Simon slapped himself for not seeing sooner that Gramps had been no different than his parents had been and for not calling him out on it. He'd thought to do so at the family's next Sunday dinner. But Gramps's words had stuck in his head for two days, and he'd begun to question his acceptance of the test results and his parents commands, to wonder if Gramps was the one who was right. He went to the Registrar that day to change one of his courses from physics, which he detested, to poetry introduction, without telling anyone.

But at the end of Frosh Week, he'd had to confess his action to Fred. He'd quailed at the thought. He'd berated himself for changing one of his science courses to a poetry class. Arts was all very well as a hobby but not as a serious subject for school. Simon knew that. He returned to the Registrar to change his course selection back. The Registrar had pulled him into his office for a private chat. Are you sure you want to change it back, he'd asked Simon. Simon had looked down and shrugged. The Registrar had remained silent awhile. Simon had explained his was to be a practical education. The Registrar had nodded thoughtfully, and then he'd suggested an English language course. There was still room in one, and perhaps that could be a compromise between practicality and artistry. And, he'd added, he would need to take an elective in the next four years in order to receive his degree. He'd arched his eyebrows and smiled. Might as well start in first year, he'd suggested. Simon had leapt at the idea. As he broke the news to Fred with Phyllis listening in, he'd used the Registrar's words about needing to take an elective, that this English language course was the first one that was available, that it had practical use, something that would aid him in promotion. He recalled his rationalization speech with pride. Fred had bought it. Phyllis had concurred since language was important to her.

Gramps's words about Simon having poetry in his heart had died within him soon after. He'd stuck the idea in the back of his mind as those of a sentimental old fool, and then under the avalanche of reading and writing and group projects of first-year university, he'd forgotten them entirely.

Recalling himself to the present winter air, Simon sighs heavily. A stream of fog blows out his mouth and dissipates in the cold air. As he trudges further and further away from his life-by-default, he recalls Gramps's words: "You are a poet my boy. You are sensitive, and we need sensitive people in the world. I don't know if you can write poetry—hell, your boyish attempts were pretty stilted and silly—but make no mistake," he'd said as he'd pointed a sharp forefinger with the hand that held his drink glass, "You are a poet." He'd nodded, as if that settled everything.

At the time, Simon had taken his words literally. But poetry was metaphor; it was picture and rhyme masking harsh observations. Gramps was calling him a poet, yet he hadn't meant poet in the way he had thought. Simon frowns and halts abruptly. A body bumps into his back and rocks Simon forward. Simon steps quickly toward the road side of the sidewalk and mutters sorry. The muffled man says sorry back, and they part. Simon stays on the edge of the sidewalk, oblivious to the large pond that fills a pothole behind him. Ice floes cover the icy water, hiding its danger to unobservant pedestrians who lurk too close. A passing woman gestures to the road behind him and says plainly, "I wouldn't stand there." Simon looks over his shoulder, sees the pond, spots a car motoring toward him and the pond at the speed limit of 50 kph, and vaults away just in time.

A great arc of ice and slush and water splashes over where he'd been standing.

Simon shivers.

He wraps his scarf tighter around his neck, sticks his hands back in his pockets, and resumes walking.

He cannot make it as a poet. Writers don't live on words alone in this country: that's what Fred had opined at the dinner table once. Phyllis had said mildly, it was good to know writers. People were impressed by one knowing writers, socializing with them, even being invited over to dinner at their houses. And knowing a poet improved one's social status. But to have a writer or poet in the family would not do, she'd finished. Gramps had snorted his coffee out his nose at that pronouncement, to Sarah's braying laughter and Phyllis's disapproving frown. In that one moment, Simon had felt apart from them. He'd clung to Fred's advice as a way to get back in to his family, the group he'd begun life in, the group he's been a member of his whole life. He hadn't been able to imagine life without his group of origin, he sees that now. He still cannot.

His family is familiar. His job is familiar. His education had given him a raft to keep him afloat in this treacherous life. Does he really know what Gramps had meant?

He doubts himself.

Why would he leave the familiar, no matter what thoughts and feelings they engender in him? He's only being weak, isn't he? Malingering in the past. Stupid at his insistence on following where his thoughts are taking him. His family wants what's best for him, as they have averred many a time. Don't they?

All of a sudden, what he's done becomes a stone in his stomach. All of a sudden, what he's done scares him. He shouldn't have left Priscilla. Fred and Phyllis don't approve of her, but they would've have come around. A promotion requires a wife, a social bee, and Priscilla is popular.

Simon isn't.

Simon stops to turn his head and look back from whence he came. If he returns to Priscilla, she will forgive him. He knows she will.

But he feels spent, too tired to retread his steps.

He feels alone here. But he is alone when with the familiar too. Neither aloneness nor familiarity is a pleasant place. He despairs at this impasse, at this seemingly impossible conundrum to resolve. He hugs himself and wants to be rid of his thoughts. His lifts his head sharply. He scans the street to see where he's come to. He's near home. All he has to do is cross the Viaduct.

Halfway across its lengthy span, his feet turn automatically into the alcove where the telescope stands for those who want to look closer into the view. He squeezes around the old telescope and looks down. He cannot see the ground very well with the bright streetlights behind him. Black shapes with grasping hands sway hypnotically below him. He sways in tune. They want him. Their whispers rise up to his ears, calling him to join them, assuring him that he will feel better, that here he is wanted, needed. Here he is not alone. It won't hurt, the whispers rustle. They lie, those who say joining the ground is bad for you. Gravity is natural. Trees and bushes cushion and care for and hide humans. How can that be bad?

"Beautiful view, eh?"

Simon jumps.

A smile so white, it blinds him to the stranger's face, greets him.

Simon is mute.

"I like to come here to see the view," the man unknown to him says.

"Not much to see," Simon strangles out.

"Sure there is. There's you."

Simon furrows his brow. Is this man some sort of pervert? He suddenly realizes that his way back to the sidewalk is blocked, that his body is up against the parapet, that the telescope is an immovable barrier before him, the man standing in the opening between telescope and parapet.

The stranger's smile widens and widens until it warms the air and thaws Simon's suspicions. The stranger's smile retreats into a closed line that hints at an inviting humour and that allows Simon to see the man's face not just his bright white teeth. The man's big eyes are open, their colour indeterminate in the artificially lit night with its harsh shadows and over-bright spaces behind him. He gazes upon Simon with compassion. Simon shuffles awkwardly when he feels that compassion.

"Don't believe the tempting lies. It's harder to see and reveal the lies that lie so sweetly, that mask themselves in an attitude of 'I only wish to help,' for those are the lies that deceive the most."

Simon raises his brows and then frowns. Who is this man? He repeats in his head the words the man had said. His brow clears as their meaning opens up to him. And then he frowns again. This man is a mind reader. Simon steps surreptitiously away from the stranger. The stranger doesn't move, but he becomes serious.

"What is life? Have you ever wondered that?" He sweeps his arm out toward the forested side of the Don Valley, where snow has brushed delicate lines along tree branches, lines Simon knows are there only because he sees them in the mornings. The stranger continues: "I drink in this beauty every day. It feeds me and sends me on my day. It readies me for sleep at night. But though it is there for my enjoyment, it doesn't exist solely for my enjoyment. And I know I cannot live there. Do you know that?"

Simon stops his slow side-stepping and stares.

The stranger says, "Why are you here at this time of night?"

Simon croaks inarticulately.

"No rush. I'm not going anywhere."

A ball bobs up into Simon's throat, and he swallows hard. The man's patient compassion, his listening stance unleashes Simon's emotions fully into his consciousness, and he cannot withstand the torrent. He hopes the streetlights don't reveal his face. But the stranger's expression doesn't change to judgement or impatience. Simon sees no pity or contempt either.

"I was checking out the view," Simon finally replies.

The stranger nods and waits.

"As you said, it's beautiful."

The stranger nods and waits patiently.

The truth crowds out all other thoughts in Simon's mind, but he doesn't want to admit that the ground was speaking to him. The man would think him mad. Yet the truth is pushing up and making itself known to him. He flashes to *The Suicides*.

"I like what Michel de Montaigne says about suicide in his essay 'A Custom of the Isle of Cea'," the man says all of a sudden.

Simon blinks rapidly and involuntarily steps back hitting the granite-filled concrete hard.

The man softens his voice and says, "Remember? De Montaigne said: 'The opinion which disdaineth our life, is ridiculous, for, in fine, it is our being. It is our all in all.'"

Simon's bowels stir, but his mind doesn't understand.

The stranger goes on, "All the inconveniences in the world are not considerable enough that a man should die to evade them and, besides, there being so many, so sudden and unexpected changes in human things, it is hard rightly to judge when we are at the end of our hope." The stranger pauses before finishing, "I have seen a hundred hares escape out of the very teeth of the greyhounds."

Simon isn't sure what to think. Who sees hares in the city? He feels the words filtering through the bars on his mind and past the waning hypnotic effect of the ground to settle into his memory.

"Beware the greyhounds of the world, I always say." The stranger inclines his head toward the far-down ravine below their feet. "It is beautiful to look at; evil to join."

Simon nods slowly.

"Come. Let's walk off this bridge of fantasy."

The stranger begins to walk toward Broadview, and Simon is pulled along like a hare on a leash. They walk side by side along the narrow sidewalk until they reach the blacktop on solid ground. They cross it in a gap of traffic turning onto the Don Valley Parkway on-ramp, ignoring the red colour of the traffic light. On the other side of the road, Simon turns to him and says, "I'm alright. I don't know what you were talking about. But I'm alright."

The stranger considers him as they stand underneath the inhospitable streetlight. "Let me walk you to the lights. I'm going that way, anyway."

Simon acquiesces, and the two men walk the short distance to the intersection. They cross it. When they reach the eastern side of Broadview, the stranger stops and says, "You are not alone. Truly, you are not."

Simon doesn't believe him, yet he finds himself nodding and feeling that in this one moment, he isn't. Then they part. And alone Simon walks home.

16

EDUCATION

Simon files in with the rest of the attendees, coffee in hand, the scarf his Gramps had given him wrapped around his neck like a tie of comfort. Chairs are arranged in rows before the short dais upon which sits a white lectern with worn edges. A microphone sprouts out of it like a wilted rose; it curves toward a man standing, waiting, behind the lectern.

Simon looks around lost. Others are sitting down with a hushed rumple of sound: small shifting of bums on seats, clearing throats, and laptops blinking open. He finds an empty seat. Simon has brought his iPad. Mr. Confabulate had recommended that he buy the newest one and get himself a Pro version of Evernote too. You'll need that app, a lot, his boss had told him peremptorily. Time to become managerial, he had said.

Simon had gone straight to the Apple store in the Eaton Centre—he shudders at the memory of entering that mall, so large, so vacuous—and had bought a black one. He'd spent a half hour setting it up and taking a gander at the Evernote app. Then he'd spent the weekend playing with the iPad, finding and downloading poetry apps and eReader apps. He was astonished at how many apps were free, and he'd gone on a bit of a spree. He'd downloaded poets rapping and had listened to them for hours through his earplugs while lying back on his couch, one leg draped over the far arm, the other drooping onto the floor. Late last night, he'd remembered he'd looked at but hadn't learnt how to use the Evernote app. He'd hastened to do so and signed up for the recommended Pro account too. He'd quickly figured out how to use the recording function.

Simon powers on the iPad, presses the elephant-head Evernote app icon, and the note he'd started for this workshop launches itself. He presses the record button and sits back, crossing his legs to balance the iPad on them and then crosses his arms.

The man at the front begins to speak. His droning words lull Simon; his eyes droop. He watches from under lowered lids that the iPad is becoming darker. He sits up hastily and grabs the iPad: he'd forgotten to change the Auto-Lock settings. He switches to the Settings app, then gets lost in the plethora of options. What is the setting called again? He can't remember. Power off? Auto off? Lock closed? Where in the multi-layered menu is it?! He spots Auto-Lock and tries that. Ah, he sighs in relief under his breath. He selects Never, switches back to Evernote, and frowns at it. Is it recording? He'd caught the iPad before it'd turned itself off, but . . . maybe not. He'd closed the program, hadn't he? He hits the record button. Nothing happens. Maybe he'd turned it off. He tries again. The blank white note stares at him. Is it recording? He shakes his head in frustration.

"You disagree? Mr., ah?"

Simon shoots his head up. Pink plays on his cheeks. He stammers, "Ah, no, no."

"Good. I'd hate for you to disagree with a basic premise of Con Fable's business principles."

Pink splays into red across Simon's face.

The man resumes speaking and points to a slide on the large screen behind him. Simon hadn't noticed the PowerPoint presentation. Maybe an audio recording wouldn't be sufficient. Can he videotape this? He isn't sure. Does the iPad have enough memory or battery or whatever it is that it needs? He isn't sure how this thing works, only that Mr. Confabulate had said it could handle anything he threw at it. He'll try videotaping. He bends his head to his task of pressing one icon after another until he finds the camera app. He takes a few pictures as his finger brushes the screen.

"Mr., ah, what is your name?"

"Simon," says Simon.

"Simon." The man pauses. The room murmurs. "Are you following this? Con Fable likes their employees to be well versed in their business practices and to be up on the latest managerial theory. Are you following?"

"Yes, sir," says Simon as he leans forward over his iPad in an attitude of interest.

The presenter lowers his eyebrows at him suspiciously then turns his back to point out with his red laser pen one line on his current slide.

Simon returns to the camera app and immediately sees the little bar to turn the still camera to video. He smiles to himself, switches the bar to video, presses the red button to record, and cradles the iPad in his arms so that it has a good view of the man and his presentation. And so that he looks interested. The woman sitting next to him leans over and whispers, "It took you long enough." He sidles a glance over to her, and she grins. He smiles briefly back and ducks his eyes forward, which meant he couldn't help but follow the presentation awhile.

"So, let's talk about Con Fable's sustainability policy." The presenter clicks the remote in his hand, and the screen changes to another gradient blue background with a swoosh of Con Fable colours across the left corner and four bullet points in pleasant cream all marching in a neat list down the centre of the slide. The presenter points to the first bullet point with his pen laser.

"Sustainable. This is the hallmark of Con Fable's sustainability policy. We are dedicated to creating a sustainable environment for our human resources in order to maximize job satisfaction and efficiency. As I mentioned earlier, Con Fable is interested in increasing productivity in order to maximize claims processing and shareholder satisfaction. We believe that creating a sustainable environment maximizes our ability to achieve these aims."

Simon begins to stare unblinkingly.

A voice at the back calls out, "What do you—"

The presenter interrupts him, "As I mentioned at the beginning of the presentation, I will take questions at the end of the morning session. Please reserve your questions until the end."

"But, I don't under—"

The presenter interrupts repressively, "Wait. Thank you."

The voice silences, the presenter continues, turning his back to the audience to point to the second bullet point. He says, "Green."

Simon blinks rapidly, trying to wet his dried-out corneas.

A whisper floats across to him from the woman who'd spoken to him before, "It gets better."

Simon doesn't respond since he isn't sure if she is being sarcastic or not. He mulls that over. He listens to her whisper repeat in his head in order to analyze its tone over and over. It soothes him.

He jerks forward and grabs at the iPad as it's about to fall to the floor. Maybe recording is an error of judgement. He can hear Fred instructing him on the first day of university about how to take notes, how to record with a small cassette recorder that he'd handed over to him. He hadn't dared tell him that tape recorders weren't used anymore. Besides which, Simon enjoyed writing. He liked the feeling of a pen scratching across the paper, the look of a notebook as it became transformed from pristine flat to puffed up and indented, with the weight of the ink curling the pages ever so slightly.

He had intended to do the same here. But Mr. Confabulate had informed him that Con Fable was committed to a paperless environment, hence his instruction to all managerial up-and-comers to use iPads. Simon had asked for permission to expense it. Mr. Confabulate's eyebrows had hiked themselves to his hairline. He'd studied him then muttered, "Take it off your taxes."

Simon wonders now if he could write on the iPad. He'd overheard another customer at the Apple store talk about purchasing a stylus but seeing the price of the iPad had distracted him. He'd forgotten about a stylus. Maybe the woman next to him can guide him.

His legs jerk, and he lunges for his iPad again as it begins to tumble off his lap. A low chuckle gusts into his hearing, and then: "Why can't men stay awake for other men's droning?"

Blood fevers his skin and floods across his scalp, giving his straw-coloured hair a pink undertone. The chuckle grows louder.

"Is there something funny about a paperless office, Ms., ah?"

"No," the woman next to Simon answers calmly. "It's a perfectly serious subject."

"Then why are you laughing?"

Hearing no answer, Simon sneaks a sideways look at her. Her lips are wiggling as she tries to regain her composure while staring full on at the presenter, who harrumphs and resumes. Simon cannot believe her chutzpah. He wishes he was so brave.

"Con Fable is committed to a paperless office because it found in its paperless pilot project they were able to save $51.63 per treatment plan and $75.03 per application. As a result, Con Fable requires all treatment providers to email their plans in PDF and will penalize any that send it in by paper. We are aware of the criticisms that email is not as secure as paper. But we believe that is exaggerated by those who are not as green-minded as Con

Fable is. Con Fable is committed to keeping claimant information secure—"

Simon chokes, and so do a couple of others behind him. He exchanges a shared amused glance with the woman. She's grinning so hard, her ears look like they'll pop off to make way for her widening lips. The presenter keeps his back firmly to them.

At last, the morning session ends. The presenter switches off his equipment with a parting word of how important it is to Con Fable to save energy, and the group swarms out like ants on a leaf hunt toward the break room where sandwiches, coffee, drinks, and water await them. The woman finds Simon hanging back at the edge of the crowd and hands him a sandwich wrapped in plastic wrap. "I hope you like tuna on whole wheat," she says. "Only the worst ones will be left by the time you get up there. You're a newbie, ain't you?"

"Yes. Thank you," Simon replies as he accepts the sandwich. He unwraps it carefully until the top end is released from its plastic bondage and bites into it tentatively.

"You're a neat one, ain't you?"

A man joins them. "Which one you got Caroline?"

"Tuna. You?"

"Egg."

"Ewww."

"You always say that!"

"Yup. Cause it's true."

He takes a large chomp into his egg sandwich and chews happily in reply.

She laughs and bites into her own. The three stand together and chew in silence awhile.

Caroline swallows and asks, "You just got promoted, Simon?"

"Yes."

"Which office you work in?"

"Downtown."

"Ah. That sucks. That means you don't get a trip out of it."

"Where do you work?"

"London."

"Head office?"

"Yup. Me and Lou here."

Simon, having just taken another bite, nods in greeting. Lou reciprocates in kind. His cheeks are stuffed like a squirrel's. He swallows hard then speaks, spitting out crumbs, "Hi. Nice to meet ya."

Simon schools his distaste and replies, "You too," as the man shoves the rest of his sandwich into his mouth. Simon hastily bites into his own sandwich to take his eyes away from the sight.

Lou swallows his half-chewed wad down and asks Simon: "This your first time to one of these things?"

"Yes."

"You don't talk much, do you?" Caroline joshes him.

He blushes.

"And you blush easily," she laughs.

He blushes brighter.

"Never mind," she says as she smiles at him. "You'll get used to us. You'll soon memorize these workshops, too. Nothing you haven't heard before, you'll find. Sometimes Con Fable sends us on team-building exercises. They feel it keeps their employees engaged and morale high. And you gotta have high morale to keep doing what we do."

"What do we do?"

"Well, we make people's lives hell, don't we?"

Simon stops chewing. He swallows his half-eaten bite. He gags as it turns to stone on its way into his esophagus.

Caroline frowns in concern as Simon gasps for air. "Are you okay?" She frowns harder as Simon isn't recovering.

"Hey Caroline. You're gonna kill him."

"No, I'm not," she says as she steps forward and around Simon to thump his back hard. A pea-sized bit of sandwich discharges out of Simon's mouth. He quickly fishes out a clean handkerchief from his pocket, wipes his mouth, and picks up the offending food from the grey carpet. He wanders through the crowd looking for a trash bin, unknowingly with Caroline and Lou in tow. He finds one and tosses in the rest of his sandwich, dangles the handkerchief over it until the projectile food falls down into the bin, and folds the handkerchief so that the dirty surface is on the inside. He carefully puts it back in his pocket. He turns around to find himself face-to-face with Caroline.

"I'm sorry. I didn't mean to offend you," she says.

"You didn't."

"You do know what we do, right? You have to have the stomach for it, and you gotta love money. And boy, do I love money. I do this job so I can keep myself in shoes."

"You got that right," Lou mumbles, sending his eyes down to her shoes.

Simon involuntarily looks down at her feet, too. They're encased in soft suede red high heels with a buckle on the outside in slightly darker red suede. Thierry. He knows from his sister the price of those shoes.

He looks back up at her. "My sister likes that brand."

"Any woman worth her salt would," she declares.

Simon doesn't know what to say.

"So what did you think Con Fable does?"

"We're an insurance company. We insure people so that when they're in an accident or a house crisis, we're there for them. They pay their premiums to ensure financial help when they need it, and we're mindful of the potential for fraud and ensuring a satisfactory return for shareholders."

"Need it." Caroline lets that phrase echo in their heads. "So who decides what they need?"

"We do," Simon says.

"You got that right," Lou parrots as he crumples up the plastic wrap from his sandwich and throws it into the trash bin accurately.

Simon continues: "We have to be the ones to decide. We're paying out the money. And we're objective." Suddenly the memory of Isaac accepting every treatment plan on his quitting day flashes into Simon's mind.

"What you thinking?" Caroline asks, cocking her head.

He shakes his head.

"Aw, c'mon. Spill."

"I don't know," Simon says reluctantly. He rolls his shoulders back and says, "Shareholders finance us, and we're responsible to them."

"Why?"

"Why?" Simon pauses with his mouth open. He has no answer.

Caroline's voice hardens as she says: "Claimants have financed us, too, through their premiums. We give them the idea that we're there to serve their needs as long as they keep up their premiums, and we don't give an inch on those, do we? We need to make sure we don't lose money, aka ensure a healthy profit on those premiums, and Con Fable's government lobbyists make sure we don't, do they?"

Simon hesitates. Despite Isaac's defiance and disturbing comments and his decision to leave Priscilla, he'd retreated back to what he knew. Fred had feted him both his promotion and coming to a decisive decision over Priscilla, and Simon had basked in the unexpected praise. He'd focussed on learning Con Fable policies, not the principles behind them. He'd done his job and done it well. But all those thoughts Isaac had stirred up and he'd set aside begin streaming into his mind.

"Cheer up," Caroline says. "As long as you're honest about what you're doing—making the stockholders happy by arbitrarily denying claims—"

"Arbitrarily?" Simon echoes disbelievingly as rage flings itself into him. "I don't deny anyone arbitrarily. I follow the rules."

"Rules. Shmules. Who set those rules? You think Con Fable set them in consultation with treatment providers and claimants? Of course not. They alone set them; they consulted with number-crunching people in the business. You gotta hand it to them, how they rationalize sickness and poverty for the sake of money for the company and the stockholders. But you know they make most of their money playing the stock market, don't you? C'mon, you must. They lost a bundle. That's why they had to lobby hard for reduced accident benefits. They were caught out in the 2008 recession, and they had to placate angry stockholders somehow."

Simon retorts, "Con Fable is committed to helping people recover and get back on their feet. It's the first line in their policy book. They're correct to ensure strict rules to guard against fraud."

"Of course," she smiles at him wickedly. He glowers back until the import of her words sink in. He blinks rapidly as he tries to process this new understanding.

"Break time is over," the presenter calls over the heads of chattering people.

"C'mon, Simon. Back to the trenches, and don't make it so obvious you're not listening this time, eh? It makes it tougher for the rest of us to doodle."

"Or play games. You gotta do it with the sound off. Turn off your iPad sound," Lou advises. "It gives you away every time."

"I don't know how to do that yet," Simon admits.

Caroline rolls her eyes. "You really are a newbie. C'mon, I'll show you how. I'll even give you a lesson on how to use the iPad the Con Fable way and then the real way." She chortles and shakes her head. Simon follows her and Lou back to the school room.

Hours later, Simon leaves the full-day workshop exhausted. He'd learnt much from Caroline, and he'd traded his brand-new business card for her been-around-the-block one. He wonders if they'll ever speak again, maybe greet each other like old friends at the next Con Fable workshop in Toronto. Somehow, thinking of attending another workshop feels unsatisfying. It makes him itch, but he doesn't know where or why. He carries his iPad in the courier bag his parents had given him as a promotion present. He lifts the strap over his head and settles it across his shoulder. He tightens his new navy blue wool scarf around his neck, that covers his Gramps's scarf, and sets off for home. He needs to think.

So many thoughts vie for his attention. He'd taken this job because he'd needed to start somewhere after graduation, and Fred had suggested it. No one counters a suggestion from his father, least of all himself. His grandfather had warned him that he was not thinking about the path he was taking. Simon had scoffed and said he could always change. But he had a girlfriend, he was entering the working world, and he needed a job, to man up as Michael used to adjure him frequently. Michael doesn't say that to him anymore, and he likes that. This job, this promotion makes him feel like he's becoming part of the world, part of something important.

But Caroline had stirred up disturbing thoughts. He doesn't like hearing out loud the whispers in his head. He wants to forget her brutal assessment of what they do for a living. He always believed that his moral values would lead him in the right direction. Gramps had laughed heartily at him when he'd first said that, slapped him on the back, and walked away, shaking his head, leaving Simon feeling frustrated and foolish.

What does Gramps know?

Poet? He's no poet! If he is, what is a poet doing in a job about money? He cannot write poetry. His rhyming falls flat on the ears. He cannot hear cadences in his head. What had Gramps meant? Gramps had shaken his head when he, Simon, had asserted he knew right from wrong and didn't need any priest or deity telling him what was right, had averred that humans had a moral compass intrinsically. Gramps's kind disbelief rankles him still. Gramps had been wrong about that, and so he must be wrong about the poet remark.

He isn't a poet.

Simon kicks at the black-topped icy mound of snow at the edge of the sidewalk. It hurts. He likes the pain. He walks hard on his hurting toes, and they burn in resentment. It's a good job he has. He's achieved a promotion; he isn't going to stagnate. He will become important, valuable to others in this job. Who is Caroline to mock him? What else would he do anyway? He has no skills, no real talents. Of what value is he? He goes to Sunday dinners, and they talk about nothing. Anytime he tries to ask questions that matter to him, they dismiss him. His interests have no value. His emotions are to be hidden like all of theirs. He'd stuffed his grief down and had felt he was doing better, like his family.

He goes to work. Elaine gossips; Isaac chatters. But there is no more Isaac. Elaine's forays into his cubicle have lessened since his promotion, and what had that social interaction meant anyway? They had sent a condolence card and flowers upon Gramps's death, but no one really talks about events or concepts or ideas or people that matter to any of them. Everyone guards their personal lives, the core of who they are. And at this workshop, Caroline and Lou had been friendly, but she would've laughed at his idea that friendship would grow. We live in a business world, that's what she would've said, and Lou would've echoed with, "You got that right." People don't mix intimately in that kind of world, he tells himself. It isn't safe. Everyone desires safety and comfort. Not Gramps. He'd strutted out into the world and made friends. He didn't care if he looked vulnerable. I been through the war, he stated once. Everything after that is easy. The problem with you young people is you've had it too easy, he'd asserted. You think the material is all that matters, and you put more stock in that than in the people around you. Your jobs, your hobbies, your bank accounts, they're all more important to you. But you forget: humans need to know each other.

What had he meant?

Simon kicks at another snowbank. His toes retreat in protest.

Would anyone remember him if he died? Would Con Fable care? They would have a line around the block of job applicants to replace him the next day. He'd seen the résumés come in to Mr. Confabulate's office, seen the pile that sits perpetually on his desk. He fishes the top one off every week to replace another adjuster who has quit or been fired.

He's expendable. Like Gramps was forgotten. You live, you die, you disappear. And for what?

A burst of cold whips across his face, and he blames that angrily for his wet eyes.

He rages under his breath, and passers-by give him a wide berth.

He barrels the rest of the way home and slams his door behind him. He locks it with a firm twist and, yanking the strap of his bag over his head first, flings off his scarves and jacket. He unties his shoelaces and kicks off his shoes. He beelines for his bathroom and opens the medicine cabinet.

Gramps's round pill box sits there.

Simon stares at it, then with a sudden movement and a growl, he sweeps it into his hand. He carries it to the dining room table. He pops off the lid, and pills bounce out and roll around. He picks one up and narrows his eyes at it. He moves his hand toward his mouth and then with sudden wrath, flings it onto the table. He watches it bounce and twist and roll. All at once, with the side of his hand, he pushes the pills together. With two of his fingertips, he counts them, pushing the counted ones off into a new pile, two by two. Eighteen. Enough.

17

JACKIE

The short days of bitter winds and grey snow have given way to lengthening days of frequent melts, thundering rain, and fly-by blizzards of wet, heavy flakes. The March birds heralding the return of the warming sun, chirp to each other in the depths of the neighbour's cedar tree. Sharp-shinned hawks, looking like innocent pigeons, wheel overhead, their short, vicious beaks pointing downward till they spot their prey foolishly peeking out from under the warmth of the neighbour's crawl space into the open lawn beside the cedar. Talons outstretched, the hawk lands on the errant mouse. A quick peck, and the victorious hungry hawk launches, mouse dangling from its beak, and swiftly disappears into the tops of the bare trees under the sharp blue sky. The sun is not yet ready to set though it's the end of another work day for Simon's family and the Con Fable team in another week since Simon had counted his stolen pills.

The workshop with Caroline and Lou has faded into memory, but the night of that day has not.

As Simon's body lies deep in the soft cushions, his eyes staring sightlessly out the window toward the soaring hawks, his mind wanders over the past few weeks. The first days after that workshop, he'd focussed his entire being on the activities of living, of diligently implementing the suggestions and recommendations promulgated by the workshop. He'd staved off the memory of that night, but now as his tired body sinks deeper into the couch, his mind sinks into the memory of counting and recounting the pills until with exasperation at himself and anger at he-didn't-know-what, he'd swept them back into Gramps's pill box, returned the little round box to its place in his medicine cabinet, toppled into bed, got up the next morning, walked to work, sat down at his desk, and for lack of any other idea as to what to do, had ploughed his energy into his new position and returned once and for all to his normal Sunday dinner role, the kind he'd had before Gramps had died. His family's relief buried his grief into a subterranean vault he'd locked against his consciousness.

Encouraged by his return to normalcy, Phyllis had begun inviting suitable young women—her words—over for Saturday tea and had expected him to turn up. Awkward conversation led into embarrassed goodbyes and false promises of keeping in touch through the social ritual of exchanging business cards while his mother looked on self-contented. As the Saturday teas wore on, Phyllis's pleasure at another good tea successfully concluded morphed into impatience with his stammering excuses as to why the latest young woman was unsuitable. She would berate him and tell him that if he wasn't going to co-operate with her efforts, she would stop. Relief would mingle with guilt in Simon, and the lethal mixture would stew then transform into resentment when she'd phone him the next day at work to inform him she'd found another candidate, that this girl was better than all the ones that had come before. He was to come Saturday for tea.

He is not the one wanting a girl in his life, Simon thinks.

His heart is telling him something else. He doesn't want to listen to it. He'd stuck it in that vault, and he resents the memory that's unlocking it. He reminds himself that if he excels at work, if Fred grins with pride at his achievements at Con Fable, if Phyllis approves of his Sunday-dinner conversation, then the stalactite-lined void swallowing him will release him.

He scans his routine in his mind. He sits down at his work computer. Weekly, he attends meetings about policy, about how to defeat difficult claimants, about legal requirements. He's taken to walking to work on the north side of the Viaduct, the peaceful side, the side with no strangers talking to him or the ground calling to him, where the view is a panorama of trees. He ignores the highway snaking out from underneath his feet and curving into the distance to the north and east. And he doesn't venture further east than his own home—except the recent outing for Greek food when his colleagues insisted on celebrating his victory over a particularly fractious claimant, a victory that Simon had brought about but which had left him feeling joyless.

Simon had been reluctant to go to that restaurant; he'd feared voicing his feelings and saying no to joining them, for celebrating with food and jugs of beer on the company tab—Mr. Confabulate called it morale building—was de rigeur at Con Fable. He feared their judgement for going against tradition. And so he'd kept quiet and went.

Once in the restaurant, sitting amidst his colleagues like a bug sandwich, watching the waiter shout, "Opa!" as he set the cheese aflame and held the Saganaki aloft to their applause, drinking his third beer poured into a frosted glass the way he liked it, he began to bask in his colleagues' appreciative favour and believe he'd been wrong. Perhaps he should be proud. Perhaps he shouldn't have stopped clubbing.

But after he'd left the increasingly noisy chatter and the furiously busy Danforth, after he'd entered his single-person apartment and closed the door on the sunless sky, doubts surfaced and lunched on his pride. And then the questions hurtled into his consciousness, questions about his victory.

Wasn't the claimant injured?

She couldn't have been that bad, he queried himself, and heard only silence in reply. He'd beelined for his fridge and drunk another beer straight from the bottle, standing there with the fridge door open, and then had fallen asleep on the couch and awoke with his mind pounding on the present. Today, though, he remembers how he became the victor. His ace was a Designated Assessment Centre, a DAC in their lingo.

He'd found a DAC who conducted acceptable expert, professional assessments in their designated centre over the course of three days, using the latest neuropsychological and functional testing, and intensive history taking. They'd arrived at the right kind of conclusion, forcing the claimant's lawyer to advise her to settle for less than they'd paid the centre and previous IMEs. The IMEs had made mistakes here and there in their reports' language. The DAC had not. A good designated assessment centre saved Con Fable, Simon thinks.

He remembers now the dénouement of her downfall and his part in it.

Mr. Confabulate had marched into his cubicle after receiving the DAC's report and told him this was the time for him to prove his worth. The report is only one salvo in their war on the claimant, he'd told Simon. The mediation is where the salvo could become fatal, and he, Simon, was going to attend the mediation as Con Fable's representative. Simon had protested.

"You're in Toronto," Mr. Confabulate had declared. "No need to send a senior representative from London. We don't require his authority. You'll do." And on that final note, Mr. Confabulate had marched back to his office.

Even though Simon knew he had no authority to settle with the claimant at that meeting, nerves jangled more and more as the day approached, for his job was to wear her down, make her feel uncertain about the merits of her case. Before the big day, Mr. Confabulate had reminded Simon how he'd lobbied head office on Simon's behalf. He'd assured them that Simon would succeed, that Simon would capitalize on the DAC and massage the IME reports to make the claimant fold. Her lawyer knew the drill, too, that a quick settlement served him and them. Don't fail me, Simon, Mr. Confabulate had repeated. Con Fable is counting on you, he had adjured Simon. Do not let me down. Simon had quailed under his boss's predatory gaze.

Memories of that mediation wash over him, and he turns his face into his couch's back.

Mr. Confabulate had drilled Simon on strategy and had drummed into him stock phrases. They'd reviewed the various levels of compensation Con Fable was prepared to accede to and at which points in the mediation he'd appear to be generous and give way. But most of all, Mr. Confabulate had hammered home into Simon's memory banks, Simon was to repeat the key points from their latest DAC. The truth of her injuries didn't matter, only the reports in their favour. Repetition made things real in the opposing party's mind. The key his boss had said, was to make her doubt herself. When she did that, she'd capitulate. Make her capitulate, Mr. Confabulate had demanded.

Simon had succeeded.

He'd received the celebratory Greek dinner.

Beer between then and now had burped his feelings out of his head.

But now the quiet of his home accuses him. The vault locking in his grief and who he is flies open. Questions break out. They pepper his mind. How will the claimant survive? How will she treat her injuries without the funds to do so? How much will she have left after lawyer's fees and disbursements? Questions, questions, questions. Questions fruited in guilt, in remorse.

He yells into the dead air of his living room: "She is not my concern! Con Fable is! My employer is! She should have had a better lawyer!" He launches himself upright in one harsh movement. He storms into the kitchen and yanks open the fridge door simply to hear the milk bottle rattle against the beer bottles. He grabs up a brown bottle, twists off its top, and drinks.

Birds bellowing into the dawn awaken him. He groans against the appearing light, and the headache stays with him all day. He rarely suffers headaches, but since the workshop, blankets of pain wrap around his temples most mornings. They have become his companion. This day, though, it's intolerable. When the day wanes to a close, for the second time since he began working for Con Fable, he boards the subway home. He leans his shoulders against the glass partition near the subway door and closes his eyes as the train rattles along the tracks eastward. At each station, bodies brush past him, purses jab his ribs, bags bang into his legs. He doesn't open his eyes. He doesn't move, for if he does, the intolerable ever-present sharp-ended pain will begin circulating. Ever since Gramps died, no matter how much he's tried to fill his prescribed role, he's hovered on the edge of life, outside his family's temper, superficially in Con Fable's circle, separated from friends, belonging nowhere. Normalcy is a mask. It's slipping, again.

The train jerks as it brakes once then harder, and he falls forward into a beefy man across from him holding a bulging gym bag.

"Sorry," he mutters.

"No problem," the man mutters back.

Simon smiles weakly; he looks past the people streaming out the open doors and spots the name of the station. His eyes widen; he squeaks and leaps and weaves through the two or three people powering their way into the subway car. His inertia carries him into the wall. He brakes his momentum with his open palms against the putrid green glass tiles. He rests his aching forehead against the cold wall in order to catch his breath. The doors chime closed behind him, and with a clunk and push of air, the train exits. The last of the exiting commuters ride up the escalator.

In the sudden hush, Simon turns around and leans his back against the wall. Across the tracks, he reads the station name on the opposite wall and remembers: this is where he'd gotten off that long-ago poetry night.

Maybe . . .

He turns and begins walking. He follows the path he found that night. As he turns onto the Danforth, the setting sun blasts directly into his eyes. He lifts one hand quickly to shade them and squints to find the coffee shop. With relief, he recognizes the front door. He reaches his shading hand out to open the door and enter the shop.

It's full.

He hesitates.

But suddenly long fingers are grabbing his elbow.

"Hey, stranger. Where you been?"

Simon looks down to see Jackie, her hair flaming down her back in straightened waves, longer than the last time he'd seen her. He smiles, "Hello," and is astonished to feel his smile flowing down into his heart, lifting the stinging loneliness up and out, like a tidal balm.

"C'mon," she tugs at his arm. "I have a table for you."

"You can't have known I was coming."

"Oh, I don't know. I had a hunch." She aims a mischievous smile up at him, then pulls him toward a small table at the front. She drops her hand from his elbow and gestures to the chair on the wall side; he squeezes past the filled table next to his and lands in his chair with a blow-out of air.

She perches on the chair across from him. "I have to go up soon," she says. "You wait here. I'll get you a cup. Espresso?"

Simon isn't sure what he wants. He hesitates, and then suddenly nods.

"And a biscotti? Guy makes the most wicked chocolate and almond ones."

"Yes. Thank you."

She leaves. A young man brings him the espresso and biscotti.

Unsure what to do, hoping she'll return, he leaves them untouched. But after a while, fearing the espresso is cooling down to tastelessness, he sips at it delicately and nibbles the biscotti. He scans the crowd unseeingly. He sips at his espresso again, places it carefully back on its saucer, looks up, and there she is: behind the microphone on the stage, not too far from him. He can see right into her eyes, see every spark of the poetry in her heart.

She winks at him, and he blushes. With a grin, she clasps her hands behind her back. Then she lets her face sink into seriousness. She speaks:

"What is this thing
That captures men's imagination
That rends them from their friends
Their girl, their parents?
What is this thing
That captures women's minds
That rends them from their friends,
Their boy, their parents?
What is this thing
That separates reason from soul
That tramples on hope, love,
Charity, and need?
It is the one who
Never falters
And always lies."

Jackie steps back from the microphone. The crowd claps furiously, enthusiastically, Simon as well, although he's puzzled as to why. What is the thing she's talking about? He's suddenly uncomfortable. He drops his hands. He shifts in his seat. The chair is hard; its edges dig into his thighs. He doesn't have enough leg room.

"Hi!" Jackie exclaims as she falls into the chair opposite him. "Whatchya think?"

Simon adjusts himself, clears his throat. "I," he articulates as he pulls his chair closer to the table. "I." He pushes his chair back a little bit and crosses his legs.

Jackie throws back her head and laughs, "It's okay if you didn't like it. Not everyone has to like my poetry."

"Oh, no," Simon hastens to assure her he liked it, but she interrupts him: "You don't know what it was about, eh?"

Simon smiles abashedly.

"It's okay. I want people to think when they hear that poem. So. What do you think it's about?"

He says: "I'm not sure."

"Well," she says as she leans forward on the table. "It's about suicide."

A long, dark well opens up inside him. "Oh," he breathes out.

"Don't you think suicide is like that?"

Simon drops his eyes to the table top and traces circles on it with his right forefinger. "Like what?" he says unconcernedly.

"C'mon, you must have thoughts about it?"

"Thoughts? What do you mean thoughts?" he says to the table.

"You know, like what do you think about it?"

Simon hears her poem ring in his head, hears the words, "always lies," echo down the hollow of his mind. He says: "I don't know if it," he takes a breath and finishes, ". . . if it always lies?" Having uttered those words, he feels stronger, certain, yet cannot stop tracing circles on the table top. He begins drawing figure-eights.

"Don't you?" Jackie asks.

"I don't think it does. I think it tells the truth."

"Really?"

"Yes."

"Why?"

Simon has no answer. No one has wanted to talk to him about death before.

"Isn't death part of life?" Jackie, the fearless poet, asks. "Yet isn't death by your own hand a lie?"

Simon stops the movement of his forefinger and looks up into her unwavering gaze. "I don't think so. I think it's more truth. It gives you absolute control over your life. You determine when life is over."

"But how do you know when is the right time?"

"You do."

"But how?" Jackie insists, leaning forward onto the table. "You can't know the future."

"You know it's the right time because the people around you tell you."

Jackie frowns at that. "I don't think so. I think suicide is the lie that comes out of your own head."

"It's the truth that comes from the environment around you. Is it really wrong to choose death when the illness inside you won't leave? The Supreme Court doesn't think so."

"The Supreme Court forgot how we strip each other's value in simply being, how we internalize the societal rubric that an unproductive citizen is better dead than being a burden, how we see the way we keep out of sight our pain and the disabled and promulgate the idea we could never live like that, and so convince us it's our own belief we want to die before we become like 'them,'" Jackie states.

"Is it really wrong to choose death when the work you do, the people you're with, wouldn't change if you were here or not?"

"What do you mean?"

"Don't we have a right to suicide when we no longer want to suffer and know we are no longer needed?"

"How do we know we're not needed? The future surprises us with its sudden twists."

Simon shakes his head.

"Could you have predicted you'd stumble into this place? You'd find me and poetry?"

Simon, preoccupied by his own point, waves away her words. He leans forward, and the backs of his interlaced hands touch the knuckles of her clutched ones. "We know when we're not needed. People tell you. They want to go out to eat, but they don't want to talk about things that matter, about me, about you, about ideas or . . . or . . . they don't notice when you leave or reach in to alleviate when the suffering becomes unbearable."

"Then you have the wrong friends. You find better ones."

With a hard shake of his head, Simon negates her assertion.

"C'mon. Of course you find better ones. Can't hang around haters, you know, Simon."

Simon abruptly asks her: "Why are we here?"

"For different reasons. I write and read poetry. I talk to people through my words. That's why I'm here."

"It doesn't make you a lot of money."

"It doesn't make me any money," she laughs openly, sitting back in her chair, dragging her hands off the table, opening up her fists, letting them drop into her lap. "You don't think this society appreciates poetry, do you?"

"So why do it?"

"Because I enjoy it, and because I need to, to breathe as me. Plus," she gestures to the people crowding into the coffee shop, "there are some who like it as much as I do. I don't need the whole world to approve of me, just some to enjoy my creative side."

Simon shakes his head.

"What do you do?" Jackie asks him.

Simon ducks the question. Shame of his job, of being from a place where money and social standing and acceptance together is the sole object and motive, of being the opposite of here, shuts his mouth.

"You don't like what you do, do you?"

"That's not the point," Simon blurts out reflexively, defensively.

"That is the point," she retorts. "That is the point. Sometimes we have to work at jobs that suck in order to support our kids. That's what my Mam did. And sometimes we have to work at menial jobs to support the things that feed us, like poetry does me, or to let us volunteer like my brother does. He and his docile collie—you ever hear of a docile collie?" she barks with amusement. "Anyway, he and she visit nursing homes. He'd do it all the time, but he needs money. Air doesn't feed a person. Or a dog!" She laughs again. "I work at, well, that doesn't matter. I work so I can recite poetry. But you . . . you, what do you do?"

"I have a right to live my life the way I see it."

"Yeah, you do." Jackie crosses her arms and stares at him, all laughter gone. Simon squirms in his chair; he plays with the spoon in his espresso cup.

"I also have the right to die when I wish," he says suddenly into their silence.

Jackie shoots forward, "No, you don't."

"Yes. I. do."

"Why?"

"My life is mine. It doesn't belong to some god, or my parents, or to you."

Jackie's eyebrows gather together and her eyes drive into his grey-green depths. "You have a point there. But life is so unpredictable. What if you die, and the next day is the day the perfect job comes your way? Or the moment that lifts your spirit and makes you revel in life and forget the pain and gives your loved one a moment of peace and joy? Or brings you the person you've longed to see?"

Simon shakes his head, "That happens in movies, not in real life."

"You don't know that. Look at Dr. Seuss," Jackie says, gesticulating, almost knocking his miniature cup off the table.

Simon grabs it while she continues unnoticing. "He was rejected sixty-seven times. What would have happened to all the kids if he had given up after his sixty-sixth time?"

"It's not giving up; it's choosing. No one else can choose better than I can for what's best for me," Simon says holding onto his cup with his hands and his eyes. "Especially when I already know I'm dying."

"That's hubris."

"What?" Simon barks.

"You heard me. Hubris. We need other people to put things in perspective for us. Suicide is a denial of the natural instinct to live and of our value to people we know and people we don't know when we don't know it. If you want to suicide, then your natural instinct is out of kilter, maybe pain is distorting it, and it's up to poets like me to show you your life is always wanted."

"Or that you're wrong, and it is right for me to end."

"No," Jackie says.

Simon has to convince her. "When Gramps died, we all went to his cremation. If Gramps's life was needed, how can we live without him?"

"We have to because we're mortal. But he fed you and walked with you until mortality took him. If he'd taken his own life earlier, what happy days, support and lessons, and the gift of just being with him would you've missed?"

Simon continues doggedly: "My coworkers sent flowers. We had a reception. People came and gave condolences. But now I don't know my coworkers anymore because I received a promotion. I still work in proximity to them, geographically, but hierarchically, I'm in a different plane. I still see my family, but we don't talk about Gramps. My friends from university have spread across the country, and we've lost touch. Where do I fit in, in this life?"

"You always fit in. You make new friends, like I said."

"It's not that easy."

She retorts, "Who said life is easy? That's why we need to sustain each other when we're living high and," she emphasizes, "dying on illness's, not our, time. The unpredictability of life and death feeds the generations that follow. When we try to control it, it locks us in to rigid lies and steals from others the sustenance of hope. It tells the young and the old that hope doesn't exist, that only helplessness exists in the face of suffering to which the only answer is self-death."

"Look," Simon says intently. "It isn't a matter of finding new friends. How will they be any different than my old ones? No one talks about Gramps anymore. How could he have mattered when he's forgotten so quickly? What is life but a wisp of smoke that puffs out and etiolates and is seen no more, remembered no more. In the face of that, why do I live?"

"You live because you're here, because justice and charity to others is needed, because those who suffer have something to teach others."

"You suffered?"

Jackie shifts back in her seat. "I don't need to have suffered to see how suffering changes others and gives people the choice to grow or languish."

"Suffering traumatized Gramps."

"But he lived."

"Yes."

"He lived with joy," Jackie muses, eyeing him closely.

Simon simply nods because he suddenly can't talk of it without her interest and energy giving him voice. He wills her to ask him how Gramps relished life when horror infested his memory forever. But she doesn't. She says instead: "You see, suffering doesn't make life not worthwhile. It makes it richer."

"It makes it harder."

"What suffering do you have?" she asks disparagingly. "I see from your clothes you're well off. You don't have to work at any old job to pay your bills. You have the luxury to find a career, work that means something."

Simon says nothing.

"C'mon you know you do. You know suicide is not a legitimate answer. Find work you like."

Simon thinks of Fred's reaction if he walked into his house one Sunday and announced he'd quit.

"My parents would be unhappy."

"So don't tell them," Jackie replies breezily as if it is as easy and obvious as putting one's pants on in the morning. "You have a choice."

Simon dismisses her words as fantastical. Fred would find out. He'd pronounce himself disappointed. Phyllis would stare at him, all hard judgement. Michael would roll his eyes and say he should try a real job then he'd know how cushy he had it. And his sister would bray about how Simon didn't have any sticking power and so how could she be the disappointment of the family. Then they would all ignore him as they extolled over Michael's residency adventures and tsk over Sarah's latest contretemps. No, he doesn't have a choice.

Yet, Simon frowns at himself, here at this table with Jackie, he's having the first honest conversation he's had about death and suicide. He regards her. She's hearing him, valuing him, not dismissing him. The vault shrinks in weight. Maybe he does have a choice. Perhaps she's right; maybe he can make new friends, lasting friends unlike his old ones.

He says, "Maybe I do."

"Of course, you do." Jackie brings her hands back up onto the table. to lean her chin on her interlaced fingers, elbows on the table. She regards him back. Unlacing her fingers, reaching one hand forward, she pats his hand. "It's been great chatting with you. I like a smart discussion. I don't get one too often. But I must run," she continues as she scrapes her chair back and leaps up. "Maybe I'll see you here again sometime?" she asks as she pushes the chair into the table and, with her hands grasping its back, stands behind it like a deer in pause before flight.

"Yes," Simon replies. His diaphragm slams up into his stomach as she flits away. He'd been serious; but she'd seen their words as mere discussion for the mind, a way to pass the time, fodder for her poetry. Nothing more. He watches her wing over to the long wooden bar to rest on it and talk to the owner Guy.

He's back to where he began when he'd first walked into this place. Does he belong in this life? He thinks of Gramps.

18

QUITTING TIME

"So I said to my patient, lie back, don't worry, this won't hurt a bit. And he replied, 'Listen sonny, I've had three of these. How many you had?' That stopped me. He had a point. So I asked him, 'What does it feel like?' He chuckled, then coughed and coughed. That put paid to his answer, and I still don't know. But I think it's important for me to know what it feels like."

"I don't think it's important to know, precisely, what it feels like, Michael. As a doctor, you must maintain an objective distance from your patient—"

"Hogwash," Sarah interrupts rudely.

"Don't interrupt, Sarah. You're neither a physician nor a surgeon and don't understand these things."

"Why do I have to be either to get it? Everyone's a patient, you know, and we all know what that so-called distance is really like."

Fred states, "Nonsense." He pauses, letting his eyes grip hers until she surrenders. He turns his spirit-sucking gaze onto

Michael. "Michael," he says. "You don't need to feel what they feel. You're going to be hurting them, and you don't want their hurt to disrupt your care. That's the consequence of going into medicine. This touchy-feely business isn't going to help you, and I, posit, will make you a worse physician."

Powerful emotions push Sarah to speak up again. "Well, I think this touchy-feely stuff will make Michael—"

While Sarah has the bit in her mouth, Simon zones out of the family conversation as he begins rethinking his planned announcement, the one about a decision he'd made after Jackie's words had snuggled into his neurons, building on Isaac's startling comments that he'd tried to bury, disturbing the equilibrium of Simon's own assumptions about his work and himself. Simon had tried dislodging Jackie's uneasy words, mentally arguing with her poem, with her words to him, and then with Isaac's resurrected words. But all those words had stretched out their little cat-like paws and dug in, insisting that he is young enough to change, to become who his grandfather, who his heart, wants him to be. Yet now with the touchy-feely conversation sniping around him, doubts trouble his decision. Those words return, kneading their presence into his consciousness, pummelling him into submission to be himself, insisting he turn that submission into the fire of desire. All he has to do is tell his family.

Maybe not.

He tunes back in to the conversation. They are discussing Sarah's latest job. No, better not interrupt her or Fred. Maybe after dessert.

While the others are focussed on Sarah, and from habit, he begins to clear the dishes when Melanie walks in from the kitchen. "What are you doing, Simon?" she asks, putting her hands on her hips.

Simon stops in the act of picking up his father's plate and blushes. "Sorry, Melanie. Habit, I guess."

"Never mind that," she says as she reaches her hands out to relieve him of his burden of plates. "You sit down, and I'll bring in the coffee." She goes around the table, picking up the rest of the plates and silverware as Simon pulls out his chair to sit back down, feeling a fool. He stalls with his hand on the back of his chair, his head down, the chiding words of Fred and Phyllis grazing him on their way to Sarah about choosing to work retail as a mere customer service rep. He lifts his eyelids and notices the serving plates sitting askew down the centre of the table filled with the dregs of their eating. Someone should remove them. Melanie will. Why can't he? He feels useless. He wants to not feel useless. He leans forward over his chair, stretching his arms to the centre of the table, and picks up the serving plates.

"What are you doing, Simon?" his mother asks him frostily.

"I thought I'd help out," he replies as he hurries out of the dining room with his cargo in hand.

"What are you doing, Simon?" Melanie asks horrified while taking the plates from him.

"That's what Phyllis said."

"I'm not surprised. Your mother won't be pleased. We must know our jobs, eh?"

Simon shrugs.

Melanie eyes him speculatively. "What's wrong, Simon?"

He shrugs again, his chest locking his words in his throat.

"C'mon, Simon. Spill. I don't want you underfoot while you hem and haw like you used to anytime you wanted extra dessert."

Simon returns her smile briefly before his lips seal up again, though he's desperate to release his words.

Melanie puts the serving plates down onto the counter then puts her hand on his shoulder. "C'mon, Simon. I won't bite. I promise you."

Her kindness rips open the lock and launches his words out of his throat, through his resisting lips, and into her listening ears: "I'm thinking of quitting Con Fable."

"Oh, I see." Melanie considers him worriedly for a minute. "Your father'll be unhappy. You sure you want to do that?"

"If I'm going to quit, now would be the best time," Simon replies, dropping his eyes to the shining floor.

Melanie squeezes his shoulder. "Yes, you got that right. Well, make sure you want to before you go telling them. You may not like where you end up." Melanie gives him one last squeeze before turning toward the counter with its weight of plates and silverware.

"I know," says Simon as he rubs the glowing mahogany flooring with the toe of his brown leather shoe. Suddenly, he knows. He will quit. He looks up and smiles at Melanie, "Thanks."

"For what?" She shooes him out, a smile on her face.

Back at the dining room table, he sits down. Melanie soon follows him with a Sachertorte. She places it in front of Phyllis, who deftly slices through its shining smooth dark chocolate surface and down through two layers of rich chocolate cake welded together with glistening apricot jam. She moves the knife over thirty-six degrees and slices again. She uses the lifter that matches the cake plate to lift out the first slice and place it on a plate. Melanie has returned with a bowl of whipping cream, and Phyllis spoons a cloudfull next to the triangle of luscious chocolate. She tells Simon to pass it to his father. He does so. Phyllis repeats the process until she has served her entire family.

Meanwhile, Melanie has vanished into the kitchen; she soon returns to the dining room carrying a tray laid out with the tea service including a pot of fresh tea. She places it on the buffet and begins serving out cups of tea. Phyllis had decided last week that they should drink Darjeeling tea after their Sunday dinner. Healthier, she'd pronounced. Watching Melanie carry cups of tea to everyone, Simon wonders if Phyllis's sleeping has worsened. That thought leads him into thoughts of whether she's missing any of her pills yet. She hasn't said anything. But Phyllis wouldn't. And maybe because she won't speak about her private affairs, he begins to question for the first time about how she's reacting to her diminishing supply. Does she think she's hallucinating? Or feeling like she's losing her memory? He doesn't want to affect her, only take her pills. But maybe he'll quit. He won't borrow any tonight. He's only borrowing, again, just in case. But he doesn't need them anymore: he'll follow Jackie's advice, and he'll forget his grief.

After Melanie disappears into the kitchen and as everyone takes their first bite of the dense torte, he pronounces, "I'm quitting."

Forks clatter onto plates, a cup rattles in its saucer, someone chokes.

"You're what?" Phyllis demands as she tries to swallow her first bite of cake down quicker. She sounds a bit strangled.

"I'm quitting Con Fable. It isn't the right job for me."

"And what is the right job for you?" Fred asks with a deadly tone in his voice. "One where you can be a poet? Or perhaps one where you can sleep in every morning? Or maybe like Sarah, you think you can live off our largesse? Well, I'm here to tell you, you can't."

"I wasn't expecting to. I've worked there long enough to qualify for EI."

"I see. You intend to live off the government's generosity instead of mine."

"It's not the government. It's my money. I paid into that fund like every other working Canadian. I paid the insurance premium. It's my turn to receive the claim." Simon hears his words tumble out of his mouth, and dread suddenly hits his stomach. Would EI be like Con Fable? They're both insurance.

His father speaks: "I heard you were up for another promotion. They think you're a good employee, one so good you deserve to be rewarded by swift promotions. I wonder what they would think if they knew they had a viper in the nest."

"I am not a viper."

"Aren't you? They've paid good money to train you. You've acted with all intents and purposes as if this is the career for you. If you quit now, you've wasted their money and my time."

"Your time?" Simon's mouth drops open.

"Yes. My time and my reputation. I've put in good words for you. How do you think it will look—how do you think I will look," he says, emphasizing the "I" word, "if you quit now. I'll look like a man who doesn't have control over his family, who doesn't know what his family is up to. You think the men on the Board will trust me after your irresponsible action? Hardly. I won't be able to ask them again for a favour and certainly not for you. This will affect Michael, too."

"Leave me out of this," Michael mutters to his fast-diminishing slice of cake so that only Simon can hear him. Sarah, too, is studiously observing her slice with its one bite forked out of it and its untouched cloud of cream next to it. Simon slides his eyes right toward Phyllis. She's nodding approvingly to every word Fred is uttering while carefully forking off a little bit of cream from its cloud to add to the small bite of cake speared onto the end of her fork. Maybe he's wrong. He'd thought this was his life, his decision. He hadn't considered anyone else.

"But that is like you, isn't it, Simon," Fred says, dragging Simon's attention back to himself. "Selfish, spoiled, indulged. You don't consider anyone else, especially us your parents who only want you to be happy. I guess with you being the youngest, we indulged you, made you think that the world revolved around you. That was our mistake. But you're an adult now. The world does not," Fred pauses on the negative word before continuing: "revolve around you. Your actions affect others. They're going to see you as disloyal, other good employers will find out, and then who will hire a disloyal employee?"

Simon simply stares at Fred. Fred unblinkingly returns his look. Simon lowers his eyes to his untouched slice, its deep chocolate colour seemingly sucking him bottomward, reprimanding him for his greed. He has never considered himself a disloyal person. In the last year before Gramps's death, he'd prized becoming the kind of person his grandfather could rely on.

A thought wiggles in: should loyalty be the sole reason to keep a job?

Simon takes a surreptitious look back at his father. Fred is surveying him disparagingly.

Simon's heart flutters, and his stomach hollows underneath the familiar stare, the one he'd seen after receiving a B in History, after coming in fourth during his last cross-country meet, after quitting running after that last meet.

"It's like your running. You failed once, so you quit. Are you failing now? Is that it? It would be just like you to quit. Or worse."

"You just said I'm getting a promotion," Simon ejaculates, raising his head and neck to look full on at Fred.

"I did. But I'm wondering now if they don't know something they should."

Shame flares across Simon's fair face. "I. Do. Not. Cheat."

"I didn't say you did. Glad to hear it." Fred pauses. He states, "I hope you aren't."

Simon clenches his jaw. He's going to quit. He is. He is. He can be brave like Isaac.

Fred resumes eating his cake. He cuts off a piece with the side of his dessert fork, but before raising it up to his mouth, he looks straight at Simon and says: "What are you planning on doing, other than going on the government teat? Do you even know what you want to do? Do you have any clue what you're good at? We know that at least you're good at this. They like your work. They want to promote you. You're making the company money, and Con Fable likes people who help their bottom line. This is good paying work and a fair job. You're keeping the economy going, and we know how important it is in these tough times to keep it going. And have you thought about that, too? How hard it is to get a job? Do you remember you needed my help to get you this job? I didn't think so. Well, don't expect it this time. And this time—if you know what you want, which I doubt—don't think of coming to me. You won't be receiving any help from me. This time, you're on your own." He raises up his laden fork and clamps his lips around it while boring his gaze into Simon's eyes.

Simon feels shot. He'd thought about all those questions, hadn't he? Maybe he'd been lying to himself that if only he quits, if only he puts himself into a survival situation, then he'll have the courage to discover the career meant for him. But sitting here now, pinned to his seat, he cannot remember one conclusion, one solution he'd devised. It's as if he'd made the decision on the spur of the moment with no thought whatsoever. He feels stupid. And alone.

"Sorry, man," Michael whispers sideways into Simon's ear as he leans forward to reach the sugar bowl on Simon's other side. Simon gazes at Michael's half-full teacup for a moment and then, with a desultory hand, picks up his fork and slices off a small piece of cardboard-tasting cake.

19

SACRIFICE

The sun stabs through the blue sky, and clouds hang above the city as if they're artistic punctuations to the light. Simon trudges alone along the holiday-quiet streets, thoughts flinging themselves around the rough inside of his skull. What is Good Friday? Why is it called Good Friday? What is good about a man hanging from a rough-hewn cross, only three nails keeping his body pinned to the wood, as his flesh and bones stretch and pull under the force of gravity until he suffocates to death?

It's hard to ponder the strangeness of Christians as they celebrate the torturous death of a man long ago. It's hard to ponder it, period. At one time, Romans lined their roadways with crucified slaves. Citizens walked along between them as if they were shade-giving trees, not grisly corpses pointing the way to the city. What kind of minds did Romans have that they thought . . . that they considered it routine to crucify in the thousands, as public spectacle? But worse, what kind of mind did that man have that he purportedly agreed to his death and willingly carried the cross of his demise to the hill where he would be executed by malice, while people spat and cursed and cheered what was to come?

What kind of mind?

A mind that knew his own purpose and what he wanted to do with his life and his death, answers Simon to himself, mourning the absence of such certainty within himself.

Simon takes in the church that has appeared in front of him as his wanderings come to a halt. The edifice stands silent, though he knows it must be packed with worshippers. His mother would be in her church right now. His father, too. They and the Sunday School his parents had enrolled him in made sure he knew every detail of this story before he was six years old. But once he hit his teens, he never went back to church—except for duty attendances—never bothered himself anymore with what they called "bible study." In his eyes, Christ's death was meaningless. Historians said that he existed, that he was crucified. Another man; another crucifixion.

Why did that man spar verbally with Pontius Pilate in such a way as to hammer shut the case against him? Why did he co-operate with mob rule? Why did he let human heartlessness drive him to that killing tree?

Christ gave the mob what they wanted.

The mob was happy in return.

Was Jesus happy to give himself over?

Simon shakes his head. How can anyone be happy to die? To die in that way?

And yet . . .

Death on the other side of one's last breath seems so peaceful, so contented. It beckons, it cajoles, it seduces that the river of needles will never stop its motion of pain. Life is pain. Only death ends pain.

Simon feels the tug.

He rubs his chest, circling his heart with his hand, the pain so much a part of him now that he cannot remember when he felt free, unburdened of it. Grief had snatched him from his complacent life of growing up, going to university, finding a job, getting married, and having kids. Grief had revealed the loneliness of his life. Grief had opened up to him the understanding of dying. Before, dying happened only after retirement and afternoons on the golf green, so far into the future it hadn't been a part of his thoughts until the day Phyllis had called him about Gramps. Grief had thrown brimstone into his life. Life is hell. There is no supernatural hell. It exists here. Now. Yet in that fictitious Jesus story, they didn't call life hell. Instead, they called "hell" the place the man went to for three days after he'd died. The words echo in his mind: "He descended into hell."

Why would he do that?

He, Simon, would not willingly have gone into this grief, this arid time of the soul, when friendlessness shrivels up desire for living. He cannot imagine what would have driven that man to do that willingly.

Simon raises his eyes up to the top of the church steeple, blinking against the sunlight. He asks himself again why that man would enable those nails being hammered into his hands, to have his feet crossed and another nail hammered through his life-toughened skin and through his resisting cartilage and through his tender muscles, pushing the delicate bones aside, until the soles of his feet were fastened securely into the splintering wood behind them. And then to be raised up, his weight pushing his feet down, while gravity reached up its inexorable fingers to pull his body down, the nails resisting as flesh tore against their metal hardness until his bones reached the bloodied iron and halted his downward progress. And all this as the mob cheered at seeing his pain, at seeing his soul cry out.

No one is so relentlessly cruel and unheeding of another's pain as a group of people, whether two or two thousand.

They said Jesus was God; so if he was God, why didn't he release himself from that excruciating, mocking end to his life? He claimed he died for the sins of the world. Isn't that what leaders who puff themselves up claim—that they're making the tough decisions for others? Yet those sorts of leaders don't die willingly. This man did. Simon shakes his head, puzzled.

Good Friday. What is good about torturous death? Simon scrunches up his eyes against the strong rays shining down from above as the earth orbits the sun and the sun appears to traverse the sky. What is good about a man dying who knew exactly who he was and why he was, who was immune to the buffeting of other people's opinions?

Simon releases his eyes from the sun's glare and searches the pavement under his feet as the questions repeat themselves, and into their repeating, insert futile wishes for such courage. What is good about death? Simon exhales gradually.

The end of life, is.

A chosen peaceful end is.

No more pain is.

And then he hears the lies, the seductive untruths, the failure of faith in hope in those words.

Simon sticks his hands into the pockets of his pea jacket and trudges on, deciding that for all the fiction around that man, he was good, like he wants to be good. At the corner of the intersection, he halts. And before he moves back into his fated life, he turns his head to look one final time at the church and the cross that adorns it. It must've been something to have known a man who would sacrifice himself like that for friends and for people he didn't know at all.

20

WINGS

Simon slits open the large envelope. At last, the lawyer for a particularly pesky claimant has sent him the claimant's government health insurance records. Dispassionately, Simon riffles through the tall stack of print-outs for a quick examination. He straightens the stack and begins to read the claimant's government-covered medical expenses carefully from the first page, marking off entries he can use. This man has been living off the largess of the government teat for a long time, which serves Con Fable well. Simon wheels his chair over to his filing cabinet and pulls out the lowest drawer. From under the hanging files, he fishes out his hidden pad of paper—the kind Con Fable disapproves of because of the wasteful use of forest resources. He wheels back to the stack of records and begins jotting down notes about the marked-off entries. To Simon, the act of writing clarifies his observations, helps him marshal his thoughts. He begins to see much possibility here: hypochondria may not be the most believable defence, but Con Fable's experts can turn this into somatoform disorder, giving it a lick of scientific validity. He pauses as he thinks back to another recent workshop he'd attended.

The leader had reviewed how to change a claimant's innocent actions, survival needs, and normal medical events into proof of fraudulent behaviour. He'd told them that people believe the powerful and the myth that the innocent can't be made to look guilty. He'd laughed at the gullibility of so many, and they'd laughed with him. Con Fable having the money, the looks, and lawyers behind them, have power, he'd chuckled. Then repeated it with a sharp forefinger to remind them not to forget it. After their lunch break, he'd described various disorders that they could use to fight claims or if needed convince juries that the claimant is faking his injuries. His stomach had bothered him the entire day as the leader had walked them through suitable diagnoses, and he'd briefly thought of quitting then.

But quitting is no more a realistic option.

Talking to Jackie had made it seem like one. She'd poked hope out of its hiding hole and disturbed him enough to try. But after that Sunday dinner, the memory of which continues to dog him, he knew quitting meant letting his family down and not being the good man he thought he was. And Gramps was. He wants to be someone worth knowing. This is his job; he will make Con Fable his career. He will buy a house, find a wife right for him, and establish himself—swanning around in a fog of confusion over what he wants to do with his life will not accomplish that. Fred knows best. Fred is pleased with him, again.

Simon's chest squeezes a burning rod up into his throat.

His stomach joins in.

He rubs his ribs, but the soothing action accomplishes nothing.

Be a man, he thinks, channelling his father. He straightens his torso, pushes his shoulders back, and bends his head over the health insurance print-outs. Soon, he is scribbling furiously on his illicit pad of paper. He will do the best job possible on this claimant for his employer.

Quiet footsteps approach his cubicle. Simon's vigilant ears prick up, and he sweeps the pad of paper underneath the now-messy pile of health insurance print-outs. He swivels his chair around as Mr. Confabulate stops inside his cubicle.

"Hi, Simon. How're you doing?"

Awful, the thought pops into his head. He firmly pushes it down and plasters a serious smile on his face. He reports, "I received the health insurance print-outs I was asking for, sir. I believe we can create a solid defence and undermine the claimant. I have diarized a meeting with our legal department to review our status of the claim."

Mr. Confabulate says, "Well done, Simon. Head office is noticing your work. You're making me look good," he grins, revealing his canines.

Simon looks away as if thinking deeply then back again. Mr. Confabulate is still grinning. Simon frowns internally. His boss rarely keeps a grin on his face or shows his canines. What is going on?

Mr. Confabulate claps his hands and rubs them together. "The numbers came into the office today. We're the best performing office in Con Fable's operations. We've increased our denial numbers by ten percent over the last quarter, and they've decided to give everyone a performance bonus. I," he points at Simon as he continues, "credit you for this fiscal improvement. I'll be recommending you for an accelerated promotion, and you'll be elevated to your own office space. With a door. How's that sound?"

Simon schools his face to show pleasure and suitable humility. Out loud, he says, "Thank you sir. I couldn't have done this without a great team."

"Of course not, of course not. But any team will work well under your direction, Simon, and I'll ensure we put you in charge of our best group of people. Here's your first managerial decision.

What do you think we should do to reward the staff for our quarterly bump?"

Simon cannot hide his surprise at Mr. Confabulate considering rewarding anyone beyond the head-office-mandated performance bonus. Seeing his boss's lowering expression, Simon turns it into surprise over being asked his opinion. Hurriedly, Simon says, "Thank you for asking me, sir. I don't think I'm qualified to answer." At the same time, he brings his eyebrows down and squares his jaw.

Mr. Confabulate seems mollified. He smiles, "Nonsense, Simon. You've earned the privilege."

"Thank you, sir." Simon pauses to think furiously. He thinks about Elaine and what she'd suggest. "How about we take them out for a pub lunch? The Irish Jig down the street serves good chicken wings, I hear, and many of the staff favour it."

Mr. Confabulate's head bounces up and down at the end of his neck, "Good, good. Excellent idea. Organize it." And with that, he shoots back to his office.

Simon has no idea how to organize a pub lunch. What does one do? Send a group email around? Elaine's voice impinges on his consciousness. She's walking past his cubicle with a coworker, grilling him about his marriage. The rumour is that his wife is unhappy with his work and wants him to quit, but he likes the steady paycheque. Elaine, of course! She'll know. After all, it is her idea, after a manner of speaking.

"Elaine!" Simon calls out as he launches himself out of the chair and out of his cubicle to catch up to their rapid steps.

"Simon?" Elaine asks as she stops and turns around. She points at herself. Her companion takes the opportunity to skulk off while her attention is occupied elsewhere. The unfortunate coworker disappears around the corner of the last cubicle in Simon's row as Simon reaches Elaine.

"Yes. You're just the person I want. Listen, Mr. Confabulate wants to reward the staff for increasing claim denials by ten percent over the last quarter. We were thinking a pub lunch. Could you organize it?"

"Sure, Simon." She smiles cheekily. "You can't do it yourself?"

"No, um, it's not that," he replies, controlling his blush. "But I know if you do it, it'll be a success. You'll carry it off flawlessly," he smiles with his mouth.

Elaine preens under the compliment, while Simon marvels those words came out of his mouth. Where did he learn how to stroke a person's ego like that? Elaine interrupts his reverie: "Sure, Simon. I'll do it. This Friday?"

"Yes," Simon nods, and they part.

Friday arrives, and precisely at noon, the office staff stop working and meet up at the elevator. They walk in groups to the pub, chatting and laughing over this unexpected recess from work, Simon lagging behind them, hands stuffed in his suit pants pockets, head down, welcoming the chill of the late spring day.

Elaine has reserved the entire pub. Simon is astounded at how she convinced the owner to close his pub on the busiest lunch day of his week. Mr. Confabulate had informed him that he does not attend such functions but expected Simon to do so. Simon isn't happy as he complies. He longs for his bed and a weekend alone. He straggles in to the busy pub behind the rest. He enters the dark warmth to find most already seated.

"Here, Simon. Over here," Elaine yells, waving to him. He gestures an acknowledgement with his head and walks over to her booth. "Take your jacket off," Elaine instructs. "We're not at work anymore. It's time to relax!" Coat poles stand at each booth, and Simon shrugs out of his grey worsted wool suit jacket. He hangs it up on top of the pile of light spring jackets hooked on it. He slips in; that's when he notices Isaac sitting across from him. He raises his eyebrows.

Isaac laughs, "Yeah, man. It's me. Good old Elaine figured the big boss wouldn't be here and you wouldn't tell. You won't, right, Simon? She misses me, man." He leans forward and whispers exaggeratedly, "I think she's short on gossip. What do you think, man?"

Simon smiles, and suddenly his muscles lose their tension. He relaxes back into his booth. He hadn't realized how much he'd missed Isaac. He quips, "I think you're right. So what is the gossip?"

Isaac bursts out laughing.

Elaine says, "You shouldn't mock me. I arranged all this, you know."

Simon stretches his hand out toward hers resting on the table but doesn't touch it. "Yes. I'm grateful. Very grateful."

Isaac eyes him and says, "Where'd this confidence come from, Simon? You gunning for another promotion?"

Simon grins.

Isaac slaps the table. "I knew it. I knew they'd slated you to be the man. When is it, man?"

"Oh. He got a promotion already. This is another one," Elaine shares.

"Two?" Isaac asks shocked. He shakes his head ruefully, "Man, they really got the hots for you. You must be saving them money left, right, and centre. So what's it like saving money on the backs of poor people?" Isaac grins while his brown irises darken into polished orbs.

Lines of tension rip along Simon's muscles and contract them again. His stomach becomes a churning maw. Simon shrugs, trying to ignore his insides, saying nonchalantly, "If they were truthfully injured, we'd be paying out their legitimate claims."

"Aw c'mon, man, you know that's not true."

"What do we know? What truth do we know?"

Isaac considers Simon skeptically. "Man, you really been drinking the Kool-Aid over there."

"Nah, Isaac. Leave Simon alone. It's his dad," Elaine says.

Simon's jaw drops.

Elaine looks smug. "I have my sources."

A server carries over a tray with a pitcher of beer and three glasses on it. She plops the pitcher down in the middle of the table, slopping a bit of beer onto the table's scratched top. Simon slides his arms in their white cuff-linked sleeves back off the wood. The server distributes the glasses and asks if they're ready to order at the same time as she pulls out her order pad from the pocket of her black Pub-logo'ed apron. "Not yet," Elaine says. The server nods, tucks her pencil behind her ear, and leaves.

Isaac returns to his topic like a terrier burrowing after a rat in its hole.

"So what do you want to do, man? This? Since I left, I never been happier."

"So why are you here?" Elaine jibes him as she lifts the pitcher up to fill her glass to the brim with beer. She pours beer into the others' glasses as they talk.

"I'm here to convert you from the dark side, why you think?" Isaac laughs.

"Haha," Elaine says. "That dark side fed you."

"Yeah, yeah."

"Seriously. Simon needs to establish himself. He lost his girlfriend, you know?"

"He did?"

"Yeah. She wasn't right for him. We all knew that."

"We did?"

"Yeah. Anyway, he's gotta find a woman for himself, now that he's going up, and he can't do that if he's going to be in some dead-end job. This job is for him, you know that. He's going places. He's going to make good money after this promotion. You'll see. Once he's in management, he'll be too swell for us. He won't need us anymore. But that's okay cause this new job, it'll be right for him."

"Hey, everyone needs someone!" Isaac counters.

"Maybe. But he won't need us. He'll be management. Management have their own groups."

"Yeah, I seen those groups. Bunch of stuck-up shirts, gotta get drunk just so they can talk to each other. That's when they're not stabbing each other in the back, pretending to be best buds."

"You're so cynical, Isaac," Elaine grins as she fist-bumps his shoulder. "Simon will make other friends, you'll see."

"You're going to have to set him up, Elaine."

"Hmm . . . I don't have to, Isaac, everyone likes Simon, even cynical you, but . . ."

Simon rubs his fingers up and down his beer glass, focussing on the feeling of the cold condensation dripping down the glass. He watches his fingers, while he listens to the two bicker about him. He experiences a strange sensation of them moving away from him as if he is on the other end of a long lens in reverse zoom. They disappear out of his focus, and he disappears from himself.

"Hey," Isaac slaps the scarred wood of the table right in front of him. "You with us, man?"

Simon blinks rapidly as he readjusts to the present. He sits up straight and grips the beer glass. He lifts it off the table to take a long draught. He sets it back down, wipes his mouth exaggeratedly with the back of his hand, and forces bon homie into his sinking heart. "Yes. I'm here."

Isaac squints at him then shrugs. He picks up his menu and scans it. He says from behind the giant laminated sheet, "Time to order, man. I'm having the chicken wings."

"They're good?" Simon asks.

"They are."

"The burger is better," Elaine ripostes. "But a man like you Simon, going up in the world should have the steak. The sirloin."

"Hey, he the man. He should have the most expensive item on the menu," Isaac shoots back. "That's not any old steak."

"I'll have the wings," Simon states.

The two shake their heads at him. "No, no," Elaine says. "Isaac is right. The most expensive item. It's," she hesitates as she disappears behind the enormous laminated menu to scan it.

"No. I want the wings. I haven't had them here before," Simon says stubbornly.

Elaine peeks out from behind the menu to object as the server arrives. Simon immediately orders wings for himself. Elaine glares at him. But Simon ignores her, turning his head away: wings is what he wants. And when they arrive and are placed before him, their skins glistening a deep caramel brown, accompanied by extra thick chili-red sauce in a bowl on the side, his mouth salivates. He picks one up delicately and gnaws slowly and with great focus on it.

21

CONTINUED

"So, whatchya gonna do, man?" Isaac asks through a mouthful of chicken meat that he's just stripped from a wing with his teeth. He keeps on stripping and chewing as he locks eyes on Simon.

Simon swallows his thin morsel and says, "I intend to keep on working. It's a good job."

"Job, schmob."

Elaine mumbles incoherently through a massive mouthful of burger. With both hands, she's clutching a stack of puffy white bun, turkey burger, tomato slices poking their red peel out toward Simon, lettuce, brie squishing out like a slipped disc, with pumpkin mayo and gloriously coloured cranberry mustard oozing onto her fingers. Isaac ignores her. Simon feels the blood rush into his cheeks under Isaac's skepticism and curses this flushing weakness of his body. Why can't Isaac drop it? He's made his decision. Fred approved. His father has been around a lot longer than he or Isaac has. Mr. Confabulate is happy at Con Fable. Elaine seems to enjoy herself. Why can't he?

Isaac shakes his head ruefully, "You got nothing, man. Nothing."

"I do," Simon splutters.

"A job at Con Fable? C'mon, a big shot like you? That's easy pickings, man. You know where you're headed: a big time executive job at head office in London. You want to live in London? Pfft."

Simon hadn't thought that far. No, he doesn't want to live in London. He picks up another chicken wing and nibbles through the glistening skin into the flesh as he stares sightlessly down at the table and thinks about living in London. He's never visited that town west of Toronto. He remembers a long time ago driving through it when he and a group of his high school buddies had gone on a road trip through southwestern Ontario one weekend. They hadn't stayed long because one of them had an Aunt who lived there, and he didn't want to bump into her. They'd cleaned out the snack aisle at a gas station and taken off.

Simon shrugs as he masticates carefully a small shred of chicken. He dips the end of his chewed wing into the bowl of sauce. Once. Twice. Thrice.

"Hey man. How much sauce you gonna put on that? Your head is gonna blow off!" Isaac exclaims.

Elaine chokes on her burger, and Isaac smacks her back. She swallows the hunk, and her eyes bulge. Her face pinks then reddens then turns puce. Simon watches fascinated, and Isaac smacks her hard on the back again, worry increasing the force of his slap.

"Drink, Elaine," Isaac commands.

She reaches for her beer glass.

"Not beer. Don't ya know anything? Here," Isaac says as he pushes her water glass toward her. Elaine lifts it up and tries to take a sip but chokes again. Isaac smacks her back again, and the water shoots out of the glass she is holding and sprays the basket filled with the carcasses of Simon's chicken wings, drowning them. A lump of burger lands in among the carcasses. Luckily, Simon is still holding his one unfinished chicken wing, and he's still dipping that one in and out, in and out of the fiery sauce. It's liberally coated.

Elaine gasps in relief and sits up. She inhales carefully. Her face calms down to its normal pinkness. "Thanks. I think," she says as she turns to Isaac. "Don't do that again."

He grins back. "Don't be so greedy. Take little bites, like Simon here." They both turn to watch Simon making like an oil rig.

Elaine cocks her head. "Isaac hit a nerve, eh?"

Simon returns her look blankly.

"I think you removed his thoughts," Elaine remarks to Isaac.

"Be nice, Elaine."

"I am. You're the one who's not nice, asking him all those questions, telling him Con Fable is no good for him. What about me? How come it's not good for him but good for me?"

"You fit in there, Elaine."

"What's that supposed to mean?"

"Just what I said." Isaac leans back toward the wall the booth is bolted to and flashes his teeth at her. She narrows her eyes back at him. They burst out laughing in unison.

Simon hears and sees all this, but once again he has retreated from them. Once again he sees them as if from afar, as if they are receding into the distance from him. All he sees clearly is the memory of the gas station in London, of a boring empty street, of small buildings and a suburban feel. It's a memory void of feeling, the antithesis of Toronto with its sunken ravines and loud downtown, with its quirky retail streets and clanging streetcars—even if he doesn't like riding them. He hasn't thought consciously about where Con Fable is taking him. He admits reluctantly, forced to because Isaac is sitting across from him and once again challenging him: he doesn't like this job. He doesn't like this way of making money. But Fred had pointed out the errors in his thinking. How does he know what's best for himself? His father does. His father has made a good living for himself and has created a safe nest for his family. He's provided for them all. And here Simon is, living in an apartment in an old house in the east end with not much in his savings to show for his efforts so far. At his age, Fred was already on the way to earning well, to saving up for a substantial down payment on his house, the one his parents and sometimes Sarah still live in. Simon waves away the pushy thought that his father had had help from his father. He'd never met Fred's father but had heard he'd made a fortune in business and had spent most of it on good living and setting his children up. Simon strains to recall what the business had been but fails. Fred had sold the business soon after his father's death. He, Simon, had never been much interested in learning about a man he'd never met.

Never met.

Is memory only good for those who've lived in your own experience? Does that mean not only will he be forgotten like Gramps by the living but also by generations to come? He will fade into oblivion, like he has here at this table while Isaac and Elaine squabble like the old friends that they are.

Isaac's questions make him itch.

Prickles flow through him as his heart beats blood through his arteries. Simon strains to blink away this flowing pain that's his constant companion even when it seems to leave like it had when he'd sat down across from Isaac. Why did Isaac have to ask him these questions and bring this needling pain back into his consciousness?

Failure shames him.

Seeing once more Fred's disdain for his doubts quails him.

His diaphragm drops into his stomach, and he wants to vomit the wings.

Simon gazes down at his right hand holding the wing by its tiny elbow, still dunking the wing in and out of the almost empty sauce bowl as most of the sauce is now hugging the puny appendage. He stops his hand's motion. Elaine and Isaac stop talking and look at the wing simultaneously then up at Simon. Their faces flash a query at him.

Simon scratches the back of his neck hard with his free left hand. Fred couldn't think less of him than he already does. Failure hugs him like the sauce does the wing. How else can he rid himself of this shame and fear but try again? Maybe this crawling pain will finally leave, too, if he takes the risk of living as himself?

Simon drops his wing into the sauce bowl and clears his throat. He looks up at his work friends. He tries to speak. But all that comes out is a hoarse cough. The other two wait. He clears his throat again. "You have a point, Isaac. I don't want to live in London."

22

FATE

"I quit, Fred."

Fred stops writing in the chart on his desk and turns surprised eyes up to Simon. "You what?"

"I quit Con Fable," Simon repeats as he stands before his father's desk.

Fred looks past Simon through his open office door. Simon twists his head around to look where his father is looking. Fred's secretary is sitting at her desk transcribing his dictation into her computer. She's wearing earphones.

Fred's growl yanks his eyes back: "What. Did. You. Do?"

"I quit Con Fable." Simon's legs begin to tremble, and he snaps his lips together in case he keeps talking and his voice begins to squeak and quiver.

Fred tosses his fountain pen on top of the chart and leans back to glare into Simon's eyes. "How dare you? After all you asked me to do for you."

"Me?" Simon squeaks. He clears his throat and protests, "But you arranged for an interview, for which I'm most grateful. But I have to decide the best job and career for myself. No one else can do that, not even you," he ends on a crack. Simon gulps, trying hard to stifle the unconscious motion so that his Adam's apple doesn't give him away. All the emotional control he'd gained at Con Fable is obliterated under his father's displeasure. Fred drops his eyes to Simon's neck then narrows them. He raises embittered eyes back to Simon's face. Simon blinks hard. His father's gaze feels like a blackened laser slicing into his pupils and peeling open a line through into his brain. Simon badly wants to sit down; his right leg shakes so hard that his knee is bending and giving way. Simon fights to lock his knee and hold him up; his leg straightens and returns to simply quivering.

"Yes, you, Simon. I wouldn't have asked, gone out on a limb for you, if you hadn't pleaded. It's all about you, isn't it, Simon? You know nothing about having a real career, the sacrifices I made for you. What kind of career are you going to have with that useless degree of yours. Now Michael here—"

Simon whips his head around quickly, confusion over his father's words adding to his dizziness, to see Michael stopped in his tracks in the doorway, his fisted hand still raised as if to knock on the open door.

"I'm interrupting. I'll come back later," Michael says.

"No. Stay here. You need to talk to your brother," Fred orders.

Michael has already turned around, but he cannot pretend that he hasn't heard his father's bellow. Slowly Michael turns to face Simon and their father. He remains in the doorway. For only for a second.

Michael lurches forward.

"Hey," comes a voice from behind him. "Why are you blocking the doorway?" Sarah emerges from around Michael and, ignoring the two frozen males, saunters up to Fred's desk. She hips Simon out of the way. "Daddy, I need money."

His stern look doesn't faze her.

"Aw, c'mon, Daddy. You know me. You know I'll forever be sucking on your money teat. So don't be like that. You and me, we have a synergy going. We can't exist without each other, kind of like Dax with that symbiote of hers. I'm that symbiote," Sarah grins. "I get money from you so that I can live in the style I'm accustomed to, and you have someone to grumble about to your buddies in the Faculty Club. Don't pretend you don't get off on me!"

Angry silence answers her. Sarah pulls her eyebrows down. Then she slowly looks, really looks at her father, then Simon, then finally Michael. Her mouth forms a moue. "Oh," she says. She rakes Simon up and down. "I see I have a usurper. What'd you do Simon? Quit?" She laughs.

"Yes," Simon replies.

Sarah's mouth drops open. She exclaims, "For real? You did that? You? No way!"

Sarah regards him with a mixture of admiration and horror then moves her stunned gaze to Fred then Michael before returning it to Simon. She says in tones of awe: "You did."

"Yes," Simon says. He suddenly realizes that his legs have stopped their shaking and that his voice has stabilized. Sarah's worse example has strengthened him. He'd wanted to burn his bridges, simply walk out of Con Fable and not talk to Fred, yet he couldn't go against his ingrained politeness and respect for his parents. Phyllis's voice in his head lecturing him to treat people with respect and to use please and thank you had made him type up a formal letter and hand it to Mr. Confabulate in person, had made him come here to tell Fred in person. But he also wrote that letter and resigned first so that his father couldn't scare him out of his decision again. He knew his father would think the worst of him because he'd made the worst decision: he'd gone against his father's wishes and his advice.

"I wash my hands of you," the older man says, his hostile tone interrupting Simon's thoughts.

"Oh, c'mon, Daddy," Sarah says. "You haven't washed your hands of me." She braces her hands on the edge of Fred's desk and leans toward him while making a pathetic face. "So why wash your hands of Simon? He's the baby of the family anyway. As you say, he's always gotten his way. Now you're going to go in the opposite direction and toss him out on his wet butt?"

"Don't be vulgar, Sarah. And it's none of your business."

"Of course, it's my business. It's all our business, right Michael?" Receiving no answer, she and Simon glance toward the doorway. It's empty. Fred seeing the empty doorway at the same time seethes at them both, "The one child of mine who is making anything of his life has left because of you two. It's not enough that you want to ruin your life, Simon, you drive away the only son that matters to me."

"Daddy," Sarah sing-songs. "That's harsh. Even for you."

"It's the truth, Sarah. Simon is a bitter disappointment. How will I face my colleague after this debacle? What. Am. I. Supposed. To. Say? Tell me that, Simon? Tell me what I'm supposed to say?"

"That your son is growing up," Simon hears himself retort at the unjust treatment.

"Growing up? Growing up!" Fred roars. "You call quitting growing up? I call that weaseling."

"I call it rising to the next level," Simon snaps, his anger like heat from the western sun melting his shame and fear into one. "Working for an insurance company is not my metier. It's not my career. And just because I'm good at it, doesn't mean it's the right career for me."

"Career," Fred sneers. "What do you know about career? You young things with your garbage degrees think you're entitled to a career? You're entitled to a job. You are not entitled to live off of other people, do you hear me?"

"I hear you. I've made an appointment with the university career counsellor."

"What do they know? They don't live in the real world. I do. I know better. I went out on a limb for you. But go listen to them. See how well they'll help you." Bitterness injects hatred into his last word.

"So why not help him, Daddy?" Sarah cajoles as Simon's grey-green eyes ignite into fires of plasma. Her words penetrate his mind. Like a boulder tossed into a river, they divert the flow of his mingled shame, fear, and anger into confusion. Her sudden interest in his welfare flummoxes him. She looks at him over her shoulder and smirks before returning her attention to Fred. Simon draws his eyebrows down and contemplates the back of her head.

She pleads, "C'mon, Daddy. Help him."

"No." Fred replies petulantly as he retrieves his fountain pen.

"Well, you can still help me. I'm right on time anyway."

Fred pauses and lifts his eyes up to her face. "I don't think so. One of you beggars belief. Two is ridiculous. Both of you are now on your own." He lowers his head and begins writing in the chart again.

Sarah throws Simon a venomous look over her shoulder. "Look what you've done," she hisses at him. "You only think about yourself. You've ruined it for me, too. Fix it."

Simon points at himself, his mouth an open question: "How?"

"I don't know," she says, turning right around and looking right up into his face. "Just. Fix. It."

Simon's head flames. Humiliation clenches his teeth and tightens his lips. Loneliness throws tidal waves against his protecting anger. "I can't," he laments. He turns on his heel and marches out, hoping his father will call him back, will say that he's wrong to disparage Simon, hoping Sarah will resume that unexpected burst of helpfulness. But all he hears as he retreats past the secretary whose eyes remain glued to her computer screen, her fingers flying over the keyboard, is Sarah wheedling again and his father's voice growing weary. She'll prevail in the end. She has the wiles and the stamina to do so. But him? He does not. He has always done what Fred and Phyllis wanted from him.

Simon feels bereft. He isn't sure what to do as his feet march him toward the elevator. He knows Isaac was right. But where does that leave him?

Simon turns into a little-used hospital hallway, past darkened patient rooms, until he arrives at the far elevators that nobody uses because they are clunky, prone to stop between floors, and distant from wards and offices still in use. He'll be alone with his heaving emotions.

Simon presses the down button. It lights up then flickers off. He looks up at the numbers. But they seem to be stuck at floor four. And both the up and down arrows are unlit. It's always a guessing game whether the numbers will be true or false, whether the elevator will be going down or up when it bounces to a stop at his floor.

Ding.

The doors slide open partway, stall, then slam into the spaces on either side of the doorway. He steps on, and the elevator car gently bounces in tune with his feet. He presses the button for the ground floor. The doors bang shut, and the ground floor button turns itself off. The elevator lurches up. Simon sighs. He wonders where he's going up to. His life was going down into an unknown pit, but the elevator wants to take him up to a phantom floor. As expected, the doors slide open onto a darkened, empty floor. He futilely presses the closed door button. It seems to keep the doors open. He jabs the ground floor button again and again as tears spurt from his eyes. Nothing happens. He stabs the closed door button hard, bending his finger.

He suddenly needs fresh air; he can't handle this cantankerous elevator anymore. He moves to step off. The doors slam together, rebound a bit, then shut violently. Simon jumps back. Tears trickle onto his lashes as the elevator drops to the bottom floor swiftly, leaving his stomach up high. Simon wipes his salted face as the elevator halts and its doors bang open. Simon hustles out, head down. The elevator closes its doors right on him. The whoosh of air fans his back.

He walks rapidly to the exit and hurtles through a glass door into the noisy cityscape outside the hospital. He'd made his appointment with the university counsellor for right after seeing his father. But he cannot face her. She'd sounded chirpy and kind on the phone. But kindness will unravel him into a mess. He cannot cope with being shamed twice in one day.

He shoves his hands into his jeans pockets—maybe he shouldn't have worn his jeans since his parents hate them—but he'd wanted to fit back into the university crowd.

Birds cheep at him as he passes straggly bushes, denuded of leaves from the recent winter but with buds bursting through their bark. He hikes along the mucky sidewalk. His polished brown shoes assume flecks of mud from the rains that have pockmarked the snowbanks after winter's last flurry. Snow and rain and snow and sun in quick succession: such is spring in Toronto. He stumbles into Nathan Phillips Square. The iconic square looks like he feels: chaotic with the detritus of a recent festival. But at least the square is heading into another new season, one of hope and renewal and the life of summer events.

Where is he headed?

Fred was right. He has no clue about his future and has expected others to pick up the pieces. He rotates his shoulders back against his pricking thoughts. The futile movement only serves to light the river of needles that surge through his arteries. He slows down and wanders up the ramp toward the rising curved towers of City Hall and halts when he reaches the plateau next to the space pod-looking Council chamber. The people around him vanish from his senses. He can't hear even the birds within his self-immolation. He leans his arms on the top of the concrete wall that looks over the square and closes his eyes. If only he could rest.

His iPhone rings.

He doesn't move.

It stops ringing, and he sinks into the morass of his mind. His cheeks sag, their weight too heavy to stay up. His eyes moisten behind his closed lids. His nose becomes stuffed.

His iPhone rings again. The familiar, unwanted sound knifes into his misery. He sniffs hard and opens his eyes. Simon retrieves the interrupting device and stares at the display. Slowly, slowly, the display makes sense: it's the university counsellor. What can he say? How can she help him? She's an amateur, like Fred had said. She'll have soothing words of no practical value. She can't help him like Fred had. Her words will not equal action on her part, and he has no energy, no will for action on his own. He will end up on the government teat.

He has nothing to say to her.

Sighing, he slides the iPhone back into his pocket, desperately wanting to obey the urge to hurl it as far away from himself as he can then run up to it and stomp on it over and over and over. Instead, he slouches down the ramp and away from City Hall toward mid-town Toronto. Simon isn't sure where he's going. He'll let his feet lead him.

He finds himself on the Viaduct. On the wrong side of it. But he's too tired to stop; too tired to look down at the ground. Yet as he walks along its endless length, he's aware of the Don Valley far below waiting for him with wide open arms budding with trees and the hint of fresh grass underneath the slippery soil. His right side tingles with awareness as he walks toward Broadview, head down. The idea of the ground gains traction and attraction in his mind. But he doesn't stop. Simply feels it.

At Broadview, the light for him is red. His feet stop moving, and he looks along the Danforth stretching out before him. He turns his gaze to look south along Broadview. He wants to go home. He wants to rest on his familiar couch. Home is haven. For now. His feet take him there.

23

COUNSEL

Simon's iPhone rings from deep within his jeans' pocket. He's huddled into the corner of his comforting couch. He's been like that for an hour and doesn't want to move. The iPhone is unrelenting. He rolls over, stretches out his right leg, and draws out the irritating technology. He scowls at the display. It's the career counsellor. She's persistent. How often is she going to call him? Doesn't she get it? He doesn't want to talk. The iPhone falls silent. He breathes out relief. It vibrates in his hand with the insistence of her ring as she calls him again. Simon clenches his teeth, but then with a sigh that draws air up from deep within his lungs, he answers.

"Hello."

"Hi," a chirpy voice answers back. "Is Simon there?"

Of course it's me, he moans to himself silently. He says politely, "Speaking."

"Hi, Simon. How're you?"

"I'm fine."

"I missed you today. I hope nothing serious happened."

"No."

"That's good. I know how busy you are. Looking for new work is so busy and exciting, new paths and new people to meet, and all that. Were you able to answer the questions we gave you?"

Simon ponders that question. The truthful answer is no; he fears where that answer will carry him. "No," he answers.

"Well, that's not a problem. I can help. I'd love to help you. Listen, I have an opening in an hour. Would you be able to come? You don't live too far away . . ."

"No."

"Great! I'll see you in an hour, then?"

Simon pauses. Is she deaf or wilfully deaf? And how late does she work, anyway? He squeezes his eyes shut, gripping his iPhone to his ear, resentment pulsing through him. He might as well go. "Yes," he says.

"Fabulous. You have the directions?"

"Yes."

"Good. Bye, then."

"Bye."

Simon presses the red hang-up icon and shoves his iPhone back in his pocket, controlled anger like a needle gun sprays through his muscle cells into his clenching fingers. Using that pain as energy, he heaves himself up off his saggy couch.

Within an hour, Simon is sitting across the desk from "Caroline. Call me Caro."

"Hello, Caro," he says, detached.

"It's so great to meet you. Tell me about yourself."

Simon's mind blanks instantly. He blinks rapidly.

"All right, no problem. Why don't we begin with your degree. What did you take?"

"Science."

Caro checks the information visible only to her on her computer screen. "Was that your major?"

"Yes." Simon knows that she knows what his major really was, nothing as vague as science. But maybe if he doesn't say it out loud, he can forget it, forget he ever thought to follow in Fred's footsteps.

Caro seems to take the hint. "Did you take just the one major? Like, did you minor in anything, maybe take a few courses in something?"

Simon closes his eyes against her obvious knowledge—it's all there on her all-revealing screen. A tide of anger slams its white-crested wave against his detachment. He slides down in his seat, sighs deep within himself. The anger vanishes. Simon refuses to reflect on why anger is appearing and disappearing so quickly within him. He pushes himself back up. He straightens his back. He replies, "Yes."

Caro waits.

Simon says, "English."

Caro nods. "Lots of people think English is no good, but I love English majors. They're so erudite, you know. They know books," she says breathlessly. "It's so much fun talking to them." She beams at Simon.

Simon evinces a small smile back at her as suppressed memories of pursuing a couple of courses roll into him. Fred had found out about that second course somehow, Simon's talk of taking that one practical course having not diverted his detecting nose. Maybe Sarah had peeked into Simon's notes, had discovered what he was studying, and couldn't resist stirring up the pot to distract from her own failing coursework. Simon cringes internally as he recalls Fred's tirade upon finding out. It was all very well to take a practical English course, but to take a literature course? Fred had spat out the word 'literature' as if it was a dirty, disgusting thing that needed to be washed away.

When Simon had refused to drop the course in favour of one that would be more useful and more fitting for a bachelor of science, in Fred's eyes, his father had informed him that he wouldn't find a job at the end of university. He'd stated that Simon was wasting the money his parents had so generously bestowed upon him. He was wasting their hard-earned labour for the luxury of a useless university degree, one that he'd begged for so that he could—. Simon's mind skips like a needle on an old vinyl record:

"Wealthy layabout."

"Wasting an opportunity."

"Many students don't have his luxury."

"Living off my teat to avoid university debt."

"Men earn their way."

Fred had demanded: "Why are you throwing away the opportunity I've given you on nonsense courses?"

Simon had had no answer.

Simon blinks, recalling himself to where he is: sitting in the university counsellor's office. Simon rubs his face up and down to erase those memories. He drops his hands to his knees and sees Caro's perky expression aimed at him. Her smile grates on his nerves. An urge, he's not sure for what, grips him so strongly, he half-rises from his chair. Caro says quickly, "You know, employers like well-rounded people like you. You would be an asset to them. You understand the practical side of life, you've shown a head for numbers—"

"But—," he says as he thumps back down into his chair. "I quit Con Fable."

She waves her hand as if to wave away his statement. She rejoins, "So what? Young people like you are finding their way. Quitting is a part of life. You want something better, right?"

Simon doesn't answer.

Caro persists, "Don't you?"

Simon nods thoughtfully.

"Of course you do. Most people stay in and grit their teeth, then they hate their job and make for a lousy employee in the long run. You gained valuable knowledge and now you're going on to fulfill your talent." Ticking off on her fingers, she continues, "You know numbers, you understand business principles after your term at Con Fable, you can write, you have some marketing education that you can turn into creative ideas because of your English courses, you know how to work with a team." She stops, leaving her right forefinger pressing her left pinky back and looks directly into his eyes. "You understand what I'm saying here, Simon? You're a catch. Now we just have to find the right kind of company for you and plant the seeds of a career. Piece of cake," she pipes. "You'll see."

Simon frowns at her. In this economy, isn't it the other way around? What has he done to be a catch?

"I saw that," Caro says with a smile. "Don't worry. I get people jobs in companies where they thrive, even in this economy, which in Canada is a lot better than anywhere else. You'll see. I'm a people person, Simon. I can work with this amazing background you've brought me, and I know how to make companies think it's their idea to hire you. I can find you something. It may take a little time," she concedes. "But it'll happen. All you have to do is go out there, make your résumé shine. I'll give you the tools, beginning with those questionnaires. They'll help me learn more about you, and then we'll meet again in a week, okay? Here's a new batch for you so you can answer them right away, here. You don't have to go home and search for the online versions." Caro's smile has not faltered once.

"Thanks." Simon takes the large envelope she hands him.

"There's a table where you can work at through there," she says pointing through her closed door and a bit over to the right, Simon's left. "When you're done, just knock on my door, okay?"

Simon nods and pushes his chair back as his heart falls. He'd envisioned taking the questionnaires home, tossing them on his dining room table with the original set, where he could forget about them then "forget," too, about his next appointment.

As if reading his mind, Caro says, "Here, let me show you." She bounces out of her chair and canters round her desk to her door, whipping it open and trotting out in front of him, her expectation that he will follow pulling him up and out of his chair. Fatigue drags at his legs as he locomotes after her. When he reaches the hallway, he spots her standing near another door a little ways down. He forces his legs to move faster and catches up. She precedes him into the room. "You're in luck," she chirps. "There's no one here to disturb you. I know some people feel these questionnaires are intrusive and don't like filling them out in public. But I assure you, no one will see the results but me, and these tables are spaced far enough apart that if someone else joins you, they won't be able to see your answers. Besides, it's quiet today. I'm sure you'll be left in peace. When you're done, just knock on my door, okay?"

Simon nods. She leaves. He sits down and pulls the sheets out of the envelope. A tray of pens and pencils await him in the centre of the table. He selects a pencil out of the tray and begins to fill in the answers as glacially as he can, pausing every time he reaches the end of a sheet.

But it isn't slow enough. Simon still finishes all the questions, still completes this step that sets him apart from Michael and Sarah in the family hierarchy, still pulls him away from Fred and Phyllis and their wishes for him. What has he done? What is he doing?

Squelching his doubts, he leaves the package with Caro and stumbles out the building. He trudges over salt-stained sidewalks, past old houses and sleek towers with their threat of falling glass, past grubby retail shops and spiffy fashion stores, all the while not sure where he's going. Simon finds himself in a small coffee shop. Scuffed tables stand here and there, and chairs are scattered around them. They're all empty but one. At it, a man with unshaved chin and a pilly beige sweater is diligently typing on his Mac Air with a lone cup of coffee and a half-eaten muffin next to his flying hands. Simon orders a dry cappuccino and retreats to the opposite end of the café from where the Mac acolyte is sitting. He looks fixedly out the window as he sips his foamy drink.

On the street, people dash past, and he registers their presence but doesn't notice them. Simon ruminates over Jackie, about how she can write poetry, about how comfortable she is in reading it to a raucous audience, about how she accepts that poetry won't feed her body but is willing to sacrifice for the gift of her talent feeding her mind. He aches for that kind of certainty.

The days plod by. Simon's appointment time with Caro arrives.

"Hey!" Caro says as she comes out to get him where he's waiting in the waiting room. Today every chair is filled with nervous mostly twenty-something graduates awaiting advice as to what to do next. He is no different.

"So," she says as they sit down on opposite sides of her desk. "I went through everything. I think we can find something for you quickly, Simon." She begins handing him one stapled set of pages after another, saying, "I have put together some possibilities for you. Here, I want you to take a look at them. Read them over; think about them. We'll meet next week, and you can give me your feedback. I have here guidelines on writing a résumé. The way I like to work is you write one up following these guidelines, then I'll edit it, point out where you need to strengthen it, and you then polish it, with options targetting different companies. We'll also work on a cover letter, and you'll do the same with optional paragraphs for different companies. Here's some tips on how to write a good cover letter. Once we've agreed on your companies and your résumé, we'll begin sending them out. I'll also set up networking opportunities for you. Volunteering always pads credentials. Companies like to see people who give back to the community. Do you volunteer, Simon?" Caro asks hopefully, handing him the last of the pages and proceeding to poise her fingers over her computer keyboard to record his volunteering experience.

Simon shakes his head. He used to with Gramps, less so in the final years of university and after he'd graduated. But since his grandfather died, all desire to continue the work Gramps had involved Simon in had died with him. Simon doesn't want to be reminded of what he used to have with Gramps. He doesn't want to remember how Gramps had used to say how lucky he felt being able to volunteer in his retirement and how that had made Simon feel lucky in the last year of Gramps's life. He doesn't feel lucky, now. He doesn't want to be in place where the people who knew Gramps, and who'd been the recipient of his friendship, don't want to talk about him, this man who'd made Simon feel important and valued, too. No one had called him from those places after they'd sent the obligatory condolence card or after a few had attended Gramps's funeral.

He nods in tune to Caro's cadence as she continues to talk without him registering a single word. He suddenly realizes she's looking at him hopefully.

"Pardon? I'm sorry I missed that last part."

She smiles, "That's okay, Simon. I know it's a lot to take in. What do you think about the list of companies? Don't worry, we have a few minutes for you to scan them and tell me your first reactions."

He stares at the top sheet in the pile in his hands. The words scatter into gibberish. He squints and focusses hard on the first name. At last, the words spring into clarity. He begins to read quickly the names and brief company summaries, ignoring the details that follow. "This one," he says, showing her the third bunch of stapled sheets.

Caro leans over her desk to squint at it. She asks, "Which one?"

He leans forward toward her and turns the summary around so that she can read the company name right side up.

"Ah," she says brightening. "That's a great company. I've placed one person there this past year, and they're looking to hire more people. They want someone who has business acumen and knows the canon, as they put it. I believe they will like you. Why don't you Google them, learn more about them? Follow the tips in writing a cover letter and customize it for them, based on what you find out. Okay?"

"Okay," Simon says, sitting back and putting the pages back onto the top of the pile on his lap as hope eases into his heart.

Simon leaves Caro's office, feeling that maybe he will find his way.

That Sunday night, he informs his family of his job progress and the company he's considering while keeping his eyes fixed on the painting of colourful slashes that hangs over the buffet across from him.

"I have nothing to say," Fred declares. "You chose to quit. You make this choice on your own. Don't expect me to help you. Last time I did that, at your insistence, you quit and humiliated me. It was the best career you could have had, and you think this company is a good substitute?" Fred blows contempt at him, stabs with his fork at a final piece of roast beef sitting on his plate, and chews angrily.

Michael shrugs, "Don't know nothing about them. I don't have time to read."

"Yes, you do," Sarah retorts.

"Not those kinds of books. They're a waste of space."

"What do you know? That's why you don't know what you're missing out on and why you're so shallow. If you read real books instead of thinking textbooks are real books—they're just boring bits of words—you'd be a real man."

Michael aims a vicious look at her, opens his mouth—

"Enough," Phyllis commands in her calm, penetrating voice. "That's a good company, Simon. I read their books, and I don't find many grammatical mistakes in them. You would do well to work there, I'm sure. But I don't know enough about them to advise you. You have a counsellor, you said? Well, I'm sure she'll guide you well. But don't expect us to know what to do for you. We gave you our best advice. There's nothing more to say."

Simon deflates. He shrinks into his chair and thinks about how Gramps would have responded. Down in his lair, he'd probably have asked him all sorts of tough questions that would've made him squirm and then bite back that he didn't know what he was talking about. Upon which, Gramps would've pointed out sharply that of course he, emphasizing himself, didn't know what he was talking about, that's why he was asking questions. And if Simon knew what he was talking about, he'd be able to answer the questions. Maybe he, Simon, should go research the answers more, come up with better ones. Then after that acerbic exchange, Gramps would've mixed him a vodka tonic so that they could discuss the whole thing better. And maybe Simon should power up that dratted piece of technology so that he could look up the answers to the questions he couldn't answer.

Gramps's voice is loud and clear in Simon's head, as if Gramps is sitting next to him.

A sparkling crash and a giggled 'Oops' interrupts Simon's internal conversation.

As he watches Melanie wiping up Sarah's spilled wine, Simon contemplates how no one is left to ask Gramps's kinds of questions. Yet he feels somehow that working at this company he's contemplating is possible, that somehow he has already had that kind of conversation with Gramps.

He tells Caro about his hopefulness at their next appointment and about what he's discovered about the company. She asks him if he believes his degree and skill set will match their needs. At her question, doubts resurface. He isn't sure. She shakes her head at him but with a smile. She grills him in a mock interview until he recognizes that he is, after all, a good match for the company. Her belief in him obliterates his doubts. Simon's face relaxes into a smile. Satisfied, Caro wishes him goodbye chirpily. And for once, her cheeriness doesn't grate on Simon; instead, it's spread into him. Simon stretches his lips wide into a grin. He chirrups, "Goodbye." Caro beams.

A week later, he has a job. No, not a job, he tells himself but the seeds of a career, as Caro had put it.

24

A NEW PLACE

Simon steps off the elevator and walks straight forward through two glass doors that remind him of the glass doors that he used to walk through into Con Fable. He blinks away the memory and pushes back his shoulders. He walks up to the receptionist. She asks in a trilling voice if she can help him. My life is full of chirpy women, he thinks.

"I'm Simon."

She cocks her head. She doesn't know.

"I'm the new marketing person."

"Oh. I'll get the boss." She punches in a code on her large telephone and speaks into her headset. "Hi, it's Sandie. Simon is here for the new job." A look of pain crosses her face as she cannot tear her ear away from the voice squawking its displeasure at top volume. Simon tries not to discern the easily heard words. The voice stops. The receptionist looks up apologetically at Simon.

"Sorry, I hafta get Clara for you. She's the head of marketing. She'll show you around."

Simon files a note into his head not to ask the boss a question that the hierarchy dictates he should ask someone else. He forces himself to stand loose while Sandie punches another number in. A few seconds later, she informs Simon that Clara will be right out.

A woman with hand outstretched emerges through the door to the right of the reception desk. "Hi, I'm Clara, I'll be your new boss."

Simon shakes her hand and says hello.

Clara gestures to him to follow her. They walk through the door she'd come through and into a large area filled with desks. Late spring sun shines through tall windows along one wall. No cubicles break the expanse. Everyone works in the open. The desks are a mish-mash of wood and metal, the chairs a range of high-end Aero ones and, he sees with dismay as Clara leads him toward it, an old-fashioned wooden one on wheels. Gramps would've liked that. It is rather romantic, he thinks. It makes him feel like he's in the heady world of words and old-fashioned values, the kind of world Gramps had related so often to him, the kind where people who liked each other spent time with each other, like in the old black-and-white films or Judy Garland movies.

"And here's your desk," Clara interrupts his introspection, gesturing to the old chair and dented ancient oak desk with a laptop sitting closed on top of it. "I assume you know Word."

"Yes."

"Good. I want you to familiarize yourself with our leading author's work. You'll be working on her account. Our production schedule has been sped up for her since we had a few problems with the editing over the summer, which put us back and has compressed our post-editing schedule. But enough of that. Although you'll be working on her account, I like my marketing department to be familiar with all our authors' works so that you know who they are and can answer any question on their books. You're a fast reader?"

"Yes."

"Good. You have an eReader or iPad?" She doesn't wait for his answer. "The boss doesn't believe in them, but even she knows we have to keep up with the times. She lets us publish eBooks, but she doesn't know we use eReaders. But if you don't have one, you must get one, otherwise you'll never keep up with our catalogue and be familiar with how they look in that format. To market our product, I like my staff to know how they look and behave. Not everyone does in this industry, but I do. Understand?" Again not waiting for an answer, Clara finishes swiftly. "Just don't tell her."

Simon nods.

"Good," Clara nods. "Your three-month probation period starts now. Welcome to First Past the Post Publishing." She leaves.

Simon lifts the laptop lid, hunts for the power button, turns on the computer, launches Word, then stops. He stares at the blank page of the word processor. What is he supposed to do? A soft chuckle hits his ear. He turns his head to see big brown eyes watching him. "Clara does that," says the owner of the brown eyes. "She expects you to know exactly what to do without her having to go to the bother of explaining it. Hi," she says pulling her rolling chair toward him with her feet and reaching out her hand at the same time, "I'm Sandy. Yes, there are two of us here. Mine is with a 'y', hers with an 'ie.' Don't get them mixed up."

"I won't," Simon returns, smiling back, reaching toward her, and having his hand shaken hard. Sandy lets go all of a sudden. Simon retrieves his sore hand.

"Here, I'll show you," Sandy says as she wheels closer to him. She nudges him aside. She pulls open a drawer and slaps out sheaves of paper stapled together. "Here's all you need to know about your job, company policy, and so on. And here are your login details," she tells him, flipping through the sheets, pausing on one, and pointing to a line halfway down a page. "You'll have to change your password. Not something stupid like your name or birthday, understand, but smart. Password rules are here," she says pointing to the paragraph below the login details. She hands the sheaf of papers to him, pulls the laptop close to the edge of the desk, and, with a few swift keystrokes, shows him how to login, where to find the manuscripts, where to find the author Clara wants him to brush up on, and how to download her eBooks so that he can read them. "You got an eReader?"

"No."

"Get one. Doesn't matter which one, just so long as you get one that reads ePub. Okay?"

He nods.

"When you get one, I'll show you how to copy those files onto it. But for now, you'd better get started. But first, change your password!"

"I will," Simon assures her.

She wheels backward to her desk. Before she swivels around to return to her work, she adds, "Oh yeah, when Clara asked if you were a fast reader, what she meant is can you read a hot thick romance in an hour. Can you?"

Simon's jaw drops. "That fast?" He blinks as the rest of her words percolate. "Is that what I must read?" Blood flushes his face.

Sandy laughs, "Welcome to our world. Nah, not hot thick romance always. But for now Shelley, our author du jour, likes to write steamy. There'll be sedate books ahead, I promise. You'll like it here, but you'll have to plough your way through one of Shelley's books every three months. That woman can write!" And on that note, Sandy grabs her desk with her right hand and pulls herself around to face her own laptop. Simon watches her erect profile and listens to her furious typing, for a moment. She's mesmerizing. Priscilla rises up in his memory and then pops like a soap bubble in the wind of Sandy's warmth.

He returns his attention happily to his laptop and begins the password change process.

25

THE RIVER RISES

The months and years flow by. Simon masters his job within his probation period. He becomes Shelley's point person for all her publicity campaigns. Sandy, at first his mentor, becomes his partner on marketing campaigns. Her good-natured ribbing and the fun they have bouncing ideas off of each other, lift Simon into the ebb of a regular life in the publishing world. Monthly, he meets with Isaac and Elaine at their pub, and soon after he'd begun working with her, he asks Sandy to join them. The laughter and chatter patter on until closing time. Each year, Simon adds an extra pitcher of beer to their menu and airily pays for the increasing cost. Isaac needles him over his thirst for beer; Elaine ignores it; and Sandy watches thoughtfully. None say anything. As he passes his twenty-eighth birthday, his stomach reflects his growing taste for beer; he takes up running to counter it. One of FPTP Publishing's authors is a fitness guru, and he catches him at the elevator for an ostensible conversation about his marketing campaign, but in reality Simon has forgotten what he knew about running and wanted a Coles notes version of what he needs to buy and how to set himself up for success. The author staccatos information at him on their ride down in the elevator, suggests joining the gym on the ground floor of the building the publisher is in, but Simon is pumped to begin his new regimen. He won't join the gym; he'll run in his new shoes and new spandex. But after a couple of aborted attempts, he realizes he needs a destination for a running route. One morning, nursing his familiar lethargic headache and being forced to half-run to work to make it in on time, and hearing the beat through the gym doors as he half-jogs by on the way to the elevators, he has a light bulb moment. He'll run to work. He'll run down Broadview to Queen and thence west to work. And he'll join the gym to use their showers to cleanse him of his sweat before Sandy arrives. He'll still be able to avoid the Viaduct, which he has since he'd snagged this job. He doesn't drive, walk, or take the subway over the Viaduct.

He and his family have an unspoken pact at Sunday dinner not to discuss his work with its undertones of refusing to look up to Fred's advice nor the fact he hasn't moved out of his apartment after he received a good raise. He tells himself he likes his neighbourhood. After his probation period ends, he jaunts east to the café and asks Jackie out. She laughs merrily and good-naturedly shares he's not her type. But she trusts him as a friend. Trust is big. It's the foundation of a friendship that can withstand the storms life whirls us into, she tells him with a smile brimming out of her eyes. He smiles back and leaves, vowing to put her out of his mind. He resumes dating through Phyllis's network, but each woman is unaccountably more unsatisfactory to him than the last. He persists, though.

As the years roll one into the other, his nights blur one into the other, and his hours at work lengthen, Jackie returns more and more to his mind until she dominates it. He has the job — career, he reminds himself — but wife and family continue to elude him. Perhaps friendship and the familiarity it brings will breed a different feeling in her for him, he muses but doesn't act upon. As the end of his twenties loom on the horizon, he berates himself for his fantasy. Jackie will always see him as a friend. He isn't her type, he reminds himself. What is her type? he wonders. No, he shakes his head angrily at himself. She'd said no. Maybe friendship isn't so bad, he thinks one frustrating warm April day after he arrives home from work and begins to open his fridge door for his first wind-down beer of the evening.

He lets go of the door handle and lets the fridge door shut itself as his right hand rubs his chest round and round. He moves to his bedroom. His hair becomes like sewing needles stitching threads through his scalp to bind his blood cells together in a wire that whips the walls of his arteries as it lengthens its reach into his heart.

With scrabbling fingers, Simon rummages around in the bottom drawer of his dresser where he'd buried Gramps's scarf the day after he'd joined FPTP Publishing. He'd decided all memories needed to be put away. But now frustration at he doesn't-know-what moves his impatient feet, disturbs his hands until he yanks open that bottom drawer. His right hand finds it by the feel of its familiar weave. He pulls it out and wraps it around his neck. It's just a scarf. Its comfort dampens the hurt in his heart, the hurt that beer and job had been suppressing into hidden places below his consciousness.

He suppresses all thoughts of Gramps as he jerks open his front door. He stomps out of his apartment and stomps down to the streetcar stop on his convoluted subway-avoiding way to what he thinks of as Jackie's café.

He needs the stress relief of a long walk from Queen to the Danforth.

No alcohol blurs the clarity of his mind emerging from its long somnolence.

He rotates his shoulders, he fists his hands, he squeezes his eyes shut and open as he fights the emerging clearness. After he steps off the Queen streetcar, he climbs the long hill north to the

Danforth, and his steps quicken as pain upon pain leaks into the spaces between his neurons while the desire to see Jackie rises. The scarf's comfort is unequal to the wire whipping his heart and releasing the pressure of the long-masked river of needles gushing mental torment and grief back into his consciousness. As he pushes the café door open to the stuffy space, irritation walks in with him. Like the first time he stumbled in, every seat is taken, every wall surface covered in leaning people, all awaiting the first reading. Simon scans the crowd for a chink he can sidle through and finds one. His "excuse me," "pardon me," open a way to the space he's spotted, and Simon squeezes himself between two tables without touching the men on either side of him to flop into the empty chair.

As he leans against the chair back, his hand brushes the ragged end of his scarf. Memories of Gramps float up into his mind; even his grandfather's scent invades his nostrils. He blinks. He must be losing his mind, and then the man next to him shifts his chair, and Simon realizes that this man is wearing the aftershave Gramps used to pat on all over his seamed face. Simon shifts his chair a miniscule amount away from the man. Yet the memory the aftershave brought on won't be moved away from.

Simon crosses his arms and grips his upper arms with his hands. This past Sunday had been Gramps's birthday. Phyllis had casually mentioned it. Hearing his name had shocked Simon and caused him to spill his wine. That had been Melanie's first mop-up of the evening. On the heels of his grandfather being forcefully brought back into his consciousness, a pang of guilt of not knowing his birthday had spasmed his heart and twisted his face. Phyllis had shot him a repressive look.

"Gramps is gone!" Sarah had shouted as if to a stupid child.

Melanie had swiftly dabbed at the wine stain on the tablecloth as she'd murmured in his ear, "We all miss him, they don't want to admit they used to forget his birthday."

Simon's heart had squeezed until pain shot outwards along his ribs and upward into his shoulders.

Fred had commanded Michael to refill Simon's glass, and Michael had grinned, "This'll cheer you up."

Simon had stared at the light-reflecting red liquid until Michael had patted his shoulder sympathetically and whispered, "We'll go to the pub as soon as Phyllis lets us go."

Simon had lifted his glass then as he longed to retreat down to Gramps's old lair. He hadn't thought of it since Phyllis had gutted and redesigned it the summer after he'd passed. Fred's mocking voice had carried across the table as Simon had drained his wine from his glass into his stomach, "Poor Simon. To be so consumed with the past. Men face forward. But I suppose it's my fault for not raising you to be a man, isn't it?"

Simon had said nothing to that. But true to his word, Michael had treated Simon to a series of vodka tonics, and they had gotten drunk on alcohol and Gramps stories, though as Simon tried to remember through the alcoholic haze that clouded his memory of that night, he'd done most of the story-telling. Michael had had few to tell. Simon tries to reassure himself that was because he, Simon, had spent more time with Gramps. Michael had spent little time with Gramps because of his intensive studies and need to get into the top medical school at UofT. Still, the division of their experiences with Gramps cleaves Simon further from his family and into a place of aloneness. He'd woken up that morning with those thoughts percolating through his headache and had stared at his swollen eyes until all thought of Gramps had vortexed back into the vault he'd had locked them in all those years ago. Satisfied, he'd run to work, his headache pounding with each footfall on the grey, cracked concrete.

And now sitting in this café, years after he'd first found it, driven there by a blizzard and grief, it's like nothing has changed. Simon digs his fingers into his flesh until the physical pain wraps the needles churning themselves through his arteries and pierces the memories that won't leave him alone.

Screech!

People slap hands over ears. Simon hunches his ears into his shoulders, not releasing his arms from his fearsome grip.

The screeching ends. Simon drops his shoulders, lengthens his neck, and spots someone at the mic. It's him. The owner. Guy is his name, Simon remembers. He's portly now, no longer simply burly. Guy chuckles embarrassedly. "Sorry about that folks. We're still having a little difficulty here with the new sound system."

"We can't hear you!" cries a voice from the crowd.

Guy lifts his head and bellows: "Is this better?"

"Yes," comes the reply from someone Simon can't see. The crowd murmurs laughter.

Guy bellows the rest of his speech, ending with, "I now present to you, Jackie." He raises his hands to applaud, and the crowd joins in. Simon stretches his lips, vigorously slaps his hands against each other, and sits up straighter and taller.

Jackie's happy face and long, blaring-red curls appear into view. She reaches toward the mic as if to test its solidity. Her face takes on a sombre cast. Her mouth moves, but Simon cannot hear her words over the crowd's shuffling and coughs and whispers.

"Speak up!" says the same demanding voice from before.

Jackie turns her head to raise her eyebrows at Guy who shrugs back at her. Suddenly, Simon is standing up and weaving his way swiftly through the crowd before the thought reaches his consciousness that after years of helping authors with their readings and book launches, he knows how to fix a microphone.

Breathless he spurts out from the crowd onto the empty space in front of Jackie and Guy. "Where's your sound system?" Simon asks.

"Hey, it's you," Guy says. "Sure, this way." Simon follows Guy to the system. He studies it and sees the problem: a connector had loosened itself a tiny way out of its socket. He smiles to himself—it's always the simplest thing—and pushes the connector firmly back in. He nods at Guy, and the two walk back over to Jackie, who's been watching them.

"Try it now," Simon says.

Jackie steps back to the microphone and grasps it. "Testing," she says. Feedback whines and rises to a crescendo. Simon hurries back to the system, plays with the gain controls, and gradually the feedback dies away. Simon nods at her again. Again, Jackie says, "Testing." But no one can hear her. Simon gestures at her to keep speaking into the microphone while he turns the volume knob up slowly, then resets the master switches.

"Can you hear me?" Jackie asks for the last time.

"Yeah! Finally, a man who knows how to do things," calls out that voice from the crowd. People clap, and Simon, blushing right into his straw-coloured hair, ducks his head and makes his way back to his chair. The man on his right pats his shoulder. "Thanks, mate," he grins. Simon smiles back.

Jackie clears her throat and says, "I'm doing something different today. This is a new path for me . . . ," she says, her voice drifting off on the last words.

She stands silently. The crowd settles down.

Jackie bows her head, her eyes downcast, and she crosses her hands behind her back. She stands silently a little longer. With a rasp, she speaks rhythmically into the microphone:

"I

Sit and weep

For the dawn to sleep

Upon the grass

So green."

Jackie pauses to take breath. The crowd hushes.

"I

Sit and weep

For the night to creep

Upon the grass

So clean."

Jackie pauses again, keeping her eyes downcast. She continues all in a rush.

"I
Sit and weep
For the day to leap
Upon the grass
So lean.
I
Sit and weep
For my dog to sleep
Under the grass
And stone."

She lifts her head. The crowd shuffle their feet. Simon looks around. He raises his hands and slams them together loudly. Over and over, faster and faster, willing the crowd to join him. The man who had praised him earlier over the microphone looks over at him as if to say, are you daft? Simon glares at him. The man hurriedly lifts his hands to clap, too. Like a flicker of flame, the clapping leaps from person to person then slowly fades. Simon is the last to leave off clapping. Jackie smiles wanly over in his direction.

"I will now do a reading from Keats. Keats used to sing me to sleep when I was a teen, his pretty poetry a rhythm in my head. In the month of April, he seems particularly dear. He'll bring the budding trees of this month into our hot little room."

The crowd waits.

"It is said that in April a nightingale built her nest in Keats's garden, and Keats felt joy in her song. I give you *Ode to a Nightingale.*²"

"My heart aches, and drowsy numbness pains

---

2 *Ode to a Nightingale*, by John Keats, from *Keats: Poems Published in 1820*, downloaded from Project Gutenberg, in the public domain. It was written and first published in 1819.

My sense, a thought of hemlock
I had drunk,
Or emptied some dull opiate to the drains
One minute past, and Lethewards had sunk:
'Tis not through envy of thy happy lot,
But being too happy in thine happiness,—
That though, light-winged Dryad of the trees,
In some melodious plot
Of beechen green, and shadows numberless,
Singest of summer in full-throated ease."

Jackie's easy voice sings on as Simon falls into the familiar words. Gramps had quoted Keats to him, he suddenly remembers. Simon himself studied Keats in Grade 12 English. But while he'd forgotten him, Gramps had been able to quote his entire poems from memory, regaling him with the 19th century poet's melodious yet dark words. Gramps's voice had risen and fallen, boomed and whispered in tune with the poem. Simon had marvelled at Gramps's ability and having that gift of just the right words to suit his mood available to him in an instant.

One day he'd said so out loud. Gramps had paused. He'd pinned him with his sharp eyes and said: "Well, why don't you memorize it for yourself, then? Our teachers expected us to memorize poetry. It's a good skill to have. But if your blasted educational system won't do it for you, do it for yourself."

Simon hadn't, though he'd kept on meaning to. Why had he forgotten all that the moment Gramps had died?

"Fade far away, dissolve, and quite forget
What thou among the leaves hast never known,
The weariness, the fever, and the fret
Here, where men sit and hear each other groan;
Where palsy shakes a few, sad, last gray hairs,
Where youth grows pale, and spectre-thin, and dies;
Where but to think is to be full of sorrow
And leaden-eyed despairs,

Where Beauty cannot keep her lustrous eyes,
Or new Love pine at them beyond tomorrow."
The words in Jackie's sad, sad voice puncture Simon's heart. Consumption was in Keats's thoughts, the fever eating him up, Simon sees. So many died of tuberculosis, Simon recalls, the tragedy of those poets smitten so young by a bacteria easily killed off with today's drugs. He frowns. His father had ranted once about how the drugs were becoming ineffective and soon we'd be back in the time of Keats. Surely that could not be.

Jackie's voice sharpens and draws Simon back.

"I cannot see what flowers are at my feet . . ."

Simon is plunged into thoughts of flowers, how Gramps can no longer see flowers or the new growth of spring, feel the hope of the coming warmth, experience joy at the last of winter's frosts being killed by the southern air. All of a sudden, none of this April day seems as sweet without the man who had made him think, who had made him, Simon, feel important, necessary to those around him and to the world, important to him—the man who is dead. Who considers Simon important now? Who puts Simon at the top of his or her list of must-see, never-leave-alone people? His friends know the persona he's built up, not the man he'd been becoming until grief had sluiced him into a river of needles nor the man who'd reached out, trying to find friendly hands to hold on to for safety as the lacerating rapids shot him to an unseen destination.

He blinks rapidly and stares toward Jackie, willing her voice to drown his thoughts.

"Darkling I listen; and, for many a time
I have been half in love with easeful Death,
Call'd him soft names in many a musèd rhyme . . ."
I don't have the rhyme in me, Simon admits. How beautiful Keats makes death. Simon for the first time in years feels the beauty of death, remembers the singsong of the ground, the stranger, and Gramps's little pill tin. In a fit of cleansing on the

day after his probation period ended, he'd thrown out Gramps's pill tin. He'd regretted it the next morning and run out in his pyjamas to the grey, plastic garbage bin. But it was too late. The bin's lid was flipped back, the bin itself askew on the sidewalk, indicating that the garbage men had been by. He'd put both hands firmly on the rim, leaned his head way in, blocking out the light, searching, searching for signs of a glint, a glint that would indicate that somehow Gramps's round pill tin had rolled out of the tightly tied up green garbage bag. Not a glimmer. Simon had straightened himself slowly and let go of the bin.

What a stupid decision that had been.

"Thou wast not born for death, immortal Bird!"

Gramps's remembered voice booms in sync with Jackie's lilting tones. He doesn't know how he remembers, yet he knows with certainty that Gramps would pause at this point in the poem. Once Simon had spoken into that pause to ask if it was true, if Nightingales lived forever. Simon had been young then, he couldn't remember how old but not yet a teen when he'd scorned his older relatives and demanded an answer to such a silly statement that a bird was immortal. Gramps had chuckled at his silliness and had heaved himself out of his chair to search the bookshelves for the Audobon collection. He had laid its heavy weight on Simon's tiny lap and told him to search. Simon knew how to spell "night" and assumed that's how the bird's name would begin. Still, he'd foolishly asked Gramps how to spell the bird's name. Gramps had raised his eyebrows. "I know, I know," Simon had sighed. Gramps and his spelling games; Gramps expecting him to use a dictionary and figure it out on his own. Simon veers into the thought: he knows who gave Phyllis her love of language that she'd then distorted into rules. He plunges back into that spelling memory. He'd succeeded on the first try, found the bird, and read about it. After a few minutes, Gramps had asked him to read the entry out loud. His easy tone had somehow halted Simon's objection before he'd uttered it. Gramps had corrected his reading, and it had been painful going. But, Simon reflects, those lessons at how to read out loud well had proven fruitful in his marketing job today. He winces at the memory of one new writer who'd spoken out her chapter at a rapid rate in one high-pitched tone. It had taken many tries, and many tantrums on her part, before he'd finally managed to turn her reading into something that people at least didn't flee from. He turns his authors into readers people want to listen to, he thinks with satisfaction.

He returns himself to the presence of Jackie's beautiful voice. He sinks into her healing cadences.

"Adieu! Adieu! Thy plaintive anthem fades
Past the near meadows, over the still stream,
Up the hill-side; and now tis buried deep
In the next valley-glades:
Was it a vision, or a waking dream?
Feld is that music:—Do I wake or sleep?"

Jackie steps back. The crowd sighs out its pleasure then applauds. Jackie bows, and Guy steps up to the microphone to introduce the next poet. Simon suddenly sees red hair in his peripheral vision. He turns his head. She gestures with her head for him to follow her out the café. He gratefully does.

Outside in the gentle warm breeze, underneath the harsh white streetlight. She asks, "Did you really like it, or were you being polite?"

Simon knows she means her own composition. "I liked it. I've read much modern verse this past few years. I—"

"Mine's not modern."

"I know. That's why I liked it. It was refreshing to hear simple rhyme."

She harrumphs. Suddenly, some self-preserving surge from an unseen well inside him pushes his lips to move. He hesitates. Does he dare ask her? It isn't his job. But his conscious mind says that maybe it would get him a promotion and . . . he slaps the other thought surging into his consciousness away.

"What?" she asks.

He licks his lips, "I was wondering if you . . . maybe you'd like to submit your poetry to my publishing house?"

"No one publishes poetry anymore."

"I think they will yours."

Jackie raises her eyebrows skeptically. He pleads at her with his eyes. She shrugs okay, whatever. He grins.

"No," Clara, his boss, says unequivocally when Simon brings Jackie's poems to her desk.

"This is good verse," Simon says.

"No one buys poetry. They want it for free if they read it."

"Poetry will expand our market."

"We have a good market position, already."

"Poetry will add cachet to our offerings and draw in a new demographic."

"We don't need it. Our market position is solid."

"It'll be a loss leader then, beautiful words to draw people in to our bestsellers."

"That's not how the publishing business works."

"We spent half a million on marketing Shelley's book—"

"It was a bestseller."

"But have we made our money back on it?"

"That's not the point."

Simon rather thinks it is.

She continues: " And what do you know about it? You've had a few successes, but I've been in this business decades, and I know how books sell and what sells. Authors like Shelley require a fitting marketing plan. And poetry doesn't sell."

"With today's POD technology, we can publish Jackie's poetry without losing—"

"POD is not good enough quality for our brand. You have a lot left to learn about the publishing industry. How long have you been with us?"

Before he can answer, she shakes her head, "It doesn't matter. You'll learn that others before you have had the same high-brow thoughts, but the book-selling landscape has changed, and poetry doesn't sell. We're in the business to publish and market authors who make us money. You stick to your job and keep learning." Clara lifts up her phone handset. Simon sighs deep within himself and makes himself walk back to his desk with a straight back. With a last look at the poems in his hand, he reluctantly files them in his bottom desk drawer and returns to booking bookstore readings for Shelley, whose pedantic words make him long for that night of Keats. How will he tell Jackie?

Jackie's sanguine when he finally admits to her his boss's decree. She places a hand on his arm, comforting him. "Hey, don't look so glum. There are other ways. I can self-publish. Technology has made it much easier. Maybe some day I will."

"But without the backing of a publisher . . ."

"There are other ways, Simon. There always are. You don't need to worry about me. I like my life. My poems are requited here," she gestures with her head toward the café. She finishes, "I'll find a way when the time is right."

She sounds like Gramps, he thinks. When a door closes, he'd intone, a window opens. God always makes sure. But Simon doesn't believe in pollyanna ideas or a God like Gramps did. Still, Jackie will try, he thinks as she walks away from him along the sunlit sidewalk. She won't succeed though. It's been years since he'd first seen her. And there she still is, working at a job she doesn't like, reading her poetry to an unappreciative crowd, unpublished. Where will it all lead?

While she remained happily still, he'd quit, found a new job, begun it with hope, only to find himself working for mediocrity. Was mediocre goods a better reason than deceitful money?

This past Sunday dinner, frustrated at letting Jackie down and seeing an excuse for him to be in touch with her daily slip away, weary of marketing a nice author whose books were cookie cutters of each other, missing Gramps's reliable and wise presence, his blood nettling him with hidden emotion-memories, he'd broken the unspoken rule and had blurted out whose campaign he was working on.

Phyllis had stared at him shocked. She'd rasped, "You can't be serious. I knew you were marketing some low brow authors, and it was better not to know, to be honest, Simon, but her?!"

Sarah had guffawed and promptly stopped under Phyllis's withering look.

Michael had looked puzzled.

Fred had taken Phyllis's cue and said, "Your mother knows her authors. We expected better from you. Well, actually, we didn't. Your quitting Con Fable told us all we knew about you." He'd stabbed his salmon steak and pulled a flake off from the whole of it.

Simon had averted his eyes from the sight but couldn't avert his ears from Phyllis's succinct skewering of Shelley and his pride: "A hewer of the first two-hundred words of the English language," she'd pronounced. "It doesn't take much of a man to market that to the masses."

He'd hoped that bringing Jackie's poetry to his boss would net him his first book, increase the stature of his job and bring him into Jackie's life-giving light. As his family had dismissed any further mention of his work and turned toward listening to Fred advise Michael on a puzzling case, Simon had desponded that his present workplace was not Con Fable, where initiative to save money had brought him accolades; this was a publishing house where everyone waited their turn and did it the company way.

Simon blinks back into the present as Jackie disappears from his view. He realizes that she will always be and only be a friend, and he can't stop wanting more. He can't stop wanting someone to love him, to put him first in their life, to cherish who he is no matter his job or status, like Gramps had. Like Priss, he thinks, forgetting in the pain rushing through his arteries how superficial was her love for him. Priss had been his last chance at marriage, at creating his own family to love him, he mourns.

Simon shoves his hands into his pockets and turns around to walk in the opposite direction, eyes firmly on the drab concrete under his feet. He kicks at an errant pebble. "Sorry," comes a mumble near him as, with head down and eyes firmly on the ground, Simon bumps into someone, man or woman he doesn't know. Simon automatically returns the apology as his thoughts tumble on. It doesn't matter anyway. He fingers his wallet in one of his pockets and the wad of Kleenex jammed up against his iPhone in the other. He yearns for a confab with Gramps, for a shared vodka tonic. He yearns for someone to commiserate with, to laugh at him, to want to be with him . . .

He lets the thought drift off. He doesn't want to be alone anymore. He doesn't want to be alone in a sea of people. Hazy-headed beer with three isn't enough, anymore. With no more alcohol fumes fuzzing the river of needles, it surges higher and higher with each pump of his heart. He wants to be with Gramps, but Gramps is dead.

The Viaduct breaks through into his mind.

He stops in the middle of the sidewalk and looks up, looks along the long straight road of the Danforth, sees the cars zooming in the direction of the far-off bridge, veering around cyclists on their way, and braking suddenly with angry red taillights for pedestrians starting and stopping and hopping as they pop out from between parked cars to dash between driving cars. He hasn't walked across the Viaduct since he began working at his new job. Why had he stopped?

He misses walking the bridge.

What is he doing? Why is he here? He's traded a life of money for a life of seeming meaning. But he's still useless.

Jackie likes him but doesn't want him and doesn't expect him to succeed. He's no knight for her. And she can't bring him felicity, he admits.

Jackie isn't the only one to doubt his facility as a man; his mother or his sister or his brother and oh very especially his father ban all talk of his life because they don't like hearing failure. They don't expect him to succeed.

Gramps had, though.

Gramps's death had lanced his assumptions about his life. The frothing river of his unheard grief and loneliness hasn't been quietened, Simon sees for the first time in years. He'd deceived himself into thinking it had by submerging it under his intent focus on his authors, by spending hours and hours making his writers succeed at their readings, by excessively celebrating successful book launches and his authors' increasing royalty cheques as a result of his campaigns. Sandy had been his partner in work, but she went home to a family. He'd never joined her; she'd never invited him to her home. They only socialize together when with Isaac and Elaine at their monthly pub nights. Barely a stopgap in his loneliness. Beer his only daily companion. By drowning in his work—and he admits, too, by finding comfort in beer—he's been able to ignore the pain that pierces his flesh with every pound of his heart against his ribs. While he's ignored it, it's been swelling in hidden caverns of his mind. Undammed, it's whirling and stabbing and swirling him down into a black maw of grief and loneliness that not only destroys joy but all desire for existence on earth, all hope, all optimism.

The pain of it stings his face like a writhing electrical wire.

He launches himself forward from his standing stop.

26

THE BEGINNING

Simon accelerates along the sidewalk, his eyes taking in the concrete ribbon before his feet as his feet eat up its length, striding left-right, left-right. Simon is unheeding of the people he brushes past as they, too, don't notice him on their own impatient way to their own destinations. Simon ignores, too, the street's giant pots of enormous upthrusting greens waving in the wind and the hopeful buds on the trees striving to live off their roots' confinement underneath the broad sidewalk. He flashes by side streets, keeping his eyes averted from the greening grass in front of their brick houses and ragged bushes. He doesn't want to witness the brave crocuses and early tulips pushing their way up into the light.

A black tide swamps Simon's mind and keeps from him the conception of life unfolding into tomorrow. He cannot hold in his mind the idea of the next Sunday dinner. He cannot imagine what the next workday will bring. The future is blank and impossible.

It's absurd for him to make plans, to strive for better work; for what will it achieve him? Life yawns an abyss of aloneness and loneliness before him. It promises the same sweet superficiality of his past, that makes everyone rub along together but promises no meaning, no purpose, no need to be.

Hope is an illusion that makes you think you're moving forward when, in reality, you're treading sludge that pins you in place.

Why remain here on this blue planet?

This grey planet.

A grey place with clouds of shallow frippery hovering around everyone. Clouds are ephemeral. You put your hand up, and your hand disappears inside their watery particles, lost to your sight, lost to you, with nothing to feel. He has no skill to penetrate the complacency of his fellow beings; yet he doesn't know how to become like them, to divest himself of this yearning for meaning, for caring connections to something, with someone, anyone, to no longer covet being important to at least one person, like he had been to Gramps and Gramps to him, because he's loved and missed and wanted to be near to as much as he wants to be with them.

How is it that others can achieve happiness in such a state but he can't? Is he alone in his angst over such an individualistic world as this, where poetry is scoffed at for its non-value as a money maker, where people are admired for being alone and unneeding of anyone but their own selves? Where grief is spurned, and mourning is judged?

No. They can't be happy. Contented. Fulfilled. They cannot like it. They must be as dissatisfied as he. But they don't want to wave their arms, jump up and down violently to disperse the clouds so that they can see what is out there, respond to his desire for intense kinship, risk the pain of feeling grief, sitting with his grief, and themselves be seen in turn.

The rapid thoughts, beliefs, judgements propel him forward. His steps quicken. His legs thrust forward farther and farther, left, right, left, right.

He arrives at the intersection of Broadview and Danforth. He halts. Hesitation grips him. A brutal gust blows his straw hair forward, toward the bridge. Fred's contemptuous voice reaches inside his head—"Life is difficult and there you quit, Simon." It stirs up his courage. Resolve straightens his spine. In this, he will not be a quitter.

The light turns green; the pedestrian light flashes to a white walking symbol. Simon crosses Broadview Avenue, with its broken-up road bed, scarred by streetcar tracks, stretching his legs longer and faster. Cars nose-to-tail growl beside him as they crawl toward the Viaduct and the Don Valley Parkway, to head downtown or toward home.

Home. The thought makes him judder to a stop at the corner. Where is his home?

Is home his apartment? The family home?

An ache burns his heart and catches at his throat. No, not his family home. He doesn't belong there, as he is, only who they want him to be. And he can't be that anymore. He looks longingly south down Broadview Avenue toward his apartment. His home?

He shakes his head. He is alone there; he is always alone there. It's not a home, it's a familiar place where he can use beer out of sight of others to hide his mind from himself. He himself, within himself, by himself, is not home. Nowhere is he home in this reality. He crosses the Danforth on his green light. And now he is on the correct side of the Viaduct.

Simon turns to his right and heads for the valley under the mesmerizing black tide whose wave rises, rises, rises in his mind. His eyes stare ahead. His mind is under the power of the tide. He doesn't feel the mist settling onto the ends of his stalky hair as he steps onto the narrow south sidewalk of the massive bridge. He stumbles on a seam in the solid poured concrete and briefly sees the Viaduct stretch before him.

Simon blinks, and he feels one with the bridge.

Simon speeds up, his heart thumping with adrenaline. Cyclists pedal furiously past the slow cars and pass Simon in the opposite direction to where he's pounding down the walk. The path he's navigating messages to him how unimportant people are in this world; how important machines are with all the space cars are given on this structure. He desires a wider path, a clearer path. But all he perceives before him is the same unwelcoming, fearful, self-absorbed people he wants to know but who fear him knowing their inmost selves. They fear knowing themselves. How can he have a full life, a life of true laughter, of joy, of meaning, of purpose, of being needed when everyone wants to skate on the surface, even when the surface is as insubstantial as this mist?

Simon blinks.

When did this mist appear?

Although Simon has allowed himself to be pulled to this place, he has been studiously avoiding looking south, to not thinking about where he's going. His feet slow.

Simon turns his head to his left and looks over and past the railing all the way south toward the deep, dangerous lake hidden behind bridges and architectural award winners, toward the mouth of the Don River, encased and forced into a channel that forever needs dredging.

The view contracts as the mist blows up into fog and obscures his sightlines. The rough railing attracts him as if it's an enormous magnet and he iron filings. He cannot see the top of Bridgeport Hospital, that renewed place of suffering that sits so close to that historic place of resentment and brutality and hatred and despair and suffering: the Don Jail.

A hard edge slams into his midriff. Simon beholds its top surface, puzzled, while he soothes his offended abdomen with a compassionate hand. What is he doing? Where is he? He stops stroking his abdomen and leans his forearms on the rough parapet. The pink stones in the railing push themselves through his jacket sleeve, through the cotton sleeve of his shirt, and into his soft skin. He leans more of his weight on the stones, wanting their edges to pain him.

A man brushes past him on the narrow sidewalk, grumbling, "You can't see anything in this, man." Simon shuffles closer to the railing, his body caressing it, his arms almost hugging it.

The ground pulls at his head. He rears back. Where is he? He must not be here. A whisper tickles his ear and draws him back: "Here is life. Here is where you want."

He swallows. Where he wants? He doesn't want to be alone in a world where love comes with strings and friendship is monthly. He doesn't want to be working at a job where he's paid to make people miserable or a place where his ideas are shot down as being those from an ignorant, inconsequential man.

Who is he?

Waves of energy flow up from the ground far below and magnetize him in agreement with his thoughts. And then a damning statement punctures his senses: "You are no different. You talk and talk about your grandfather. But you don't have the courage to be him or be with him. What are you?"

What is he?

He is unutterably alone, divided from the world. He is in his head. He fears to feel — like the others he's been criticizing.

Loss hurts. Feeling it hurts. Being controlled hurts. Emotions hurt. Striving for freedom to be who he is hurts.

A couple stroll past him, chatting, the fog billowing around them. One of them brushes his back and doesn't notice.

He's invisible, Simon thinks as he senses the couple walk away from him.

A blob of lead gathers itself inside his stomach. His arms ache with desire to hold and to be held. His neck and shoulders tighten and rise up toward his jaw as his eyes burn with unshed tears.

"Come," whispers the ground hidden by the fog. "Come. I will hold you. Come. Join your grandfather."

Unbidden comes the Star Trek line: resistance is futile. He wants to be with Gramps again, to be where he is treasured. He so very much wants to. He wants the kind of love the ground promises, the kind that used to feel solid beneath his feet, that he hasn't felt since Gramps died.

"Yes," whispers the ground and beckons through the fog. Simon stares down, hypnotized by the sense of it. The ground reaches up its hands to grasp either side of Simon's skull and yanks hard.

The cords of Simon's neck tighten; his veins pop out. He forces his eyes to lift to where the disappearing horizon should be, scanning for an anchor, seeing only a blurred outline of the financial towers while he feels his head lowering. The fog thickens, coating his skin with moisture.

He doesn't want to go.

He doesn't want to stay.

The loneliness nourishes the blob of lead in his stomach and grows it into a viscous pond that imprisons his heart.

Another person walks toward him, footfalls muffled. Simon feels the person's presence, the physical energy of the woman as she glides past him in the fog. She doesn't slow down, doesn't hesitate, doesn't look. The only one who cares is the ground.

He drops his eyes and cranes his neck over the parapet.

The wind blows a hole through the low-lying cloud. Way below where Simon stands, the grass grows verdant, the bushes with their sprinkled white buds wave languorously on either side of the swollen Don River over which he's standing. He shuffles back the way he came, down the sidewalk, away from the murky river, retaining his grip on the granite-studded concrete, uncaring that the roughness scrapes at his sensitive palms.

When Simon sees that he is right over the ground, between highway and river, he comes to a standstill once again. No water near him at all. No highway or road or path either.

His eyes transform into green-flecked pebbles. They leave sight of the present, of all surroundings but the ground. Simon straightens himself to his full height.

"Yes!" declares the ground. "Come!"

Simon steps back and feels the edge of the sidewalk underneath his right heel.

Simon rocks forward on his right foot, shifts his weight to his left, and pushes himself off his left foot.

"Yes!" chortles the ground.

Simon places both hands on top of the railing and vaults over.

"Yes," sighs the ground orgasmically. And the fog closes Simon off from sight of it.

Simon falls, feet toward the happy ground, his face toward the murderous Lake Ontario.

A shocked cry zips over his head, "A man just jumped!"

A scream rends the air above him.

Simon falls into the closing fog, the low cloud obscuring his vision of sky and ground, of life and death. Is this what death is like? A vanishing into nothingness? He closes his eyes in relief.

Upward wind blasts chill up his pants legs and flings open his eyes. The sun slashes a hole through the fog and paints faint white-gold on the river on his right side and the waters far in the distance to the south. That sunlight painting holds his gaze. He loses breath in awe of its beauty. Desire to drink it in revives in him. Knowledge he won't be able to in mere seconds throws a sob up out of him.

Why did he jump?

He plummets further into the clarity of air.

Simon's heart slams his ribs with regret.

He watches Bridgeport Hospital ascending in the distance as gravity pulls him downward. *I don't want to die!* he screams silently. Tears burst from his eyes.

Cries above him multiply. Horns honk and brakes squeal.

He feels the energy of the bridge disappear behind him as he falls past the curving steel struts and into the hollowed out spaces underneath the Viaduct's span. Too late, too late thoughts swallow him up. His shirt rises up past his scarf. His scarf ends fly up past his eyes. He is temporarily blinded. Why can he not see? What is he doing? He doesn't want to be doing this. His scarf whips past his head. He only wanted the pain to be gone. He only wanted his grief to be heard.

Simon can see.

The ground rushing toward him.

He only wanted to be free to be himself. He only wanted to be free from the penalty of rejection.

Simon hurtles through a rebirthing bush, its greening branches grasping and scratching him, and sinks into the grass, into the April rain-soaked soil.

He doesn't want to be dead.

Simon lands.

There is no pain. No more lead blob. There is nothing.

He cannot move. He cannot feel his legs. The ground holds him triumphantly in place as sirens from the city scream toward him, threatening anyone who gets in their way.

Gramps materializes before Simon's startled eyes. His heart leaps, and his mouth reflects his joy. But then he is back in his lonely place, for Gramps is a ghost, a far-off apparition who stands and weeps.

Suddenly, love, as if it was a material presence, rushes toward him, surrounds him, blinding him in its strong golden light. In response, sobs of joy, of deep longing met, erupt from Simon's core. He doesn't know or care if they're wracking his body physically or only his mind. The love, like energy with mass, is all that exists. The love tightens its hold yet doesn't hurt his broken bones, his shattered organs, his ripped muscles, his whipped heart. It doesn't adjure or criticize. It doesn't tell him to shut up already about his grandfather or tell him not to talk about such a morbid subject or inform him that the time for grief is over, to get on with his life. It doesn't tell him his choices harm others or washes their hands of him. His arteries pour the river of needles out of him as the love turns off the needling pain forever. This presence that makes him weep with all the force of reconciliation met doesn't tell him to focus on what is important or or how lucky he is to have a father or compare him to another. Instead, it cradles him and lets him feel. It speaks to him through his mind, flooding every neuron with kindness, seeking his heart through his healed blood as his heart continues to pump stubbornly.

Simon senses Gramps move toward him through the dazzling light that rocks him as a mother rocks her baby, as a father holds his child. Gramps kneels down and leans toward him through the light to look deep into Simon's eyes. "Oh, Simon. What have you done?"

At the same time as Simon wonders, "Not an apparition?," he feels: there is no criticism, only sorrow from this relative for the man who felt driven to jump. Simon wants to reach out and touch his Gramps and be touched in return so badly. Yet he cannot move. His torso has no feeling, either.

The pain of living is nothing compared to the regret of chosen death, he belatedly understands as the future he couldn't see when above the ground unfurls its hope and beauty and vitality and excitement before him now so clearly.

Cries run toward him. "Over here!" a deep voice yells.

"Where? I don't see him," a higher voice replies.

"In the bushes," the first voice yells back. "He landed in the bushes."

Love continues to soak into Simon, and he cries out. Gramps stretches insubstantial arms toward Simon and hugs him gently. Gramps lays his mass-less head on Simon's and kisses him softly. Forgiveness flows through Gramps and into Simon. And stays. Simon weeps. Still, he cannot hear his own tears flowing, cannot hear anything emit from himself; all he can hear is Gramps's voice and those far-off cries racing toward him. So close now. Deep wanting pours out of him and toward him as the strong light brightens.

His loneliness had been so unbearable he'd been unable to endure it. And so why could this love—this overwhelming, gentle, demanding love—not have made itself known to him earlier when he'd needed it so much? Why now? When his blood is soaking the lying ground? The love conveys to him the idea: "I am always here. You didn't seek me."

What is that supposed to mean? Simon asks with a spurt of vituperation. Gramps, with his head still against Simon's, laughs into Simon's stuck-out hair. "That is life, Simon, speaking to you. You needed to challenge it to live."

"Why now, Gramps? Why now?" asks Simon as he suddenly falls back into despair.

"Because you looked in the wrong places and didn't believe. In death, you will always meet life. But life demands you keep seeking, Simon, to persist and endure, as me and my family did. Why didn't you hear when I told you those tales in our lair? Oh, Simon," Gramps strokes Simon's face and continues talking. "Life is hard, my boy, I know, but you must've known always that you and I would be together. Waiting is frustrating, Simon, I know, divided by the two substances of our realities, but it's sweeter the meeting when we let patience claim us so as to experience our future and become fully ourselves before rejoining. Oh, Simon, the promise of nothingness, of peace in chosen death is a false one. I love you so much. But I don't want you to be here with me just yet."

Simon tries to comprehend this criticism that isn't criticism but soothing sadness that washes away his own despair and lifts him up, wanting him to live, too. Too late, too late, he wants to live.

"Only know," whispers his grandfather as he lets go. "Some things are not meant to be understood, only known."

Relief surges through Simon.

"He's sitting up," says the suddenly close female voice with astonishment. "Max, his eyes are open."

"Dead people have open eyes, too, Marge. And that's how he landed. Sitting up."

"Don't think like that," she admonishes him. "We're here to save no matter what the odds. You need a vacation, Max. You've seen so much death, you can't tell it from life."

"You got that right. What number makes this jumper? Why can't they put that damn barrier up already? So much talk meaning nothing." The man pants as he skids to a halt on the fog-slicked grass and drops a heavy case on the ground. "He looks more shattered than the last guy, who died. So much blood."

"Hush. He can hear us. He needs to know we want him to live."

The woman kneels down in front of Simon and searches deep into his pupils.

For the purposes of this story, the Prince Edward Viaduct or Bloor Viaduct does not have its Luminous Veil. After much debate, the Luminous Veil was added on in 2003, changing the Viaduct from being the second most fatal standing structure in the world, after the Golden Gate bridge, to having zero suicides. The design of the Veil was completed for the Pan Am Games in 2015 with the addition of artistic lighting. The Distress Centre signs remain near the bridge, and the TTC has signage so that anyone with the urge to suicide can call someone for free and know that they are not alone.

Toronto
416-408-HELP (4357)
https://www.torontodistresscentre.com/

Canada
1-833-456-4566
http://www.crisisservicescanada.ca/
Centre for Suicide Prevention: https://www.suicideinfo.ca

United States
1-800-273-8255 (TALK)
https://suicidepreventionlifeline.org/

International
International Association for Suicide Prevention's list of crisis hotlines: https://www.iasp.info/resources/Crisis_Centres/
Zero Suicide Initiative: https://zerosuicide.sprc.org/

258